The Adventures of a High School Scholar

"Believe in yourself and follow your dreams."

Jukwan Brooks

Published by: Better Knowledge LLC

Cover Art by

Jukwan Brooks and Joshua Allen

Edited by

Steve Seward

Table of Contents

Introduction

Allen is an 18-year-old kid in his senior year at Terry High School in Macon, GA. He is an A- Honor roll student and has the highest GPA out of everybody in his school. He is already getting scholarships offers to colleges thanks to his good grades. Even though he is well-known at school, Allen doesn't have a lot of friends and hardly doesn't have a social life. He is a smart guy, but a kid that is trying to find his true passion in life. He tries to live in the dreams his parents' vision for him. Although deep down he knows he must live in the dreams that he visions for himself. Through this book you will see how Allen finds out who he truly is, finding his purpose, and how just by him walking into his calling helps transform the lives of the people around him. Welcome to "The Adventures of a High School Scholar". I hope you enjoy this inspirational novel that you are about to dive into.

6

Chapter 1: Trying to Find Myself

It's a Friday sunny afternoon in March of 2020, a pep rally is going on in the gymnasium at Terry High School in Macon, GA. As graduation is two months away. The students with the highest GPA's are getting honored. Principal Davenport calls Allen's name as he has the highest GPA out of anybody and has officially been named the Valedictorian for the Class of 2020. Principal Davenport says, "And the student with the highest GPA and the Valedictorian for the Class of 2020 is Allen Callahan." Most of the crowd cheers for Allen while Blake, one of Allen's classmates, yells out an offensive remark. Blake has always bullied him since their elementary school days. He yells out, "Nerd!" Half of the crowd starts laughing at Blake's statement towards Allen. Allen keeps a smile on his face despite the negative attention that has come his way.

After the pep rally is over with, he is congratulated by his best friend Paul. Paul and Allen has been best friends since they were three years old. He daps up Allen and says, "Congrats my guy, forget what these people say bro. Enjoy your accomplishments, what you got plan on doing tonight?" Allen says, "I got to go to work tomorrow morning, so I'm going to be in my house all night." Paul wants Allen to get out more, but he respects his friend's decision. "I had wanted to celebrate with you, but we will do it another day."

Shanice, who was just named the Salutatorian of the 2020 Class, goes over to Allen to congratulate him. She taps Allen on the shoulder and says, "Congrats Allen, I knew you would have the highest GPA out of everybody." Shanice is Allen's crush, all the guys in the school is crazy about her. As they love her black and brown curly hair, her light brown ebony skin, with her beautiful brown eyes. Plus, she is the most intelligent girl in the whole school. As everyone loves her personality and is in awe of her beauty. Allen has had a crush on her since they were in the third grade. The two of them have developed a great friendship over the years due to them performing in Theater Arts together. Allen hopes that one day Shanice be his girlfriend. He nervously responds to her, "Thank you very much, congratulations to you also." "Thank you, I will talk to you later." After Shanice walks away, Paul says, "Look at you, got the hottest girl in the school giving you props." "I'm just blessed to be in her presence. Well, it's the end of the day, it's time for me to get home talk to you later."

After school has ended, Allen drives home in his 2006 Honda Accord and is greeted by his parents and his younger brother as he walks inside his house. On the outside looking in, Allen comes from a great family. Allen's Father (Al) is the president of National First Bank in Macon, GA. Allen's Mother (Imani) is a doctor at Mercy Hospital in Macon, GA. Allen has one younger brother named Jalean who is six years younger than him. All of them stay together in a beautiful light brown house in the suburbs of Macon. Allen walks inside his home as he is automatically greeted by his mother. Imani has always been a loving mother to him and his brother. As she wants the best for her kids. She says to him, "Glad to have you home son, how was your day?" Allen says, "It went great got an award today for having the highest GPA in the school. And I have been named the Valedictorian of my senior class." Allen's Dad jumps up out of his kitchen chair when he hear the news. He says, "That's my son just like your old man can't wait to see you graduate proud of you. That's what happens when you stay focus on your academics." Al is super hard on Allen as he wants him to mainly focus on his education. And to go to college and have a successful career in his field of study. Jalean comes from his room and says, "The only thing he needs now is a girl." Even though the brothers throw jabs at one another, they do love each other. Allen responds back to him, "And the only thing you need to do is learn common sense." Imani laughs, "Okay Kenan and Kel it's time to eat dinner."

The Callahan's family sit down for dinner. While eating, Al asks Allen if he has decided which college he wants to attend. "So, Allen you have two months left before the school year ends. Have you decided which college you want to go to?" Ever since he was a little kid, Allen's parents has told him he needs to go to college to be successful in life. Right now, Allen isn't sure what he wants to do in life. He has five scholarship offers from Georgia Southern University, Georgia State University, Kennesaw State University, Georgia Tech, and University of Georgia. Before he decides to even attend college he wants to find his calling in life. He wants to know what was he put on this planet to do. "Honestly pops I don't know, I got to do more praying and meditating about my decision." "Well, I hope you get a scholarship offer from Seward University the best college in the world." Seward University is Allen's parents' alma mater. Imani says, "Son just do what you feel in your heart. With your final year of High School close to being over with, how do you have plan on ending the school year?"

Allen wants to end his senior year of school in a great way. "Honestly having some fun doing stuff I could tell my future kids about." "Enjoy these last couple of months while they are here. Go out and explore anything you want." Al interjects as he disagrees with his wife's statement. "That sounds fun and all but remember what we always taught you stay focus on your education and GOD. Because when you graduate that's when the real world is going to start. You want to be a success story, not someone that get fully distracted by their hobbies and what their friends are doing." Allen's Brother, Jalean says, "And also stop being scared and go for what you want." Imani yells, "Jalean!" "I'm just being honest Mom." Allen takes into consideration the advice his family has given him.

Before going to sleep, Allen plays with his guitar and starts writing down in his journal what he wants to have in the future. He writes, "Thinking about my life trying to figure out which direction I want to go in. I don't want to let my parents down I want to make them proud of me. At the same time, I want to be happy in life. I don't want to live an ordinary life of just going to college, then graduating and getting a job afterwards. I know I am meant for more than that. Also, I have two months before I graduate from High School I want to be viewed as somebody important not as a nerd. Someway or somehow, I'm going to make my final year of High School one to remember. The key question that I need to answer is who am I? And what is my purpose in life? When I look at my life, I honestly don't know who I should be. Or what is my calling in life. I know once I have those questions answered I will be ok."

The next day, Allen goes to his job at Rick's Grocery Store. Where he has been a store clerk for two years. Allen walks into the breakroom to clock in for his shift as he is greeted by Mr. Jimmy, his manager. Mr. Jimmy says to him, "If it isn't one of my favorite employees how are you doing today, Allen?" Allen says, "You know what they say boss another day another dollar." "Yes, sir indeed, Kevin is in the back working on the truck with all the products that came. I want you to help him with that today." "Sounds good."

Kevin is Allen's favorite co-worker and one of his best friends. Allen views him as a big brother, he is three years older than Allen. He always give Allen the best advice. As the two have been working alongside one another for two years. He sees Allen walking to the back of the supply room. Kevin puts his hands up with excitement as he says, "Look who it is my boy Al coming through how you doing my boy?" He and Allen dap one another up. Allen says, "Doing great, it's time to make some money. How many pallets came through on the truck?" "About 16 pallets and some of the guys who worked on night shift got half of it done. We are going to finish the rest before the end of the day. So, let's get started, so Bossman don't be on us."

While stocking groceries, Kevin ask Allen about his plans after he graduates High School. "So, how's school going?" "It's going ok I'm getting acknowledge for my accomplishments in school. I was officially named valedictorian yesterday. Receiving offers from colleges, but I'm still trying to decide what I want to do in my life." "Well, I can tell you one thing it isn't working here. A lot of these people are going to be here for the rest of their lives. Not you though you are a gifted kid, you were designed to make a big impact on this earth. Don't get caught up in working job to job for good money. Go for what you truly want in life, life is too short to be living a lie. It's all about truly living, meaning living in the dream we see for ourselves." With the advice Kevin has given him, Allen starts thinking more about his skills and future. "I appreciated man you always keep it real with me. I just got to find my purpose."

While working, Allen gets approached by a beautiful girl who he knows very well. The beautiful girl walks up to him and says, "Hey Allen, how are you doing?" He gets excited and quickly turns around as he knows that elegant voice from a mile away. With a smile on his face he says, "Hey Shanice, I'm doing great. Can I help you find anything in the store?" "No thanks I'm just getting some stuff for a party I'm throwing tonight at my house. I would love for you to come join us it's going to be a fun time." Allen is shocked and flattered that he was invited to a party, especially by Shanice. "I would love to come I get off at five o'clock what time the party starts?" "It starts at nine you will love it. I want to see you there we need to start hanging out anyways." Allen is overjoyed and happy hearing her say they should hang out more is music to his ears. "I will be there, and I will bring my dance moves with me." Allen shows Shanice some of his dance moves. She starts laughing. "You are too funny I got to go I will see you later tonight."

After Shanice walks away, Kevin walks over to Allen and talks to him. He says, "I see you playboy doing your thing. She fine bro, you trying to make shawty your boo thing?" Allen reflects on his crush on Shanice. He says, "I been eyeing her since we were little kids. I just haven't found the courage to approach her. She's the girl I dream of being with, but I don't know if she would want me." "Why would you say that? You are a good dude, educated, a great actor, and can play the guitar very well. And being accepted in four colleges she would be a fool not to get with you." Allen tells Kevin and sadly reveals what he thinks of himself. "The reason why I think that is I'm not the most athletic guy. Even though I'm well known, most people in my school see me as a nerd, I don't know if she sees me the same way. If she gets with me, I want her to be proud of the guy I am, not ashamed of the person I am." Allen is 6-2 weighs around 170 pounds and has arms like a Slim Jim. "You got to gain some confidence in yourself and love who you are. Speaking of which, Ashley come here for a second."

Ashley is Kevin's and Allen's co-worker. She asks the guys, "What's going on what you guys want?" Kevin puts his hand on Allen's shoulders and says, "So our boy Allen has finally been invited to a party. And the person that invited him was his crush." Ashley is happy to hear this as she wants Allen to enjoy life. "It's about time you get out and have some fun in your life.

You only live life once. Is this the first party you will be going to?" Allen says, "This will be my first party in High School, I haven't been to a party since the 7th grade. I got to go since Shanice invited me, but I got to decide what I'm going to wear." Kevin says, "You got to wear something that stands out that shows off the true you." Ashley says, "You got this Allen just be yourself. If she doesn't like you for you forget about her." Allen decides he's going to be himself and decides to make a great appearance at the party.

After taking a nap after getting off work, Allen prepares for Shanice's party. While preparing for the party, Paul comes over to help him with his wardrobe. He looks at Allen's closet and is surprised by his clothing selection. Paul says, "My guy you got to go to the mall these outfits aren't cutting it. It's like something my dad would wear." Allen lowkey dresses like it's still 2010. He look at his clothes and says, "I don't dress that bad, but with what all the clothes I got. What would be the best thing for me to wear?" Paul looks in Allen's closet and picks out a shirt and pants for him. "I would go with the blue polo shirt and black skinny jeans it fits your style and personality. I also got some great news. My band has a gig, but we need a lead guitarist for our band. Was wondering would you join my band, and could you play for us next Saturday?"

Paul has a band called "The Believers" as they perform R&B and Rock music. Allen loves playing the guitar, he's been playing since he was a kid and writes music. This isn't Paul's first time inviting him to be in the band. However, since Paul does need a guitarist for his performance on Saturday, Allen decides to help his friend out. He is down to be a part of Paul's band, he just knows he must keep it a secret from his parents. As he knows they will be totally against it. Although he has incredible musical talent, he has never performed music in front of a crowd. He's taken part in a few stage plays during his time at Terry High School, but music is something far more personal, it's his safe haven. He only plays in front of those he feels truly close to. Every lyric he writes and every chord he strums is a reflection of his heart and soul. He cherishes his music deeply, guarding it with everything he has.

"I will be glad to join the band you know I always got your back. The only thing I'm nervous about is playing in front of a crowd. I feel like I would be sweating bullets." "First off, I'm glad to have you joining the band. You are the best guitar player I know and a gifted writer. You must come out of the shell you are living in. So why not come out your shell doing what you love. And doing it with your best friend." Allen must admit to himself that Paul has some good talking points. Even though he's a bit scared about how the performance might go he decides he's going to go for it. "I will do it just for you, but if I pee in my pants, it's your fault." Paul starts laughing. "You are going to be fine; you are the Prince to my Morris Day. We meet on Monday for rehearsal at 4 pm be there." "I appreciate the words of encouragement. How do I look in the polo?" He shows off his outfit for the party. Paul gives Allen his approval. "Looking like a million bucks my guy. Now let's go to the party."

Allen arrives at Shanice's party as Paul decided to join him. Almost everybody at their High School is at the party. Paul looks around the party and says to Allen, "She has her house pack even if you don't get with Shanice. You better get with some of these girls that's up in here." Allen says, "Well they got to like me first." "They will just be yourself."

Allen and Paul walk around the party as they are greeted by Shanice. She hugs Allen and says, "Allen, I'm so glad that you are here. And good to see you too Paul." Allen says, "Thank you for inviting me it means a lot." "You are welcome, you always be working; you need to have fun in your life. It's our senior year we must enjoy it while it lasts. Speaking of which, I want you to dance with me come on!" Shanice grabs Allen's hand and takes him to the dance floor. Allen dreamed of being with Shanice and now he is dancing with her. It looks like Allen's dream is slowly turning into a reality or so he thought, Shanice is impressed by his dance moves. "Allen, you got some great dance moves on you."

"What can I say I watch a lot of "Stomp the Yard" growing up. Call me Chris Brown Jr." Shanice starts laughing.

While dancing with Shanice, one of the guys her and Allen goes to school with interferes with their dancing moment. The guy says, "Excuse me bro as I cut in to dance with the lovely lady." The guy takes Shanice by the hand and dances with her. Instead of standing up to the guy, Allen walks away. Paul, who is watching the whole thing, slap his own forehead. He says to himself, "What's wrong with this boy?" Allen walks over to him; "You just going to let bro take your girl like that?" Shanice walks away from the guy and goes back to Allen. Allen says, "I am not stressing it, I can at least say I got a dance with the hottest girl in our school." Shanice taps Allen on the shoulder and says in his ear, "You are the only guy I want to dance with." Both Allen and Paul eyebrows rises. Allen is surprised that Shanice came back to him. "Well, let's dance the night away queen." They both go back dancing together as everyone is centered around them. Both of them are laughing and smiling at each other. Sparks are beginning to spark between the young scholars. Towards the end of the night, the DJ plays Ed Sheeran's "Thinking Out Loud". Allen and Shanice hold each other tightly as they slowly dance to the song. As Allen is holding Shanice, a part of him hopes that they both find love with each other. Little does he know Shanice is feeling the same way. She doesn't want to let go of him, if she had it her way she would be in his arms all night.

While Allen is bonding more with Shanice, Paul is drinking beer with some of the guys on the other side of the house. He enters multiple drinking challenges with the guys. He wins all of them, he has people cheering him on and women all around him. He feels like the biggest man there. After winning the last challenge he decides to do a cartwheel and a backflip. When he lands back on his feet he grabs his stomach. In a sorrow voice he says, "I don't feel so good. UGH!" Paul throws up in front of everyone. Blake looks at him throwing up. He says out loud to everyone, "The geek takes a leak down goes nerd! Down goes nerd!" A couple of the people at the party start laughing along with Blake.

One of Allen's classmates runs up to him and Shanice to tell them about Paul. He says, "Sorry to interrupt you guys, but Allen you need to come get Paul. He just threw up everywhere in the front yard. Allen and Shanice run straight to where Paul is at. He is laying down on the concrete as he is very weary and tired. Allen picks up Paul from the ground. Blake looks at him helping Paul from the ground. "There you go weak man, go ahead and pickup your geek man." Shanice says out loud to Blake, "Blake do us all a favor and shut the hell up!" Allen says to her, "I'm sorry about this Shanice, do you mind if I take him to your bathroom?

To get him cleaned up and then I will take him home." "Sure, thing let me show you where it at." Shanice takes Allen and Paul to her bathroom. "Thank you so much, again I apologize for the mess my friend caused." "It's cool don't stress accidents happen. Tonight was a fun night; you are great to be around. One thing I noticed is, I follow you on social media, but I don't have your phone number. Do you mind if I have it." Allen quickly gives his phone to her, so she can put her number in it. After she types her number in, she gives him her phone as he type his number in. Once he is done, he gives her phone back to her. "We're officially locked in thank you for inviting me. I had a great time tonight." "I'm glad that you enjoyed yourself, we are going to hangout again. Text me when you get home, both of you guys have a blessed night!"

When Shanice walks away, Paul whispers, "My job is completed." Allen laughs and says, "It definitely is you showed out tonight. You are preparing for college early." Paul laughs. "Hey, you got to have fun some time. I see you got the digits though my guy. I can tell she likes you just be patient and take things slow. In the meanwhile, from all the phone numbers I got I'm going to be hitting up Shonda, Donna, Rolanda, Dina, Tina, and Maria." Allen laughs. "Alright Playboy Paul we taking you back home sir. I'm going to spend the night at your spot to make sure you fully good. And so, your parents won't find out about this." "That's cool with me let's hit the road jack."

After arriving at Paul's house, Allen helps him go to bed and gives him a bottle of water. He pulls out an air mattress from Paul's closet and lays on it. Right before going to sleep, he texts Shanice, "That he got home safe." She texts back, "Perfect, thanks for coming I enjoyed our time together. Until next time Mr. Callahan (She sends him a wink-eyed emoji)." Allen smiles as he can't wait to see how things are going to go between him and Shanice.

The next morning, Allen is up early reading scriptures from a Bible app on his phone, while he is reading Paul wakes up. Paul wakes up a slight headache, he still is feeling the effects from his drinking last night." Allen says, "Rise and shine sleepyhead how are you feeling?" Paul says, "I feel like shit right now. What time it is?" "It's 8:30 AM." "Perfect I got time to prepare for church. You can wear one of my sport jackets and shirts also. My parents leave the house at 8:00 AM to go to my grandparents' house. My mom texted me to let me know she cooked breakfast for me and you. And our plates are in the oven." "That's perfect, I will eat breakfast then I will get ready."

When Allen and Paul walk into church, they are greeted by Allen's parents. Imani says to the boys, "Well hello guys, did you have a fun time last night?" Allen says, "We had a great time doing bible study last night mom." Al can tell Paul had fun last night by the way he looks. Paul is wearing dark sunglasses to hide his pink, tired eyes. Al says sarcastically, "I can tell son, Paul it looks like you just came from a party." Allen and Paul starts laughing. Paul says, "Oh Mr. Al, you're so funny. Well service has started let's find our seats." Everybody sits down and enjoy the wonderful service at church.

After the service is over with, Allen and Al goes to speak to his Uncle Dennis. Al and Dennis have been best friends for thirty years. Due to the tumultuous relationship Al had with his biological father and losing his mother when he was thirteen, Dennis's father Bill and his mother Jill adopted him when he was sixteen. Bill was the pastor of Mount Reunion Baptist Church for thirty years. When he passed away last year, Dennis became the pastor of the church. The Callahan family is proud to see Dennis's progression as a pastor. Al hugs Dennis and sarcastically says, "Pastor that was a great sermon you preached today. Pops and mom would be proud." Pastor Dennis says, "Appreciated brother, that means a lot coming from you. Mr. Allen how you been doing?" Allen says, "Been doing great just can't wait till my final year of school to be over with." "What is your plan once you graduate?" Before Allen gives an answer, Al interjects. "Well Allen is getting a lot of scholarship offers from a lot of colleges. So, he is going to be going to a fine college in a few months."

Allen's Dad wants him to go to college. While Allen is still trying to find out what he wants to do in life. His Uncle Dennis gives him some great advice. "Well, I will give you this advice Allen. Follow the footsteps, GOD provides for you. And all things that is guaranteed for you will come in your path. I believe and know you will do great things nephew." Allen takes his uncle's advice to heart. "Appreciated Uncle Dennis, everything will work itself out."

After church, Allen has a one-on-one conversation with his Father back at their house. Al tosses some mail towards him. He says, "I know while you were at Paul's house you had got some mail." Allen opens the letter and it's a scholarship offer from his parents' alma mater Seward University. He takes it as him just getting another scholarship offer. However, he fakes an exciting reaction as he knows what this moment means to his father. Allen says in an exciting voice, "Wow a scholarship offer from Seward University me and you been talking about this since I was a little kid. Our dreams are turning into a reality old man." "I'm so proud of you son, I been dreaming of this since the day you were born." Even though, Al is very excited for his son. Allen is still unsure about what he wants to do in his life.

The next day at school it's announced that prom season is around the corner. Principal Davenport calls Allen into his office to talk about prom season. Allen heads to the principal's office as he wonders why he is being called to the office. He walks into the office. Principal Davenport, who is sitting at his desk says, "Well if it isn't Mr. Valedictorian how are you doing sir?" Allen says, "I'm doing great sir, I'm not in trouble or anything am I?" Principal Davenport laughs and flaps his hand. "Not at all, I wanted to talk to you about Prom coming up. Have you thought about signing up for Prom King?" Allen starts laughing as he thinks of the idea of him being Prom King. "Sir look at me who will vote for me as Prom King. I'm no Michael B. Jordan; I'm more like Carlton Banks compared to all the other guys here." "You can't be so down on yourself. You are the smartest kid in this school. You are very well-mannered and a gentleman. What makes you think you are not good enough to be Prom King?"

Allen gives his opinion on why he feel like he wouldn't be the best candidate. "Granted I am an intelligent person, but my fellow peers don't see me as a powerful influencer. The athletes and jocks is who everybody looks up to." Principal Davenport reassures Allen he's someone that people can look up to. "I understand your point, but you can change that. You can have young people looking up to great scholar students like yourself. A wise man once said don't be of the world, be the man that can influence the world with his own mind. In life, we are told that we need to participate in everything the world wants us to do. But why not just be ourselves and inspire people with our own personality. And don't care what anybody has got to say. Do you believe in GOD?" "Yes, I do." "So why not love and be the person he designed you to be."

This has Allen thinking with a new mindset that instead of following the crowd, he can be the leader of his own crowd. He loves who he is, he shouldn't care what people think of him. Because he knows his worth and value. "Thank you for your advice it has got me thinking with a new perspective in mind. And I will sign up for Prom King, but I'm scared to be super outspoken." "Just be confident on who you are and showcase everything that is inside of you. Plus, I'm going to help you out anyway I can. Always love the person that you see when you look in the mirror, because that young man is a superstar." The advice Principal Davenport has given Allen has helped build his confidence. And has helped him not to worry about what anyone has to say about him. From now on, he's going to showcase all the greatness that GOD has instilled in him. "Thank you, Principal Davenport, I greatly appreciated."

After talking to Principal Davenport, Allen goes up to the signup sheet in the middle of the hallway to sign up for prom king. Seeing him sign his name on the sheet leaves some of the students in the hallway stunned. Blake is shocked as he sees Allen signing up for prom king. He walks over to the signup sheet and says, "What in the Revenge of the Nerds is going on here?" He taps on the signup sheet with his finger. "Sir, this is a paper to sign up for Prom King. Not to sign up for the chess club." Allen doesn't back down to Blake and says, "Dude I got eyes and common sense which is something you lack." All the students make a woah sound as Allen makes his statement. Blake is stunned to see Allen respond back. "Okay Mr. Geek, I'm going to be prepared for you."

After his confrontation with Blake in front of the whole school, Allen goes to talk to Paul. Paul looks at him, stunned as he is surprised and proud to see him standing up for himself. He asks, "What has happened to you? It's like you turned badass overnight." Allen says, "What can I say I have been giving a new light. And I'm just living in it. I was advised by Principal Davenport to run for Prom King. At first, I was against it, but Mr. Davenport made me realize I can be an inspiration to our fellow students. By just being myself and not trying to be like everybody else. I can help inspire people that is scared to be themselves." "I love this new energy you have about yourself. I hope you bring this wonderful spirit towards the band today." "I'm not Van Halen, but I plan on impressing them with my great guitar skills. Is everyone in the band cool people?" Paul starts laughing. "You will find out how they are."

After talking to Paul, Allen heads to class. While in his Creative Writing Class, he talks to his literature teacher, Ms.

Maggie, about his valedictorian speech. Allen says to her, "I want my speech to be one that is impactful and inspirational. What is the best way to do that?" Ms. Maggie gives Allen great insight into how to make the speech the way he wants it to be. She says, "It's simple in the speech showcase the lessons you learned during your years of schooling. And speak on how it made you into the person you are. And how you and your fellow classmates should utilize what you all learned during your twelve years of school and how to apply it to your new chapter in life. We are going to go over this together up until graduation I got you." Trying to write this speech makes Allen realize he needs to do self-reflecting about his own life.

After school is over with, Allen heads straight to Paul's house for rehearsal. Paul says, "Yo, you made it everybody this is Allen. He will be the new lead guitarist for our band. Allen, this is Joe and Claudia. Allen is the best guitar player I know, and he is one hell of a writer." The rest of Paul's band stares at Allen. In Allen's mind he's not nervous, he just can't wait for the opportunity to play his guitar for the band. Joe who plays drums and produces music for the group says, "Let's see what you got Allen." Allen pulls out his guitar and plays Poison's "Every Rose has it Thorn" for three minutes.

After Allen gets done playing, he gets a standing ovation from everybody except for Claudia. Paul asks the members of the band. "So, what you guys think about my boy?" Joe says, "Dude you are a freaking rockstar." Claudia says in a snarky voice, "He's ok let see how he does in front of a crowd." Allen takes it as a challenge. He says, "I can show you way better than this." Claudia starts laughing. "You're funny." Allen gets to know more about his new bandmates. "Where are you guys from and how you know Paul?" Joe, who produces songs for the group and plays bass guitar for the band says, "We have known Paul for a few years. We all met one another at a Kid Cudi concert years back, ever since then we have been friends. We decided to create our own band last year called The Believers. Paul is the best keyboard player I know, and I am on the drums." Allen points at Claudia. "So, I'm guessing you are the singer of the group?" "You are correct, I like to call myself the muse of the group. I write majority of the songs for the group. Paul mentioned you are a songwriter. So, I would like to link up with you to write some music." "We will most definitely do that. About to say do you guys do a specific genre?" Paul says, "We can do any genre that's how great we are. The main genre we do is R&B and Rock. The song we have plan on performing Saturday is going to be Nivea's "Complicated". Joe says, "It will show off Claudia vocals and I believe it will show off your great guitar skills." Paul says, "Speaking of which let's go ahead and practice."

The band practices and hang out for one hour. Claudia says goodbye to Allen after practice is over with. She says, "Goodbye Allen can't wait to see what you got on Saturday." After practice ends Paul talks to Allen one on one. He asks, "So what do you think about everybody?" Allen says, "They are very chill and cool people. I like the both of them, they have their own personalities. But what's good with Claudia? It seems like she was on my case in there." Paul laughs. "Claudia is a bit feisty, but she just testing you out. I forgot to tell you we do get paid for our gigs. We get $200 dollars a gig, we split that money so all of us get $50 dollars each." Allen loves the sound of this as he will be making extra money. "That sounds good getting extra money in my pocket. Where do you guys play at?" "We play at PJ's Lounge it's a spot where everybody in town hangs out at. It's not a dangerous place it's a safe place to go to. I think you will love the atmosphere of the place. I can't wait to see what you got plan for Prom." Right now, Allen has nothing planned for Prom. "I got to plan everything out, but I hope I do win Prom King."

After returning home, Allen has dinner with his family. While eating dinner, Allen announces to his family that he is running for Prom King. His family is surprised by this news. Jalean starts laughing and says, "And I'm running for president." Al and Imani laughs after Jalean says that. Allen then says in a serious tone, "No I'm serious I'm running for Prom King." Imani is happy to hear that her son is running for Prom King. She says, "Son that's amazing I'm proud of you. Like I always tell you, you can do anything you put your mind to." While Allen's mother is supportive, Allen's Father has a very stern look on his face. Al says to him, "It's good to participate in school activities but remember education first son." "Yes Father."

Before going to sleep, Allen write down his plan for the next few months. He writes, "Within these next few months I feel like I'm going to transform into a new person. With me running for Prom King I hope I can be an inspiration to shy and timid people like myself. Also, I hope to find my purpose in life, I can't wait until I find it. Whatever this road takes me to, I pray it takes me to a great destination that leads me to my destiny."

The next day at school, Allen is approached at his locker to be the lead actor in a play by Shanice. She says to him, "Hey Allen, how are you doing?" Allen says, "I'm doing good I must say you are looking very beautiful today." "Appreciated me and everybody in the drama club would love for you to be the lead actor in the Dirty Dancing play. It's about time you have a leading role in a play. You are the best actor I've ever acted with. Plus, we are doing a play that involves dancing. Seeing the way you dance at my party, I believe you will be a great leading man for us. So, tell me what you think?" Allen is excited about this opportunity as other plays he has played in, he has been a supporting character.

He is excited to finally be cast as a main role in a play. Allen happily accepts Shanice's offer. "Well Shanice lets have the time of our lives. I will be happy to accept the leading role. Who will be the leading lady in the play?" Shanice spins around and points to herself. "Yours truly, we will meet up on Monday for rehearsal see you around Allen. And congratulations on signing up for Prom King." Shanice hugs Allen and walks away as Allen is left smiling from ear to ear. First, signing up for Prom King and now getting a lead role in a play, it's like he's living in a dream right now.

After class ends Allen goes to his job. While stocking groceries, he and Kevin talk to one another. Kevin asks, "Playboy Allen what you been up to?" How was that party you went to?" Allen starts laughing and says, "A lot of stuff has happened since Saturday. First with the party it went well. I had a great time with Shanice, me and her danced with each other the whole night, it was magical. When me and her were looking at each other eye-to-eye and holding onto each other, it felt like it was just me and her out there. And I got her phone number. I hope things prosper between me and her." Kevin is happy to hear this as he hoped that Allen would get closer to Shanice. "Player, Player, I see you my boy. Did you spend most of the time at the party with her?" "Yes, I did even when another guy stepped to her, she left him behind and came looking for me." "Man, she likes you bro, you are in there." "With that being said, how should I proceed with things?" "Just take things slow to tell if she heavily interested in you, if she truly likes you for who you are, she is going to want to get to know you more. As she want the vibe that you have about yourself around her."

"That's good to know I appreciated it. I also decided to join Paul's band. They needed a lead guitarist, so I decided to help them out." Kevin is happy to hear Allen showing off his talents. "It's about time you start using your musical talents. You can play the hell out of a guitar. When do you have your first gig?" "This Saturday at PJ's Lounge at 9 pm. I would love for you to be there." "Say less, I will there brodie." "Thank you, you are one of my biggest supporters thank you for always being there for me." Kevin pats Allen on the back. "No problem, I know how it is I wished I had a big brother or a mentor to look up to when I was growing up. You are like a little brother of mine; I'm forever going to lookout for you." "Appreciated seriously, I'm also running for Prom King and I'm about to play a leading role in a play at my school." Kevin leans back smiling as his homeboy is doing big things. "You done became a superstar overnight I'm proud of you. You are stepping into a new stage in your life. Don't matter what happens, always remember to stay true to who you are. Now let's get to work before Bossman come around the corner complaining."

While working the guys start freestyling. Kevin raps, "At the job trying to make this paper, so I can ball out like I'm playing for the Lakers." Allen raps, "I'm on the grind trying to shine manifesting in the future. Stocking Groceries, but me and Kev going to be stacking money in a few." "The ladies going to start acting brand new, still going to be the same old G we are one of few that use the brain to maintain progress." "On the road to victory we don't accept defeat the only words we are accepting congratulations you made it." "You're the Talib Kweli to my Mos Def."

As the guys get done rapping, a girl with black hair wearing a Sade black tee and gray sweatpants with white shoes on starts clapping her hands in their direction. She says to both guys, "I must say you guys got some bars it's like I was listening to a Black Star album." Allen is surprised to see Claudia at the store. He says, "Claudia, what are you doing here for?" "Well first I needed to get some stuff for my apartment. Second, I didn't give you my phone number." Kevin sees Claudia talking as he wonders whose the beautiful girl Allen is talking to. He says, "Sorry to interrupt, but Allen who is this beautiful lady that is in our presence?" Allen introduces Kevin to Claudia. "This is Claudia she is my fellow bandmate; she's the lead vocalist in Paul's band. Claudia this is my good friend Kevin." Kevin shakes Claudia's hand. "Nice meeting you queen." Claudia is flattered by Kevin's charm. "It's nice meeting you to king, we might need you on a song, I heard you spitting some fire bars earlier." Kevin smiles. "Well, I am true to this, not new to this plus whenever I'm around someone that is fascinating like yourself, I get encouraged to show off my skills." Kevin and Claudia stare and smile at each other for a second, as Allen can see the chemistry between them. "I love it follow me on IG; I would love to talk to you so more." Kevin follows Claudia on Instagram, and she automatically follows him back. "That's perfect where I will give you guys some space to talk. It was most definitely an honor and privilege meeting you Ms. Claudia." "Likewise, Mr. Kevin."

Kevin walks away as Allen and Claudia talk among themselves. "I see my boy lowkey got you blushing over here?" Claudia starts laughing. "No! not one bit sir. On the real though, I just want to connect with you artist to artist. I get a good vibe from you, I believe you are a great addition to the group." Hearing this from Claudia makes Allen feel great. It makes him feel like he's important to the band. "I appreciate that it means a lot to me, we are going to make great music together. Let me give you my phone number." Allen and Claudia exchange phone numbers. "Thank you, Allen, well I'm not going to hold you have a nice day." "You to Claudia."

After talking to Claudia, Allen goes back to talking to Kevin. Allen walks over to him as he is looking at Allen with a smirk on his face. "What's up with that smirk on your face?" "Claudia is one fine lady, them brown eyes of hers is what got me smiling. It's good though she is trying to connect with you, that will help create better chemistry in your group. I forgot to ask how do your parents feel about you being in a band?" Allen's parents don't know anything about him joining Paul's band and he wants to keep it that way. His parents doesn't use any social media, so he doesn't have to worry about them discovering him performing on the internet. "They don't know nothing about it. My mom, I know she would be cool with it. Although with my dad, I know he would not like it. He would be like Allen you wasting your life away being in a band." "Your Dad seems like a very strict person." Even though Allen's Dad is strict with him he knows his father just wants the best for him. "He's really not, but his main thing is he want me and my brother to get a job that pays well." "I'm going to give you this advice. Not telling you to disobey your parents, but don't live your life with regret. Go for everything you want in life. Life is too short, to not be the person you want to be." Allen takes Kevin's advice to heart.

It's Thursday afternoon while in Gym class, Allen is invited to play basketball with the fellas. Rick, one of Allen's classmates goes over to him and asks, "Allen you want to play ball with us?" This stuns Allen as he has never been invited to play basketball with the fellas. Even though he might not be the best basketball player he decides to accept the offer. Allen says, "Sure I'm not the best, but I will go for it." Allen plays 5 on 5 with his classmates. He is guarded by Blake. Blake holds the basketball and says, "This game is all about using your body not your mind Steve Urkel." He shoves the ball at Allen. Rick yells out, "Let's play ball guys!"

The guys start playing and Allen gets to a slow start. Fisher one of Allen's teammates says, "Little boy you shooting like a little shrimp." Blake says out loud, "I told your he can't play." Some of the guys start laughing at Allen. This starts lowering Allen's self-esteem. When negative thoughts start clouding his mind he gets motivation from a teammate. Rick pulls Allen to the side and says, "Forget what they are saying about you and forget what Blake said. You are the man always know that and don't hold back show everyone in here who you are."

After the pep talk, Allen's mind and body is uplifted. Once he starts back playing, Allen starts hooping like he is Kyrie Irving. As he dazzles the crowd with his moves, Blake starts getting jealous of him. As Allen goes for a layup he is clotheslined by Blake in mid-air. Everyone in the gym stops what they are doing after seeing the clothesline. After hitting him in mid-air, Blake goes over to Allen who is laying on the ground and says to him, "You must go in stronger than that Slim Jim. Allen gets up and pushes Blake. Students come up closer after seeing the push as they feel a fight is about to happen. He yells at Blake and says, "What the hell is wrong with you?" Blake starts pushing Allen and laughing at him. "What you going to do about it?" Allen starts pushing back which leads to Blake trying to hit him. Allen ducks his big fist. When he comes back up, he punches Blake with full force knocking him out. All the students in the gym make a woah sound. Allen is stunned by what he has done. "Oh shit, I can't believe I did that." With Allen knocking Blake out what will be his consequences?

Chapter 2: Breaking Out

After Allen and Blake fight, they are both escorted to the principal's office. Allen is holding his fist with some ice as it hurts from punching Blake. While Blake has a bruised eye, Principal Davenport tries to get to the bottom of how this fight happened. He asks the guys, "Ok who started the fight?" Allen says, "We was playing basketball, and I went for a layup. And then Blake clotheslined me in mid-air. And when I got up, I pushed him. That's how the fight started." "Blake why did you clothesline Allen in midair?" Blake gives an excuse and says, "I was moving too fast, I was doing my best to make sure he didn't get a basket." "Well according to students in the gym you was laughing at him when he fell to the ground. In all honesty, I would've done the same thing Allen did. Blake, I am suspending you for two days." Blake gets upset and jumps up from his chair. "Brent Faiyaz over here the one that knocked me out. He needs to be suspended also!" "Blake go home!"

After Blake leaves the Office, Principal Davenport talks to Allen. "Off the record, I do see why you did what you did. Although you did knock him out, his eye looks like a blueberry. I'm going to have to suspend you for one day. I'm against violence, but I'm proud of you for standing up for yourself. I feel like you are becoming the person you were destined to be. Next time, when something like that transpires don't result in violence.

Your Mom is outside waiting for you. See you on Monday, Mike Tyson."

As Allen walks outside of the school, he sees his mom who has an unpleasant look on her face. He says in a sad voice, "Mom." Imani says in a firm voice, "Get in your car Allen and follow me home!" On the car ride home, Allen wonders what his parents will do to him.

After getting home Imani talks to Allen about his fight. "Principal Davenport told me what happened, I understand you was frustrated after you fell, but you can't be getting into fights. You have a lot of scholarship offers, don't mess that up over a fool. Mr. Davenport said it won't mess up your scholarship offers, but when something like that happens, you can't result to violence." Allen completely understands he should've walked away. He got caught up in the moment, he hopes his mother doesn't tell his Father what happened. "I know Mom, I'm sorry I lost my cool for a moment. You are not going to tell Dad about this, are you? Because he would lose his mind." Allen's Mother decides not to tell Allen's Father, as she believe Allen has learned his lesson. "I don't have plan on telling your father what happened. We will just say that they gave you a day off." Allen is relieved that his mother isn't going to tell his father what happened. "Thank you, Mom, I greatly appreciate it, I got to prepare for work tonight. I'm going to go and take a nap."

After waking up from his nap, Allen gets a call from Paul. He answers, "What's good Paul?" Paul is surprised just like everyone at school that Allen knocked out Blake. He says, "I can't believe you knocked out Blake. The whole school is talking about it. If you wasn't famous before you are now. I heard Blake got suspended did they suspend you also?" "Yeah, I got suspended for one day. I just can't go straight to violence when something like that happen. I lost my cool bro." "I bet it felt good knocking him out." Allen did feel good when he knocked out Blake. Blake always made him feel small so to knock him out made him feel powerful. "I'm not going to lie it felt super good. I been waiting to do that for the longest time." "Well, the bright side of this is you can practice with us tomorrow to prepare for our performance on Saturday." "What time do you want us to meet?" "We will meet up at 12 noon tomorrow, I usually go to lunch around that time." "Bet I will see you then."

After getting done talking with Paul, Allen eats dinner with his family. Al asks Allen, "So Allen how was school today?" Allen is nervous about how he will answer his dad's question. He says, "It went well I played basketball with some of the guys. I had to show off that jumper you taught me." Al smiles and laughs. "If you did that, I know you did great. Granted, you can't do it like your old man. I'm proud of you son just don't do anything foolish." "Yes sir."

After dinner, Allen goes straight to work and meets with his manager. He says, "Hey, Mr. Jimmy, you wanted to see me?" Mr. Jimmy starts smiling at Allen and says, "Yes, I did, please have a seat. I'm proud of the way you have been working for us. Everybody here loves you, which is why I want to promote you. I want you to be the co-supervisor of the stock crew. And the promotion comes with a $4 dollar raise to your hourly pay."

Allen is ecstatic to be offered a job promotion. He has been working for the company for two years and he finally got a promotion. "Thank you so much! This is one great surprise I wasn't expecting. I'm curious about being a co-supervisor who will be supervisor alongside me. Kevin walks into the room and says, "You are looking at him." Allen smiles and hugs Kevin as the two friends are moving on up together. "We are a dynamic duo like Kobe and Shaq." Mr. Jimmy smiles proudly at the guys. "You two are the best stockers here. Grateful to have you guys here, now get to work."

The guys start working and talks about their lives. Allen says, "I'm happy for you Kev, I know this means a lot to you." Kevin responds with tears in his eyes, "It's something I wasn't expecting I thank GOD for blessing me. I'm one step closer to getting a house with this promotion. I'm just glad I'm getting my recognition. And I'm grateful to have you by my side, little bro. So how was school today?" Allen knows Kevin will be intrigued by how his day went. "Well, I ended up getting suspended today." Kevin is shocked by the news as he knows Allen isn't a bad kid. "You suspended what did you do?" "I knocked out this jerk name Blake at my school. He clotheslined me in mid-air while I was going up for a layup while playing basketball and then we started pushing each other. He swung at me first he missed. Then I swung and connected." Kevin leans back as he has his hand over his mouth. "Look at you Jake Paul Jr, I hate that you got suspended. Although I'm glad you finally showing people you not a person to be messed with." "I let my anger get the best of me, but that punch felt good. Let's forget about that you still coming to my gig this Saturday?" "I wouldn't miss it bro, now let get all of this product unloaded."

After getting off work early in the morning, Allen runs into a classmate while walking to his car. The classmate yells out his name. He turns around and sees the person yelling out his name is Shanice. Allen says, "Shanice it's so great to see you. You here to get some groceries?" She responds, "Yeah, I had plan on getting some groceries. I'm also about to go to Waffle House and eat breakfast. Do you care to join me?" Allen doesn't hesitate to answer. "I will definitely love to join you."

Allen and Shanice arrives at Waffle House. Shanice wants to know how Allen is doing after the fight. She says, "So I heard what happened yesterday, how are you feeling?" Allen says, "I feel a lot better, I let a naïve person separate me from the person that I am. The good thing about the situation is I get a day off because of it." Shanice starts laughing. "At least you can bring light to a dark situation." "I hope the situation doesn't make you look at me differently." "It doesn't it just shows you are somebody that stand up for themselves. I have a lot of respect for people that don't let anyone run over them. So, what you got plan on doing since you don't have to go to school?" "I'm supposed to go to practice with my band today." Shanice's eyebrows rises hearing that Allen is in a band. "I didn't know you was a part of a band. What is your role in the band?" "I'm the lead guitarist in it, but I really know how to do anything when it comes to music. I guess you can say, I'm a musical genius." This has Shanice more interested in Allen. "So that mean you can sing also?" Allen starts laughing and smiling from ear to ear. "Well, I'm no Luther Vandross." Shanice with her dimples popping says in a sweet voice, "Sing something for me." Even though Allen is usually well-reserved he decides to sing for Shanice. "You putting me on the spot, I think I can do something."

Allen starts singing Joe "I Wanna Know". His voice woos Shanice as her eyes starts sparkling. She puts her hand over her heart as she is moved by Allen's singing. "I didn't know you could sing so well. You are a man that has many hidden talents." "What can I say I was bless with many great gifts. You know, me and my band are performing tomorrow at 6 PM at PJ's Lounge. Would love for you to come see us perform." Shanice is excited about the invitation as she really wants to see Allen perform. "I would love to see you rock the stage; I will be there cheering you on." Allen is excited that Shanice will be coming to see him perform tomorrow. "Great can't wait to see you there." "Well, I got to go to school, see you later Rockstar." Shanice gives Allen a kiss on the cheek and walks out of the restaurant. Allen is ecstatic that Shanice will be at his show and that she gave him a kiss.

When Allen gets back home, he is greeted by his father. Who is happy to see him. Al says, "Son, I got some great news, you have been invited to go to two college tours. And the first visit is to my alma mater Seward University next weekend. We are going to make this a father-son road trip. Other than me acting like a little girl over the news how are you doing?" Allen says, "I been doing good, I just been promoted as co-supervisor for my stock crew." Al is proud that his son is making moves. "My boy I'm so proud of you, you are prospering like a rose in a garden. I know this is only just the beginning. Did you get a pay raise with your promotion?" "I sure did I'm getting paid four dollars more." Al high fives his son. "Let's go boy! That's my son! You be doing what I taught you? On keeping money in your checking account only for bills and expenses like Gas and eating out. And the rest of your money you put in your savings account." "Yes pops, I got a good amount saved up." "I am glad to hear that. What else has been going on?" "I just joined the Dirty Dancing play at my school. I am playing the lead character." Al isn't a big fan of his son doing theater arts. Although he knows how much his son always wanted to land a lead role in a play. "That is so delightful to hear son. You're doing great things, remember to stay focused on what truly matters. I'm headed to work have a great day son."

After talking to his dad, Allen goes to sleep. After taking a long nap, Allen prepares for practice with his band. He arrives at Paul's house he is greeted by Claudia. She says to him, "Are you ready to rock out tomorrow?" He responds, "I'm a bit nervous performing, but I'm prepared to rock out the crowd." Paul sees Allen and yells out, "Gervonta Davis! I mean Allen my brother how are you doing?" "I been doing good ready to rock out how long will practice be?" "At least an hour or two let's go ahead and get started."

The guys have excellent practice for two hours. Paul says, "You guys did an amazing job we are going to rock out tomorrow. Allen what you plan on doing for the rest of the day?" "Well, I would try to hang out with you, but I know you got to go back to school." As Paul and Allen is talking, Claudia steps into the conversation. "Allen if you want to you can hang out with me for the rest of the day." "I will be glad to hang out with you."

Allen and Claudia go to a Chinese Restaurant downtown for lunch and have a lengthy conversation. Claudia says, "So, word on the street is you knocking people out. Allen laughs and says, "In the famous words of James Brown papa don't take no mess." Claudia laughs at Allen's joke. "All jokes aside I just learned in life you have to standup for yourself. I done let people push me around too much." "I guess that goes for me to?" Allen laughs. "Well, I know you be joking with me, with the small jabs you throw." "I was joking with you when we first met. I know Paul told me you could sing and play instruments before we met. Why do you seem scared to perform in front of an audience though?" Allen loves playing music, but he is scared the crowd won't be accepting of his music. "What happens if the person in the audience don't like me? What will be the best advice you can give me for that?" "Believe in your talent and know that you are great no matter what anyone has to say. The words that you sing and the sounds coming from the instrument you play can save someone's life."

Allen is grateful for Claudia's advice and at the same time he wants to know more about her. "Thank you for the advice. Since you are asking me 21 questions tell me what got you into music?" Claudia decides to open up to Allen. "I been in music all my life it's where I run to when I'm happy or sad. I started getting into music when I was 5, my parents put me in piano class. Ever since then I have been in love with it." "What's your favorite song?" "I have a lot of favorite songs; I will say my favorite is India Arie's "Get It Together". I'm a huge fan of neo-soul anything that has great rhythm and melodies always bring comfort to my soul. To me music is somewhat like a doctor, it heals people from broken places. And it enlightens the soul where it is vulnerable at."

Hearing Claudia talking about her love of music leaves Allen in awe of her. He wants to know more about her. "I'm curious tell me your life story Claudia." Once he says that she takes a glance out of the window. Her life story is something that is very personal to her. She can tell Allen is a good person that truly cares about people. Because of that she don't mind talking about her life story to him. "Since you want to know about my life come with me to the park across the street." "I got all day so no problem."

Allen and Claudia go to the park and walk around. Claudia tells Allen her life story. "So, I'm not from Macon, Georgia like the rest of you guys. I'm from Miami, Florida, born and raised. I was raised by my parents, I'm the youngest out of two children. It was just me and my sister. I had the perfect childhood up until I was 14. I lost my dad in a car accident; my life went downhill from there. I started going through depression and even thought about suicide at one point. Through all the turmoil, music was my saving grace. I graduated in the top 15 of my class. When I graduated, I wanted a change of scenery, so with my mom's blessing I decided to move to Macon, Georgia. I am staying in an apartment by myself; I'm a manager at Grant's shoe store down here. I decided to follow where my mind and heart lead me to. So that's why I'm down here." Allen is surprised and finds it fascinating that Claudia followed her dreams. "I got to say it's beautiful hearing the journey of your life. And that you chose to follow what you felt in your heart to do. I am curious about what made you fully open to me about your life? That was some deep stuff you shared with me." Claudia stops walking and looks directly at Allen. "It's because of the vibe I get from you. You have a caring personality. Plus, the guys know my story also, I thought you should know since you are our new bandmate now. Anytime you have a question or just want to talk I don't mind listening." "I appreciated I will say next time we meet up we should have a writing and jam session." "I would love that well I will see you tomorrow rockstar." Allen and Claudia hug one another as they have gotten closer with each other.

After hanging out with Claudia, Allen goes back to his house and watches Purple Rain. In his mind he is going to rock the stage like he is Prince tomorrow night.

It's Saturday evening, it's time for Allen to head to PJ's Lounge for rehearsal. As he goes to rehearsal his dad stops him.

Al sees his son with a guitar around his back and is curious about where he is going. He says, "Son, I see you have your guitar with you where are you headed to?" Allen says, "Me and Paul are going to have a jam session at his house. You already know I learn from the best so I'm going to rock out tonight. You never know I could be one of the greatest artists in music history." Al smiles and laughs. "I taught you well son you play the guitar better than most, but always remember your poppa is the best. Just don't get caught up in it like I did. It's all for fun, but it's nothing you can make a true career out of. And you are going to be one of the greatest architects of all time. I love you son be safe and don't have too much fun.

After talking to his dad, Allen goes straight to PJ's Lounge. As he arrives the whole band is excited to see him. Paul sees Allen walking in the lounge and says, "Here he comes." He gives him a hug. "Mr. Rockstar are you ready to rock out tonight?" Allen is sweating bullets as he is thinking about being on stage. He says, "I'm nervous bro what happens if the crowd doesn't like me?" The members of the band calms Allen down. Joe says, "Buddy you must chill relax you play some of the best music I ever heard. If people don't like your music something is wrong with their ears. Enjoy the moment of just performing, we are going to amaze the crowd tonight." Claudia says, "Allen you are one of the best guitarists I ever heard. Remember to believe in your abilities and your talents." Paul says, "Remember what we discuss last week you are the Prince to my Morris Day. We shall be great, and we shall show these people who The Believers are. Now let's get to rehearsing guys."

The band practices for 30 minutes. After rehearsing the band wait for their name to be called for an hour. Allen is getting tired of waiting for the band to be called. He asks his fellow bandmates, "Do you guys always have to wait this long for your name to be called?" Joe says to him, "Welcome to the performing life rookie." Claudia says, "We are usually the last ones to perform so we be in the back chilling." Paul says, "Like my mother always tell me the best is saved for last." Claudia starts singing "A Thousand Miles" by Vanessa Carlton. Paul makes sound effects with his voice. Allen starts playing his guitar while Joe starts beating on the wall. The guys have a full out jam session before their performance.

While still waiting, Allen takes a lookout in the crowd and sees there is a whole bunch of people out there. Allen gets nervous and his stomach starts hurting. He says, "I don't feel so well." He runs straight to the bathroom and starts throwing up. In Allen's mind he wonders whether he should go out there or not. He knows he is great at playing the guitar but is scared to make a mistake. And he doesn't want to be embarrassed in front of the crowd.

As he is cleaning himself up from throwing up, an unexpected guest steps into the bathroom to check up on him. He is surprised and says to them, "Shanice what are you doing here?" She says, "Well the time I walked in the lounge, I saw you running back here. I wanted to make sure you were fine. With what I see in the toilet you don't seem to be." "I'm just so nervous this is the first time I done ever played music in front of a crowd before." Shanice leans down to where Allen is at and holds his hands. "Listen to me you are great at what you do. If you wasn't you wouldn't have the opportunity that you have right now. This is just like the stage plays we do together, you are showing the talent you have been blessed with. I believe in you and I know you're going to do well. You can inspire people with your talent Allen, don't let that go to waste. It's time for me to know who Allen Callahan is."

With the advice Shanice has given him, Allen is motivated to show off his skills. "I'm acting like a wimp, but you are right it's time for me to show off my talents." Shanice puts her arm around Allen and holds his hand. "And I am right by your side; I will be cheering you on in the crowd. Now clean yourself up and get ready, you got this."

After cleaning himself up, Allen steps out of his shell and is ready to rock out the crowd. He walks towards the band and says, "Your ready to blow this people away." Paul looks at Allen and can tell he's ready for his moment to shine. He says, "Hell, yeah let's do the damn thing." As the guys walk from backstage the host of the event introduces them to the crowd. "Ladies and gentlemen, I will love to introduce you to The Believers."

As Allen steps on the stage, he looks into the crowd, and he sees Kevin. The main person he notices is Shanice, which gets him excited. Seeing Shanice at his performance gives him a lot of confidence. In his mind he must put on a great show for everybody. Claudia does an introduction for the crowd. She says to the crowd, "How's everybody doing tonight?" The crowd cheers heavily and says, "Good!" "Great to hear we love you guys; I would love to introduce our new guitarist, Allen; he is the most phenomenal guitarist I know. He is going to have you guys in awe." Claudia looks back at the band. "With that being said, let's rock out band. Claudia starts singing Nivea's "Complicated". As Paul starts playing on the keyboard, Allen starts playing the guitar. He looks at Claudia while she is singing; her voice bring butterflies to everyone's soul in the building. While he is playing, he looks at the crowd and sees the smile on everybody's faces. This brings so much excitement to Allen. As Claudia sings the last verse of the song it's time for his guitar solo part. As Allen's part comes, he goes to the front of the stage and lets loose on the guitar. The riff and the melody from his guitar has the crowd boosted up. In Allen's mind, he's no longer scared. He says in his mind I'm going to show these people what I'm made of. Allen's guitar solo lasts one minute, but within that minute he amazes the crowd with his talents. It's almost like listening to a guitar singing like Celine Dion. After his solo, Claudia gets close to Allen and sings the hook of the song. Allen and Claudia have a great connection on stage. From the view on stage, you would think of them both as a younger version of Sade and Stuart Matthewman together.

After the performance, the band gets a round of applause. Kevin yells out, "Allen you a bad boy!" Shanice yells out, "You go Allen!" All the shyness that Allen has had before has drifted away from his body and mind. After the performance the band goes backstage and celebrate. Paul hugs Allen and says, "Bro you did amazing on stage today." Joe says, "Them riffs from your guitar gave me chills man. You got something man I don't care what nobody says never put that guitar down." Claudia hugs Allen from behind and says, "You are something special." Allen turns around and says, "Thank you I can honestly get use to this." After being on stage, Allen has grown a big interest and passion in music.

The guys go into the crowd and is greeted by their supporters and new fans. Kevin greets Allen and bows down to him. He says, "Man you showed off, I knew you could play but jeez. You had that guitar singing like Mariah Carey." Allen thinks about Shanice and says to him, "I had a great friend that made me feel comfortable to show off my talents in a big way." As Allen is talking to Kevin, Shanice walks up to him and hugs him. She says, "OMG you were amazing on that stage Allen." "Well, I'm glad you was entertained by me and my band members. And I'm happy that you came to see me play, Hopefully I left you impressed." Shanice smiles and swings her body back and forth slowly. As she was impressed by Allen. "You did impress me Mr. Callahan. Stay showcasing your greatness everywhere you go. I was wondering could I get your autograph and maybe a date?" Allen is stunned not only did he just overcame his fear on playing music in front of a crowd. The girl of his dreams asked him out on a date. He is on cloud nine right now. Before Allen could give an answer, Claudia steps into Allen's and Shanice's conversation.

"Sorry to interrupt, but Allen we all are going to get something to eat at Tay's Steakhouse just wondering would you want to come with us?" "Sure, let me introduce you guys to one another. Claudia, this is Shanice. Shanice this is Claudia, Claudia shakes Shanice's hand and says, "Hey nice to meet you about to say, you can come with us to dinner also." "I will be glad to join you guys, I must say you have a very beautiful voice. In my opinion your singing enlightened everybody here." Claudia is flattered by Shanice's statement. "Thank you, but I have to say that's really thanks to Allen. He is not only a great guitarist, but a great friend. Well, I will see you guys in a few." After Claudia walks away, Shanice waits for an answer from Allen. To see if he would want to go on a date with her. "Claudia seems like cool people, but you didn't answer my question would you like to go on a date with me?" Allen agrees to go on a date with Shanice. "It would be my honor." Shanice is excited that Allen agreed to go on a date with her. "Great well I'm going to go home real quick. I will see you in a few at the steakhouse."

As Allen packs his guitar and puts it in his vehicle he is stopped by an unexpected guest. A man walks up to him and says, "Well done Allen seeing you performed on stage tonight reminded me of how your father was back in the day." He notices the voice right away but is not 100 percent sure it's the person he believes it to be. As Allen turns around, he is left shocked. He says, "Uncle Dennis!"

Allen is shocked and surprised to see his uncle. Dennis smiles and says, "The one and only I know you probably thinking to yourself what is Uncle Dennis doing here. Well, I come here every Saturday to enjoy the beautiful music that is played here. Plus, when I was younger, I used to play here myself. I'm not going to lie; I wasn't as good as you. I knew your dad could play, but you have him beat." "He taught me everything when it comes to playing a guitar. I know his main thing is he wants me to focus on college. He doesn't want me to have any distractions along the way. Please don't tell him I was out here performing. He would have a raging fit." Dennis knows Al would have a fit if he knew his son was performing at a bar. Mainly due to stuff that happened in his past. "I won't tell your father, I saw you. Always remember to do what you feel in your spirit. I know you will be at church tomorrow; I want to have a meeting with you one-on-one before service. And before you say it again, I won't tell your father about our encounter." "Sounds like a plan, well I got to meet up with my band for dinner but thank you for coming out. And I will see you tomorrow at church."

After talking to his uncle, Allen heads straight to Tay's Steakhouse for dinner. Once he arrives, he talks to Paul first in the parking lot. Paul waves his hand towards where Allen is at and says, "Allen come over here let me talk to you for a minute." He runs over to Paul in the parking lot and says, "What's good?" Paul pulls out fifty dollars out of his pocket. "Here is your cut my friend. Thank you for doing this for me. How did it feel performing on the stage?" Even though he thought he would be nervous Allen loved being on stage. "Man at first, I was nervous and scared, but thanks to Shanice I gained a lot of confidence and belief in myself. When I got on the stage, I just let it rip. The adrenaline you get on the stage is one of the most amazing feelings in the world. When is our next show?" "We supposed to have one in two weeks. For that one I would need you and

Claudia to write a song. With both of your music intelligence I know you can come up with something masterful." "That's no problem I gotcha.

"I know Shanice was looking at you like a large chocolate milkshake tonight." Allen starts laughing. "On the real though, I can tell she was feeling you up on that stage. You might get your dream girl after all." "I hope so it will be like hitting the lottery." "I hope it works out for you. Question for you, what are you doing next weekend?" "I'm supposed to be going on a college tour with my dad next week. It's at his alma mater Seward University in Dalton, Georgia. We are going to be up there on Saturday and Sunday. Hopefully we will have a great time." Paul has an interesting look on his face. "Interesting well hey be careful up there. We need to go inside, I see everybody else is already walking inside."

The guys walk inside the restaurant. Allen sits across from Shanice and Claudia while Kevin is sitting next to him. Shanice asks Claudia, "So Claudia how long have you been singing?" Claudia says, "Since I was a young kid music is something that I'm passionate about. It's my dream to be a songwriter and a musician for a living. I just feel like in life you should always do what you want." "I one hundred percent agree you are great at what you do. So, I know you will excel well. Allen I'm curious what made you join the band?" "Paul said the band needed a

guitarist, so he picked the best one he knows." Shanice smiles at
Allen. "I would say the most handsome guitarist I know." Allen
smiles and brushes his hair. Kevin and Claudia sees that Shanice
has a romantic interest in Allen and decides to leave the table.
They both want them to spend time together. Kevin says,
"Claudia, if it's fine with you I love to talk you one-on-one. I want
to get to know more about you." "Vice versa, on my side let's go
to another table and talk. Shanice it was an honor meeting you.
We will talk to you later Allen." "It was an honor meeting you to
Claudia."

After Kevin and Claudia leave, Allen and Shanice have a
one-on-one conversation. Shanice says, "Well it looks like I got
that date I wanted with you after all." Allen says, "Well like my
mom always tell me anything that is meant to be shall come to
pass. How do you feel about the Dirty Dancing play? And with
this being my first lead role in a play what advice would you give
to me?" Shanice gives Allen some great advice. "This is like my
fifth play; I have ever been co-lead in. This one I'm super excited
for as Dirty Dancing is one of my favorite movies of all time. This
is going to be a great play that I believe will create great
opportunities for you and me. I'm going to give you this advice
since I know this is your first leading role. It's your time to shine
Allen. We have been in plays together, you're a great actor, it's
time that you be the main character for once. Just like you did

tonight, give it your all and show everyone what you're made of. Nothing is ever perfect, I made mistakes on stage, but I don't let it bother me. You should never care what anybody has to say. You are smart and a very admirable person. When you are on that stage just do you. Plus, I'm going to be by your side you don't have nothing to worry about." Allen is becoming the person he was designed to be. He still got to fully grow out of his shyness. He is glad that Shanice is trying to help him out with that.

Allen and Shanice talk for a couple of more minutes before they leave the restaurant. Allen walks Shanice to her car as they both say goodbye to one another. "Well Allen this was one magical night. You are great to be around; I can't wait till we start practicing for our play." "It's been wonderful being in your presence, I got to take you out by myself. And thank you for the advice you gave me. I believe we are going to do great at the play. Hopefully, I don't drop you when I have to pick you up." Shanice starts laughing and pushes Allen a bit. "If you drop me, we fighting, I'm not Blake you not going to knock me out." Allen starts laughing. "You could knockout anybody out with those beautiful brown eyes of yours though." Shanice starts smiling and stares beautifully at Allen. "Speaking of eyes, you have something in yours." Shanice leans in and kisses Allen. Butterflies starts jittering in his stomach. This is Allen's first kiss ever, and he is getting it from his crush. In Allen's mind right now if I'm dreaming don't wake me up. Shanice feels like she shouldn't have given Allen a kiss. "I'm sorry I hope I'm not doing too much." "No, it's okay." Allen kisses Shanice back as they both are enjoying this passionate moment. He puts his hands on Shanice's soft cheeks as they smile at each other. "That was wonderful I want us to stay getting to know each other. I like you more than just a friend, Shanice. I have to be honest with you, hopefully you feel the same way." "I do; I want to spend as much time with you as possible." "I'm glad to hear that, listen I must go, I will see you at school on Monday. Text me when you get home." Allen goes in his car and drives off with the biggest smile on his face.

As he walks in his house, Allen is joyfully dancing and singing Ray J's "One Wish". As he is singing in the living room lights turns on which rattles him. And somebody starts walking towards the front room. Al walks in the room and says, "It looks like somebody had a fun night I have never seen you this happy. What did you do tonight?" Allen decides not to tell his dad about being in a band but does plan on telling him about his first kiss. He says excitedly, "Dad, I got my first kiss tonight from Shanice who I go to school with." Al starts smiling as he knows how it is to be a young man getting his first kiss. "Having your first kiss is something you will never forget. Do you have feelings for the young lady?" "I have had feelings for her since grade school. This might be one of the best nights of my life. I feel like a rockstar."

Al rubs his son's head and smiles. "Alright young king go to bed we have church in the morning."

It's Sunday Morning, Allen puts on his black suit and tie proudly as he thinks about last night. As he walks into church he is stopped by Paul. Paul says to him, "Mr. Rockstar, how are you doing?" Allen smiles bright as the sun and says, "I got my first kiss last night and it was from Shanice." Paul smiles and hugs Allen. "My boy look at you man. I'm happy and proud of you, hopefully she plays a string on your guitar." "Hopefully so, this past week has been crazy man. It's like I'm living in a movie." "It really has been it's like Diary of a Wimpy Kid. I'm curious with you going to school tomorrow are you scared if Blake might do something to you?" After knocking out Blake, Allen isn't worried about anything pertaining to Blake. "I think he got my message and clear to not mess with me. I'm just going to stay doing me."

As Allen and Paul walk into church together, they are approached by Dennis. He says to the young gentlemen, "Young rockstars how are you doing this morning?" Paul says, "We are doing good ready to receive some Holy Spirit." "That's what I love to hear. You mind if I speak to Allen privately real quick." "No, I don't mind."

As Paul leaves, Dennis and Allen have a one-on-one conversation. "Like I said last night, you was amazing. You have a GOD given talent when it comes to music, we must showcase them off. Never be afraid to show off the gifts, GOD has blessed you with. I decided to give brother Dwyane the day off from playing the guitar. Because we have a young great guitarist who needs to showcase his great skills." Allen looks around the church and wonders who the great guitarist is. Allen asks, "Where he at?" Pastor Dennis looks directly at Allen. "I'm looking right at him; I got a guitar picked out for you in the back. You have a special talent and people need to see that. I got to go to prepare for my sermon. Can't wait to see you rock the stage." Allen is shocked that his uncle wants him to be the lead guitarist for today's church service. He isn't nervous at all even though he is curious how his parents might react.

Allen goes to the practice room to meet with the church choir. As he walks into the room the church choir is excited to see him. Sister Angela says, "Allen we are so excited to have you with us. We are going to get you up to speed on things." Allen practices with the choir for 45 minutes. As church starts, Allen's parents look for him. Imani asks, "Al have you seen Allen?" Al says, "No, I haven't seen him, Jalean have you seen your brother?" Jalean says, "No." Al sees Paul and goes over to him to ask where his son is at. "Paul, have you seen Allen?" Paul looks straight at the stage and sees Allen with a guitar in his hands. "Yes, there he goes right there on stage with a guitar."

Allen's parents and his brother are surprised to see him up on stage as the lead guitarist. Jalean says, "What is he doing up there?" Imani and Paul looks at him proudly. While Al says under his breath, "Don't mess this up son." The choir starts performing and Allen amazes the church with his guitar play. Allen's parents, his brother and Paul looks at him proudly. Allen looks at everybody in the church with a smile as he amazes them with his talent.

After service, Dennis approaches Allen and his parents. He says, "Al and Imani you guys should be proud of Allen he did an amazing job on the guitar this Sunday. Reminds me of how you use to play back in the day Al." Imani says, "We are so proud of him." Al says, "He got skills like his old man, but I am curious Allen how did you end up on the stage?" Allen looks at his Uncle Dennis and is scared he might blow his cover. "Brother Dwyane wasn't feeling so well. So, I asked some people here who would want to play, and Allen volunteered." Allen adds, "Something in my spirit told me to volunteer to play guitar for service today." Imani says, "Well, you picked the best of the best." Al says, "Well, I glad he's showing people how us Callahan's get down." Allen is glad that his uncle covered for him as he doesn't want his parents to find out about him being in a band and performing at live venues.

A couple of hours after church, Allen goes to work. As he goes to the back of the store to stock groceries on a cart he is greeted by Ashley, his co-worker. She says to him, "What's up superstar I hear you are becoming a big name." Allen starts laughing and says, "Kevin told you about my performance yesterday." "I knew Kevin was going to be there, but a lot of people is talking about you on social media see here look." Ashley takes out her phone to show Allen how much recognition he is getting. As his social media following has gone up. Just last week, Allen was afraid to show off his talents. Now that he has shown people his gift he is getting recognized for it." Allen spins around and smiles. "What can I say, I'm just great at what I do. I love the support I have been getting lately. Who would have ever thought?" "I'm not going to lie you surprised me shrimp. I'm happy for you well let's get to work before Bossman walks through."

Allen heads out and starts stocking groceries. While stocking groceries, an unexpected customer approaches him. The Customer asks him, "Excuse me can you point me where the potato chips are?" Allen says, "Yeah sure there are on Isle 2." As Allen turns around, he sees that the customer is Blake. This is their first time seeing each other since their fight. How will this conversation go?

Chapter 3: Making Changes

Allen and Blake see each other face-to-face for the first time since their fight. He has no idea what Blake has on his mind right now. He is no longer scared of Blake. He says to him, "I'm at my job right now, I don't want any issue with you." As Allen thinks Blake is coming to start something, it's the complete opposite. Blake says, "I'm not here to start any issues with you, I just want to apologize for the many times I have bullied you. I deserved to get punched for the way I treated you. Life has a way of humbling you, any who I must go I will see you around Allen." Allen is surprised to hear words of sincerity from Blake. He still has plans on watching his back when it comes to him though.

As Allen's 2-9 pm shift is over with he talks to Kevin before leaving. Kevin daps up Allen and says, "John Mayer Jr, how is everything going?" Allen anxiously can't wait to tell Kevin everything that's been going on. He says, "Well I officially got my first kiss last night." Kevin starts smiling. "Look at you my boy playa, playa. Was it with Shanice?" Allen looks at Kevin with a smile and his eyebrows rises. "Yes, indeed it was, I have been dreaming of kissing her since freshman year. Last night was probably the best night of my life." Kevin is glad to hear that things are excelling in Allen's love life. "Playboy Allen, I see you I'm glad that Shanice is recognizing the star that she has in front of her. Remember to take things slow." I'm going to, I believe it's going to work out for me. How is everything going with Claudia?" "Me and her are actually going on a date this Friday. We are going to watch some movies together. She's cool people I love her energy. Me and her both are taking things slow." "I love to hear that, I hope it works out for the both of you. Well, I got to get home and prepare for school in the morning."

As Allen walks into his house. His father yells out his name, "Allen meet me in the garage!" Allen is nervous to see what his dad might want with him. He walks into the garage; he see his father with a guitar. "Have a seat son let's talk." Allen's mind is lowkey popping up in the air as he wonders what his father wants to talk about. Al looks at the guitar as he reminisce about his younger days. "I have had this guitar for about twenty-five years. I used to play with this when I was in a band during my time in college. I used to love playing it and being in front of the audience. However, it also led me to playing it in places that I shouldn't have been as a young man. Which brought a lot of destruction into my life. Watching you today at church reminded me a lot of myself. You are great at what you do. Here's my stance on you playing music. You only play for GOD and in the church. Don't play at a bar or a club. If you decide to go along that path, you will not be living under my roof. So, do we have an understanding?" Allen hears his father but decides in his mind he still going to be in "The Believers". He must keep it a secret from him. "Yes sir." "Good now, I have everything worked out for you for your college trip at my alma mater. We are going to have a fun time. I know I'm hard on you son, but I just want the best for you. Well, I will let you get some rest son have a goodnight."

As Allen lays down in his bed, he reflects over this past week. He has slowly transformed into a new person. He still thinks to himself has he finally found his true calling in life? With him coming into his true self how will he be received by his peers at school?

Chapter 4: Shining Star

This past weekend was probably one of the best weekends of Allen's life. As he is about to walk into school, he wonders how he will be perceived. He walks into the school, and he isn't treated like the nerdy kid he has always been treated as. Instead, he is treated like a superstar as everybody in the hallway daps him up. Everyone in the hallway shouts out his name. Girls stopping him from left to right.

He sees Paul in the hallway and goes to talk to him. Allen says to Paul, "Bro what the mess it's like my life changed overnight. I'm being treated like a celebrity up in here." Paul responds, "People are just finally recognizing your greatness. It's about time people opened their eyes when it comes to you. Hey, you still going to Seward University this weekend, right?" "Yeah, me and my father."

Paul has an idea for Allen's College trip to Seward University. "So, I was seeing that close by Seward there is a lounge call Lakeside that is doing Open Mic on Saturday. The band who wins the open mic wins $500. So, I was thinking the band should perform what you think?" Allen likes the idea except for one problem. "I love the idea except you know my father isn't going to allow that to happen." "Don't worry I got a great plan. First, me and the group will get an Airbnb for the night. Second, I can come on the campus and fake like I'm there to hang out with you. Or you could get one of the college kids on campus to take you to the bar." "I'm going to go with the latter option. Which song you guys want to perform?" "I want you and Claudia to write a song together and I want you to be the person to sing it." Allen laughs at the idea of him leading a song. "You joking right?" Paul has a great vision when it comes to Allen's involvement in the band. "Nope, you have a great mellow voice. I want to make you the lead vocalist of the band alongside Claudia. You showed people how great you are at playing the guitar, it's time you showed people how good you are at singing. Show off your full package." "Alright bet, I guess we start practicing tomorrow." "Yes sir, talk to you later."

Allen goes to class and is being treated like a celebrity. He is getting compliments about his guitar playing. And is getting recognition from his female peers. As he walk to one of his classes two girls walk his books to class for him. Even though he is getting attention like he never has before from the ladies he only has his eye on one girl.

After their Literature class, Allen talks to Shanice at her locker. He says, "Well hello ma'am you are looking marvelous today." Shanice says, "And you are looking very handsome today are you ready for rehearsal today for the play?" "I am I took the stage in front of everybody before, so I definitely can do it again."

Shanice is happy to see Allen's growth. "I'm happy that you are growing out of your shyness. And remember what I said before I'm right by your side, so you don't have anything to worry about. You are going to do a great job." "I have to go to my other class; I will see you in a few." The attraction grows between Allen and Shanice.

Before Allen gets ready to go to his first practice of the Dirty Dancing play he is called to the principal's office. Allen walks into the office and is greeted by Principal Davenport. He says, "Allen, please have a seat. I have heard you have been making a great impression on a lot of people with your guitar play. Which I am happy to hear, glad that you are showing off your talents." Allen says, "Well I'm grateful that I had the opportunity to do it. If you told me this past week, all this stuff would be happening in my life I wouldn't believe you." "Well, when you move one step forward in life blessings will come your way. Always remember this Allen, never be scared to go for what you truly want in life. You live one life don't live it with regrets. Now you go ahead and have a great practice today." The advice Principal Davenport has given Allen builds more confidence within him. From now on, anything that is set in his mind he is going to go for it.

Allen arrives at practice, and he sees some of the people are doing leg exercises. The director of the play approaches Allen and asks, "Hey are you, Allen?" Allen says, "Yes ma'am I am." "Great my name is Gabrielle I'm the director of the play. We have your wardrobe in the back. Go back and get dressed for rehearsal. And once you get done join the crew and do some leg exercise. We mainly doing that, so it helps you glide and move around when you dance." "Ok sounds good."

After Allen gets dressed, he starts rehearsing with the crew. When Allen first starts rehearsing, he stumbles when it comes to his dance moves. Gabrielle yells out, "Cut!" She continues to say, "Allen you moving too fast with your steps. Let me show you how to do it." Gabrielle gets on the stage to help guide Allen. "Slow your pace go with the rhythm of the music. Remember you are the star we all are following you. So just take your time and lead." The crew goes back to rehearsal and Allen starts to impress the crew. And when it comes to rehearsing his scenes with Shanice, he is magnificent. The great chemistry they have off-stage is showcasing gracefully on stage. Watching Allen act is like looking at Tom Cruise act in a movie scene.

After the rehearsal, Gabrielle approaches Allen. She says, "Allen you did a marvelous job remember you're the star, this play is going to be great thanks to you." Allen says, "Appreciated thank you." After his conversation with Gabrielle, Shanice comes up from behind Allen and lightly punches him in the shoulder. She says, "Well, well you did a great job Johnny." "And you did a great job too queen. My moves was okay, but yours were excellent. And Principal Davenport, I'm surprised to see you in the play." Principal Davenport is playing Shanice's Dad in the play. He says, "Well Allen I was a good actor in my high school and college years. Some of my peers called me the next Denzel." Shanice asks, "So what happened to your acting career?" "Shemar Moore is what happened, I went out for a movie role and lost it to him. I was supposed to be kissing Nia Long on screen. Instead, I became a principal of a High School, but I love you guys though. I'm going to talk to Gabrielle both of you did a great job."

After Principal Davenport leaves, Shanice asks Allen, "So what are you doing after this?" Allen says, "Going to bed, I got to prepare for work tonight. I want to take you out what are you doing this Friday night?" Allen is curious about what Shanice will say. "Oh nothing, hoping to go on a date with this guy at my school by the name of Allen." Allen is happy about Shanice's answer. "Well, I got good news Allen is going to pick you up at 7 PM for your date on Friday." "Well, I can't wait." Shanice gives Allen a kiss. Which brings more excitement to him. "Well, I have to go I will see you tomorrow, my great knight." Allen is super excited that he has landed a date with Shanice.

Later that night, Allen goes to work, and he is in for a surprise. He walks into the break room and is greeted by his manager Mr. Jimmy. He says, "There he goes the best stocker in the world has walked in the building how are you doing?" Allen responds, "I'm doing great can't complain." "That's good listen I hired a new stocker to work with you and Kevin." Allen is happy that a new stocker is joining the team. As it helps take the load off him and Kevin. "That's whatsup that would be a great help for us. When does the new guy start?" "Tonight, he's actually in the back stocking groceries on a float let me introduce you to him." Mr. Jimmy and Allen walk to the stockroom and Allen is shocked to see who the new stocker is.

"Allen let me introduce you to Blake, Blake this is Allen." Blake has a smile on his face and says, "Me and Allen know each other we go to school with one another." Allen has a shocked look on his face. "Well, that is great he is going to be showing you the ropes here. Allen is one of our night crew managers, you are in good hands with him. Well, I shall get going Kevin should be here in a few minutes."

As Mr. Jimmy leaves, Allen thinks to himself about how the work relationship will be between him and Blake. Blake says to Allen, "Like I said before I'm not here to cause any issues. I'm here to make some money." Allen doesn't trust Blake, he wants to know why Blake picked on him. He asks, "I do have to ask why the change of heart? You been picking on me since grade school why you want to be cool with me now?"

Blake reveals the truth reason. "The main reason I bullied you because I was jealous of you. Ever since we were kids you seem like a person who always had everything together. I wish that was the case for me. And because you never fought back until Thursday when you knocked me out. I love my face bro, I'm not trying to have a whole bunch of scars on it, but also due to my suspension I have had time to reflect. I have always admired you; you are the smartest person I know. With me the only thing I have ever had is my skills in athletics, that's how I always impressed people. Without it, I wouldn't be popular at school. I deal with a lot of stuff that people don't know anything about. All I'm trying to say is when it comes to me and you, I just want to put the past behind us." Blake reaches out his hand as Allen looks down at it. "What you say let's be friends leave the past in the past."

Allen hears Blake's truth; hearing Blake talk reminded him of himself. He decides to forgive him and accepts his friendship. Allen shakes Blake's hand. "It's all good let's go ahead and get started." The guys stacks the groceries from the back on a float and take them to the isles in the store to stock. Allen teaches Blake how to stock groceries and teaches him the fundamentals of the job.

As Allen is teaching Blake a better way to stock groceries. Kevin walks in the store. He says, "Allen my boy what's going on?" Kevin and Allen dap one another up. He sees Blake stocking groceries. "I see we have new fish in the building. What's your name newbie?" Blake introduces himself to Kevin. He says, "My name is Blake, me and Allen actually go to High School together." The name Blake sounds familiar to Kevin. "You know it's funny you say that I know Allen knocked out a boy with the same name." Allen chimes in and says, "Kev it's the same guy." Kevin leans back and gives a funny shocking look. "Well, I be dang, your cool now?" "Yes, we are, I'm not here to cause any issue. Just here to do my job." "Good to hear welcome to the family. Now let's get to work." Allen and Kevin both train Blake together and bond with him also.

As their shift is over with, Allen asks Blake how he likes the job. He asks, "So how you think your first day went?" Blake says, "It went well, I learned a lot of great things watching you and Kevin stock. I really didn't know you was a fun person to be around. Maybe me and you can hangout sometime." "I wouldn't mind at all. Well, I got to go get some sleep talk to you later." It's funny how life works once were enemies now are friends. Allen and Blake have formed a great friendship with each other.

Around 12 PM, Allen goes to Paul's house for rehearsal. Paul daps up Allen and says, "Mr. Superstar, how's life going?" Allen laughs and says, "I will tell you all about it after practice." The Band practices for one hour. After practicing, the guys have a meeting. Paul tells the guys the weekly plan for the band. "Alright guys first off good job on Saturday. We are going to do a great job this Saturday at Lakeside bar. The band that wins the Open Mic wins $500. So, we shall bring our best to the stage. Now we need to start writing original songs for the band. As I want to perform them on stage this Saturday. I want Allen and Claudia to write a song for us on Saturday. And they both will be the songwriters for the band. And I want Allen to be a co-lead vocalist alongside Claudia. As he will be singing lead this Saturday." Claudia says, "It's about time, we can hear Allen's vocals. Allen come at my house at 6 pm tomorrow and we will write some music together." "Sound good, I will see you then."

After the meeting, Allen talks to Paul one-on-one. Paul says, "Big Al what's going on bro?" Allen tells Paul what's been going on. "So first as you know I am in the Dirty Dancing play. It's going well, I'm going on my first date with Shanice, Friday evening. I hope it goes well." "You and her already had your first kiss so the hardest part is out the way. Just take her out and get to know her. It seems like you living the dream." "I will say somewhat, I feel like I'm still living in a shadow. Hiding from my parents that I'm in the band. The day I can be myself is the day I will honestly be living the dream. Also, you will never guess who's my new co-worker is." "Who?" "Blake." Paul leans back in his chair as he is surprised by this news. "Well dang, you knocked out the man now he is working with you. The universe works in funny ways." "I know I'm training him, but I got a chance to get to know him. He even apologized to me for bullying me." "Well, you know in life GOD do put people in situations to help change their character."

Paul tells Allen about his scholarship offer. "I know I just got a college offer from Georgia Tech for engineering. I might skip college though music is what I truly love. I want to have my own label one day. Be like Rick Rubin, I want to invest in people and make them into stars. That's why I'm hard on you. You have talents and gifts that many people wish they had. Don't waste them away, we shall be great. Allen all we must do is believe in GOD, believe in our dreams and work hard. And everything shall fall into place." "I hear you bro, we shall do great things my friend."

After leaving practice, Allen heads to school to prepare for rehearsal. While heading to the auditorium, he passes the gym and sees Blake working out. Allen approaches Blake to speak to him. He says, "What's up Blake." The other guys in the gym look at Allen and Blake to see how the conversation will go. Blake gets up from lifting weights and daps up Allen. Which leaves some of the guys in the gym shocked. Blake says, "Wassup Allen, how are you doing?" "Doing good about to prepare for rehearsal for the Dirty Dancing play." "Ok Mr. Superstar you about to lock lips with Shanice." Allen laughs. "Yeah, I guess you can say I'm a lucky man." "We got to get you working out with us. You always got to stay bettering yourself, especially your physique. If you ever feel like working out hit me up." "Most definitely, I will see you tonight at work."

Allen heads to the rehearsal and meets with Principal Davenport. He says, "Mr. Davenport you mind if I talk to you for a second. He responds, "I don't mind what you want to talk about?" Allen is trying to take two days off from school. "I was wondering could I miss Wednesday and Thursday. I'm caught up in all my work and done with most of my classes for the year. I will be here for practice on those days. I'm working nights until the play is over with." "Let me call your mother to see if she's ok with it." Principal Davenport steps away to call Allen's mother. Allen hopes his mother allows him to take some time off from school. After two minutes, Principal Davenport walks back over to him. "Your mom is ok with you taking those days off. Make sure to get some rest during that time."

After the rehearsal, Allen goes home and takes a good nap. As Allen wakes up, he is greeted by his brother Jalean. He says, "Hello dork." Allen responds, "Hello wimp what you want?" Jalean wants Allen to do something for him. "I want to learn how to play guitar like you and Dad. Pops is always busy, so I'm wondering if you could teach me. I want to be able to play for the talent show at my school." Allen feels honored that his brother wants to learn to play guitar from him. "When you get home Friday night, I will teach you some things." Jalean starts smiling as he finally gets to learn how to play the guitar. "Thank you so much and you did an awesome job playing guitar at church last Sunday." "Appreciated little bro."

Later in the day, Allen goes to work and bonds with Blake while stocking groceries. He says, "Blake tell me about yourself. Tell me your life story." Blake usually don't talk about his life to people, but he knows Allen is a sincere person. Due to that, he decides to open up to him. He says, "Be prepared to hear a movie, I was born to loving parents, had a great childhood. Until I was 10 years old, my dad lost his job and became an Alcoholic. When my dad drank, he would turn into a different person. If I didn't get the correct grades or did not do my best at sports. He would beat me; the same thing happened with my sister. Eventually he and my mom got a divorce, I haven't seen him since. Ever since my parents' divorce, I been the man of the house. Some of the anger I have displayed at school comes from my home environment. I got so much hate in me I hope one day; I will be able to let go of all of it."

Allen is stunned and saddened to hear all the turmoil that Blake has gone through. "I'm sorry you went through all of that. Something I learned from church is release all pain and anger in your heart so you can find peace within yourself. Which in return will help you be a better man." Blake takes consideration to Allen's advice. "I hardly never been to church, but I might take your advice. Thank you for listening to me, you are one of few people who know my story." "No problem, man, if you ever need anybody to talk to, I'm here for you." "Thank you it means a lot to me. What about you tell me your life story?"

Allen tells Blake his life story. "I was raised in a religious household. Raised by my father and mother. I have one younger brother named Jalean. My father is the president of National First Bank down here. And my mother is a doctor at Mercy Hospital. My parents always wanted me to stay focused on my studies, especially my dad. He's a great man, but he doesn't want me, or my brother distracted when it comes to our education. I have been working here since I was sixteen. Been here for two years, it's a great job everybody here is like family. I recently joined a band called "The Believers"; my friend Paul is the leader of the group. At first, I was scared to join the group. I was very shy of performing in front of the crowd. I decided to overcome my fears and showcase my love of music."

As much as Allen is amazed by Blake, Blake is amazed by him also. "Look at you I might be talking to the next Lenny Kravitz." Allen laughs at Blake's comment. "So, music is your passion?" "I guess you can say that it's something I love; I love creating music and creating something that will make people feel good." "So why not do that for a living? Granted you are super smart; you can get a high paying job with your intelligence. Although I always feel like you should do what you love. Either way you are going to do big things Allen." The advice that both guys have given to one another has made a lasting impact on them both.

It's Wednesday evening, after the rehearsal Allen heads over to Claudia's apartment to write a song for the band. Allen knocks on the door. Claudia goes to the door and asks, "Who is it?" Allen responds, "It's the Prince to your Shelia E." Claudia opens the door and smiles. "Well hello my Prince." Allen intimates Prince. "OOH-woo, hello my friend I got to say you have a beautiful place it smells like peaches in here." Claudia laughs. "Thank you as you can see, I have been doing some writing, but since you are singing, I wanted to know what you want to sing about. I feel like for a song to have meaning you have to speak from your soul."

Allen has a great idea of how he wants the song to be. "You know lately, I just want to be free and be able to be myself and live my truth. I want to reveal to my parents that I am at a crossroads in my life on what I want to do in my life. So, we should write a song that is like John Mayer's "No Such Thing" and 3 Doors Down "Let Me Be Myself." "Well, what we are about to write is going to be something magical. Let's make it happen sir." Both Allen and Claudia combine their writing talents and write a beautiful song within thirty minutes.

After writing the song, Allen and Claudia are prepared to start singing the song. The song is titled "I Just Want To Be Free" Allen starts playing his guitar and singing the song. "Got a lot on my mind, trying to figure out how to play this game called life, everybody telling me boy you are blessed, they don't know this young man is stressed out, trying my best to find the real me, I feel like this version of me is a Mr. Pretend, everybody see me as a smart man telling me after you graduate boy get that degree, I think to myself I just want to be free." Allen and Claudia start singing the hook twice together. "I just want to be free of the judgement and negativity, I want positivity to be around me, I want to be the person that I vision, I just want to be free and be me." Allen sings, "Tell myself don't get caught up in deceiving, you got to stay believing. Parents want me to go the route the universe tell the kids to go, I want to go to the true destination that is laid upon me, trying to be a true star asking myself how far can I go, don't want my dreams to fall apart, don't want to be the old man on his death bed with what ifs or regrets, Want to be the man that departs this earth knowing he accomplish everything he were set out to do, I shall go for my dreams and believe, Old man says youngin hold on you shall rise and your light will sparkle."

Claudia sings, "Trying my best to stay holding on, telling myself I shall rise, when I fall, I shall get back up, I pray that one day I see that great sunlight." Allen and Claudia sing the hook twice one last time. "I just want to be free of the judgement and negativity, I want positivity to be around me, I want to be the person that I vision, I just want to be free and be me."

After singing, Allen and Claudia both lay down on the floor. Claudia is amazed by the song her and Allen wrote. "Dude that's a fucking hit; we just created something special. I can tell from the lyrics and the way you singing this is something you going through right now." Allen confides in Claudia. "It's like everybody see me as the genius that should go to college. Granted I'm smart as hell. I'm starting to realize that I'm not the person people see me as. I want to be me; I want to be the person that I'm supposed to be. I'm scared of how people might react, especially my father. Just can't wait till the day I'm free from living a lie and being my true self."

Claudia gives Allen some great advice. "You are great and the most amazing guitarist I have ever played with. I'm not telling you to disobey your parents but follow your dreams. Be who you want to be, forget what anybody else has got to say about it. I believe in you Allen, you are going to do great things just believe in yourself."

He decides to ask Claudia's input on Shanice. "Thank you, Claudia, I greatly appreciate it. So, what do you think about Shanice?" "She seems like a very sweet person. I can tell she truly like you. She was looking at you like you was a piece of cake on stage. Have you taken her out on a date yet?" "I'm taking her out this Friday. This is the first date I have ever been on. Do you have any suggestions?" "Just be yourself, I saw you two together y'all have great chemistry. Just go out and have a fun time everything will be fine. Since we're talking about love interests, I'm going out with Kevin this Friday. Do you have any suggestions for me?" Allen is excited to hear about Kevin and Claudia's date. " I'm glad to hear that you two are trying to get to know one another. The main piece of advice I will give is just be genuine with him. I know that will mean a lot to him." "Thank you I believe that both of our dates will go well." Allen appreciates Claudia's advice and friendship. "It will thank you, I know we haven't known each other for a long time, but you are a great friend." "Vice versa Allen, thank you for being you." Allen gives Claudia a warm hug. "Well, I shall get going, I'm going to talk to Paul about the song. Have a nice night, Claudia."

The next day, after dinner Allen asks his father for some advice. He asks, "Dad you mind if I talk to you really quick?" Al says to his son, "Sure let's head to the man cave." Al and Allen drink some sweet tea together as they have a deep conversation.

They both go to Al's man cave. "So, what is on your mind son?" "I have my first date tomorrow with Shanice. I was wondering could you offer me any advice." Allen's Dad smiles and brushes his head. "This remind me of my conversation with your grandpa Bill, when I had my first date. I will say this be chill you already got the date. So, you don't have to overdo it when it comes to making an impression. She already likes you because she took the time to go on a date with you. Just go out and have fun, just no funny business remember stay pure. I know your hormones are probably high now that you got a girl interested in you. You must remember to control them. GOD created sex to be special for a husband and wife. Not for a friend, boyfriend, or girlfriend. When you have sex, it creates soul ties with that person."

"What are soul ties pops?" "Soul ties are an emotional bond that is created within physical intimacy aka sex. When that bond is created, an attachment takes place between you and that other person. Both men and women might not want to admit, but when you have sex with someone it makes you want to get closer to the other person. Your flesh wants to stay connected to their flesh. When you do that outside of marriage it can cause chaos in your life. The main reason is because you just created a bond with someone that isn't your wife. Sadly, when that happens it can create toxic relationships, but most of all it can keep two people together who probably wasn't even meant to be husband and wife. This isn't something I'm preaching or teaching, it's something I have lived through. I don't want you to go through it. You have your own mind, body, and soul son, you must use it wisely. As followers of Christ, we must honor GOD in all things even in our relationships.

The biggest key thing in a relationship is to put GOD first before anything. If you truly have a woman that's a follower of Christ, then you have someone you can grow with. A man leads the relationship he is in; a woman is supposed to follow his lead. And GOD will reveal to you if this girl is meant to be with you. I know you're young, but don't date someone because it makes you feel better as a man. Pursue and date someone because you see them as a person that will be a great companion along your journey in life. Make sure that she has a mindset of putting GOD first in her life and that she is living in his truth. By doing that, both of you will be on one accord. Then, as you learn more about her ask yourself, can I live my whole life with this person? That's how I knew your mom was the one for me, I knew I could spend the rest of my life with her. And that I wanted her in all the days of my life. You must have the same mindset with Shanice as you get to know her."

Allen appreciates his father's advice and plans on using it. Also, he decides to pick his brain on playing in a band that is not church-related. "Thanks for the advice pops I'm definitely going to use it. Pops, if me or Jalean was ever offered to be in a band that is not church-related. How would you feel?" Al gives him his full honest response. "I would be against it, if it doesn't have nothing to do with church. I don't want you guys participating in it. Plus, I know from personal experience being a part of a band can make your life hell. If you guys live under this roof you won't participate in no such thing. Any who, I can't wait for our trip this Saturday. I booked our rooms earlier today. We are going to leave Saturday morning and probably come back that Sunday evening. Once you walk on Seward University, you will absolutely love it." "I can't wait it's going to be great."

Later that night, Allen goes to work and is greeted by Kevin who is his night shift partner for the night since Blake is off. He says to Allen, "What's good Allen? You got an extra step in your walk. What's been going on with you?" Allen smiles and says, "First, I got my first date with Shanice tomorrow. Kevin is excited that Allen is finally going on his first date. He gives him a fist bump. "I see you, my boy. Just remember this stay true to yourself." "Trying my best it's tough. I'm conflicted about being the person my parents want me to be. Then actually being the person, I want to be." Kevin cautioned, "One thing my Momma always told me the truth shall set you free. You going to have to tell your parents the truth sooner or later." "I know me and my father are going out of town on Saturday to go to his Alma Mater for my college visit. At the same time Paul has set up a performance at a nearby lounge near the college campus. So, when I get down there, I got to find a way to sneak out and meet the band. It's like I'm playing cat and mouse at this point. I'm just scared to tell my parents; I don't want them to disown me." Kevin is very transparent with Allen. "You are in a tough position, you have to ask yourself whose dreams matter the most to you, your parents' dreams or yours?" Sooner or later, Allen is going to have to decide if he is going to live his life for himself or for other people.

92

Chapter 5: Getting Out of the Shadow

It's Friday morning, Allen arrives back at school and runs into Blake. Blake says, "Allen what's going on man. How many classes are you attending today?" Allen responds, "Just three, what about you?" "I got two then I'm done for the day. About to say after you get done with your classes, you should workout with me in the gym if you want." "Sure thing."

After his classes is over with, Allen goes straight to his locker. While at his locker, Shanice spins herself towards him as she is excited for their date. She says to him, "Well hello handsome, I can't wait for our date tonight." Allen says, "I can't wait either anytime I can be in your presence is a huge blessing in my opinion. We shall dazzle the night away; I'm going to catch up with you later."

After talking to Shanice, Allen goes to the gym at the school to workout with Blake. He daps up Allen and says, "What's going on man, it's about time I get you in here. Let's workout and let's get something to eat afterwards." For one hour, Allen and Blake works out in the Gym. Allen doesn't work out a whole bunch due to that he does get a bit tired during the workout. However, his former foe-now-friend is motivating him to push through. And teaching him the importance of working out.

After working out, the guys go out and get something to eat. "So, are you ok after the workout?" Allen feels like he was just hit by Ray Lewis. "My body is sore, but I will be alright. I honestly don't see how you do it." Blake laughs. "You just got to get used to it. Remember practice makes perfect. You will get there with no worries. So, your first date is today are you prepared for it?" "I am it's going to go well; I thank GOD that I got a date with Shanice. I have been dreaming of dating her since elementary school. Now I'm finally taking her out, I feel like a main character in a 2000's Disney Channel movie." "You funny bro, other than that what all you got plan on doing this weekend?" "So tomorrow me and my father are going to his alma mater Seward University. I got a scholarship offer there so I'm going to check the campus out. Then later in the evening, my band and I got a performance near the campus. So, I'm going to be super busy this weekend." "I can tell music is your passion, I will say this follow what you truly want in life. And when you go out on the stage show them people what you are made of." "I most definitely will Blake thank you for the words of encouragement. Cheers to our success."

After having lunch, Allen goes to Joe's house to practice with the band. And to record the song he and Claudia wrote together. Paul talks to the band before practice starts. He says, "First of I got to give a round of applause to Allen and Claudia they wrote and created an amazing song. Thank you, Joe, for allowing us to use your studio to record the song. This song I believe will inspire and impact people in a great way. Remember band we are legends; we shall put on a great show. Most of all we are legends whose voices will be heard. Let's go ahead and get started." The band practices for an hour and a half. They sound so in tune together.

After practice is over with, Claudia goes to talk to Allen. She says to him, "What's up tiger are you ready for tomorrow?" Allen responds, "I can't wait to rock the stage. Got to find a way to escape from my dad tomorrow. Either way it's going to be a great Saturday that's all I'm going to say." "Well, when it comes to your dad, I believe Paul has created a great plan for that. We are going to have an amazing time on stage tomorrow. Never forget the power you have inside of you."

After talking to Claudia, Allen goes to talk to Paul. He says to Paul, "Paulie tell me what your plan is to help me go out and perform with you guys tomorrow." Paul has an excellent plan for Allen. He says, "Your dad isn't the only person with connections at Seward. I got a homeboy up there by the name of Josh. I told him you are coming up there. I sent him a picture of what you looked like. He wanted me to give you, his number. He said text him when you get ready to meet us. And he will take you to us." "Sounds like a plan where you guys going to be staying at?" "I rented out an Airbnb for us. Going to throw a kickback afterwards. But any who the big date is today are you prepared?" "I am who would ever think I would have a date with my dream girl. It's going to go great. I got to get home to teach Jalean how to play a guitar talk to you later."

Allen goes home and teaches his brother to play guitar. The brothers bond together over their love of music. It takes Jalean a moment to know the notes he's playing. To be like his father and brother he knows he would need more lessons. The main thing he loves about learning to play the guitar is getting to hang out with his brother. After Allen gets done teaching him, Jalean asks him, "How did I do?" Allen says, "You did good for a rookie. You need more lessons it takes time to learn how to play the guitar. I got you I will teach you everything I know." He brushes Jalean's head as Jalean lays his head on his chest.

A few hours later, Allen gets ready for his date and talks to his mom before he goes. Allen shows his mom his outfit and asks, "Mom, how do I look?" Imani loves what her son is wearing as he has on a blue-buttoned down shirt, white pants and white air forces. She says, "You look outstanding my son. You are going to sweep Shanice off her feet." "Is that what Dad did to you?" "When he was younger your father was super fun and could do anything to impress people. On our first date, we danced the night away to Faith Evans "Kissing You." It was a magical night; that started the beginning of a beautiful love story." "I got to see the dance moves mom." Imani takes Allen by the hand. "Follow my lead son." Allen and his mother dance as she teaches him dance moves. "Mom, you got some great moves on you." "What can I say momma still got it." "What is the best advice you will give me on my first date?" "Be yourself showcase who you are. Be transparent with everything you say and do. And just know she is nervous just like you. If she truly likes you, she will respect you for the man that you're. When me and your father were in college together, he would put on this persona. Everyone liked it except for me. Because I saw right through it, me and he didn't like each other until our junior year of college. Once he fully showcased who he truly were that's when I started liking him. Stay true to who you are son."

Allen appreciates his mother's advice. He decides to ask an interesting question pertaining to his dad. "Dad told me his guitar playing led him to the wrong places. What did he mean?" Allen's Mom explains a small part of the reason. "Your Father was in a band called "The Phoenix" when we first met. They was well-known around Seward University. As success started to grow your father got caught up. It put him in a dark place which almost destroyed his life. But it's not my story to tell it's his." This makes Allen wants to know more about his father's past. "Something I'm definitely going to ask him about, but I shall go wish me good luck."

Allen drives to Shanice's house to pick her up for their date. He arrives at her house and knocks on the door. Shanice's Mother answers the door and says, "Hello, how can I help you?" Allen says, "Yes Ma'am I'm here to pick up Shanice for our date." "Oh, you are Allen please call me Ms. Lisa; she has been talking about you nonstop please come in."

Shanice's Mother yells out for her daughter. "Shanice, Allen is here to pick you up!" Allen bonds with Shanice's parents as he waits for her. "She told me you are the valedictorian for you guys' graduation class, you play the guitar and is the leading actor in her school play, you are like a rockstar." Allen laughs. "I know your parents are proud of you. What are the secrets to your success?" Allen gives a great answer. "Showcasing all the gifts that GOD has blessed me with. And following everything the Holy Spirit tells me to do. One thing I have learned in my life is when you follow GOD you can never go wrong." Shanice's Mother is impressed by him. "You are a wise, young man Allen. I can tell by looking at you and hearing your great wisdom that you are going to do great things. You are right when we follow GOD everything that is meant for us will come to pass. Never give up on your dreams and follow the pathway GOD lead you on." Shanice's Mother advice brings fire to Allen's soul. The advice is something he needed to hear. "Thank you, Ms. Lisa, for your advice I greatly appreciated it."

Shanice's Father comes downstairs to greet Allen. He shakes Allen's hand and says, "Hey, I'm Shanice's father, Greg, it's an honor meeting you, Allen. So where are you taking our daughter tonight?" "I'm taking her to Tay's Steakhouse for a bite to eat and chat. I will have her back home on time. Shanice is a wonderful person, I'm just glad to be getting to know her." "Our princess is a bright young lady. She told me a good amount about you Bon Jovi Jr. I'm impressed by your accolades and talents. I'm curious what do you want to do in your life?" Allen feels led to play music full-time, but he still not 100% sure. "To be honest with you Mr. Rogers, I honestly don't know. That's one thing GOD is slowly revealing to me." "You are young you got your whole life in front of you. Don't be in a rush, what truly is for you will come towards you. Stay walking in the right pathway. The same goes for you dating my daughter. GOD will reveal to you both if he wants your to be together. Stay doing what you doing and never lose focus." Shanice's Father likes and respects Allen as he hope that he follows what he feels in his spirit. Shanice's Mother says, "I hear footsteps coming this way." Shanice walks downstairs looking stunning in her outfit. As her beauty is striking Allen in a heavenly way. She says to him, "Well I see you met my parents. Mom and Dad, Allen here is a great guy as you can tell." "I most definitely am, you ready to go beautiful?" "I shall follow your lead good sir." Allen and Shanice arrives at Tay's Steakhouse. How will this first date go?

Chapter 6: The First Time

Allen is on his very first date. He's sitting across from the prettiest girl in his eyes. He hopes he makes a great impression on her tonight. He asks Shanice, "So are you excited for our play next Friday?" She says, "I most definitely am I was thinking we should give everybody a sneak peak of what we have in store." Shanice goes to the Jukebox in the restaurant and plays a song. "Come dance with me Allen." Allen gets up and dances with Shanice. They dance for four minutes to Maroon 5 "She Will Be Loved" they both gaze into each other eyes and amaze everybody in the restaurant with their dance moves. After dancing, Allen whispers in her ear, "Well, well you sure do get some great moves ma'am." "Well, I just follow the steps of a good fellow."

Allen and Shanice sit back down and have a detail discussion. Shanice asks, "I'm curious when did you begin eyeing me?" Allen reveals how he feels about Shanice. "I have been eyeing you since elementary school. All these years I have been scared to express my feelings to you until now. When I'm around you my heart skips a beat, seeing your smile brightens up my day. When you invited me to eat at Waffle House, I saw that as an opportunity to get to know you more. I'm glad I took advantage of that, I'm glad we are finally connected. What about you how long you been eyeing me?" "I have been checking you out since last year. It's more than just your physical, I'm attracted also to the person that you are. I have always seen you as an intelligent person and I admire the man you are. I am a huge fan of yours Mr. Allen Callahan and I would be glad to be the lady by your side." Allen touches Shanice's hands and says, "I would love to be the man by your side." They both look into each other's eyes and give each other a kiss. "So, I'm guessing that's what heaven taste like?" Shanice smiles and responds, "I will say close to it.

So, what big plans you have this weekend?" "Well, me and my dad are going to his alma mater Seward University. I got a scholarship offer there so we going to check out the campus." "That sounds fun, I'm curious what are your plans after you graduate?" Allen takes a minute to answer the question as he himself don't know the answer. "To be honest with you, I don't know. I could go to college and be a successful architect or professor. By doing that, in the world eyes my future will be guaranteed. I know in my heart; I want to do something that I truly love. One thing I learned from my mom is that life has its own plans. You never know where it takes you but just enjoy the memories that come with it. And learn from the situations that is put in your pathway. I just hope, I be happy wherever GOD leads me. What about you what is your plans after you graduate?" "I got plan on going to University of Georgia to take up Psychology. I want to be able to help and heal people, it's a great passion of mine. That's something that I love to do is to help people. And I know GOD will reveal to you on what he wants to you to do. Just know I'm here to support you." "Well with your beauty you can heal anybody's soul. You truly healing mine right now." Allen and Shanice kiss one more time.

Shanice has a present for Allen, she pulls out a bracelet out of her purse. "I made this bracelet for you hopefully you like it. Allen holds the bracelet, and he is amazed by it. Especially the message that is displayed on it. The message reads, "You are a star that will always shine bright." "I deeply appreciate this, I definitely will be wearing this bracelet everywhere I go." Shanice gives Allen a hug and a kiss on the cheek. "All of those words on the bracelet is true. You are someone special Allen, I hope and pray that is something you never forget." This means a lot to Allen, not only to be seen but to have the girl of his dreams seeing greatness in him.

Allen also tells Shanice about him performing tomorrow night at Michael's Bar in Athens, GA at 8 PM. "Also, The Believers the band I am in, we will be performing tomorrow I know it's far from here, but you should come see us perform. I will be singing and performing, so your guy will be rocking the stage in a big way." "I do have to meet up with a friend of mine early in the day. Although I will try my best to see my man perform." Allen leans back in his seat and smiles. "Your man, I'm your man?" "Yes, you are I just don't kiss anybody plus we have a beautiful connection. One that, I believe can blossom into something special." "So, in that case we are officially boyfriend and girlfriend?" "I'm happy to be your girl, Allen." It seems like things are finally falling into place for Allen as he got his dream girl. He and Shanice kiss the rest of the night away.

It's Saturday Morning, beautiful sunny day outside. And Al is super excited to be going back to his alma mater for his son's college visit. He has all his Seward University clothes on. Imani laughs as she looks at her husband jump around in his gear and says, "Al, you out here jumping like a bunny. You are super excited about this trip. And you cooked pancakes you hardly ever cook." Al responds, "Well, first off, I do cook a lot. Imani looks at Al with her eyebrows up. "Ok only on occasions, but when I do I throw down. I'm super excited to be going back to be going to Seward, especially with my son. I had great memories there; it was where we first met. I have been in love with your fine self ever since. I want Allen to experience some of the great memories like I did up there. I know I'm hard on him Imani, but I just want him to be better than me." "Our son is a bright young man who is going to amaze the world with his brilliance. It's time that you reveal to Allen what happened to you when you was in The Phoenix at Seward. And all about your past life he has the right to know." Al decide it's right for Allen to know the truth.

Al goes into Allen's bedroom and wakes him up to go to Seward University. He shakes Allen and says, "Wake up sleepy head it's time for us to hit the road, I already got your clothes pack and got a plate of breakfast made for you so giddy up cowboy." Allen had never seen his father this happy before. This is going to be one trip that will change Allen's life forever.

Allen gets up and gets dressed and he makes sure to pack his guitar. Before leaving the house, he calls Paul to tell him he is on his way to Dalton, GA. He says, "Paul me and my father are on our way to Seward right now." Paul responds, "Gotcha me and the rest of the band should be in Dalton by 3'oclock. When you get there, text Josh, so he can link up with you. Today is going to be a magical day in our lives. If people don't know the name Allen Callahan they are going to know tonight. Try to be at the Airbnb by 5'oclock so we can practice before our performance." "Gotcha Bossman I will see you in a few."

Before Allen leaves, he says goodbye to his brother and his mother. He gives his brother and mother a hug. Allen says to Jalean, "Alright knucklehead, I will see you later on." And he says to his mother, "Alright Mom wish me well, I love you. I have never seen Dad this happy before he been smiling like the Grinch all morning." Imani says, "This is something your father has been dreaming of since you was a baby. Showing his son his alma mater. I believe this trip is going to do both you and him good. At the same time, when it come to you picking out a college pick which one you feel like is best for you. I love you son have fun this weekend."

Allen and his father head to Seward University. On the way there, the father and son duo bond together. Allen asks his father, "What should I expect at Seward?" Al says, "You are going to experience amazing stuff and amazing people. When I went to Seward, I made great connections and friends for life. That is also where I met your mom. Being at Seward changed my life forever. I believe this is going to be a day that will have a lasting impact on your life son. So how did the date go between you and Shanice?" "It went very well we decided last night to officially be boyfriend and girlfriend. It's funny pops I dreamed of this girl being mine since elementary school and now I finally have her. I hope I don't screw it up."

Al gives Allen some relationship advice. "One thing I learned when it comes to relationships is taking it one day at a time. Enjoy every moment with your significant others, the good and the bad. Because each moment has either a wonderful memory or a lesson. Me and your mother were friends for a year before we dated. It was a time in my life when everybody walked away from me, but she stayed. She helped mold and build me up at my lowest. That was one of the things that showed me she was the one. Before we ever thought about taking vows, she was there for me at my worst. Now this is your first relationship, and you are just eighteen. Don't put too much pressure on yourself. You should invite her to church one Sunday would love to meet her." "I will Dad thanks for the advice."

After driving for two hours the guys finally arrive at Seward University in Dalton, Georgia. Al is super excited as they pullup in the parking lot. He and Allen gets out of the vehicle as they look at the university from the parking lot. Al says, "Welcome to the great Seward University my son. It has changed a bit since I been here, but the place still is beautiful." As Allen looks around the front of the campus, he falls in love with the scenery of the campus. As he and his dad walk towards the front of the campus they are approached by the Admissions Officer and fellow parents and students. The Admissions Officer speaks to the parents and students and says, "Welcome everyone to Seward University we are so glad to have you here. We are a precise university that takes pride in the principles that we teach here. Like this gentleman right here that has all our gear on." The Admissions Officer points at Al. The Officer asks Al, "Are you a Seward Alumni sir?" "Yes, I am and proud of it, Class of 1997. Representing the blue and black everywhere I go." "That what I love to hear. Well, ladies and gentlemen let's start this tour around this legendary campus."

As the tour starts, Allen sends a text message to Josh (Paul's Friend) that he is on campus. Josh responds in a text, "What's good my guy, Paul sent me a picture, so I know what you look like. I will meet up with you at the front of the campus after the tour is done. Let me know once you guys get done."

As Allen and his father walk around the campus. He can see that his dad was a huge name during his time on campus, Allen sees a picture of his father on the wall of former Class Presidents and says, "Pops you was class President?" Al smiles as he looks at the picture of himself and says, "Yes sir memories Class President of Seward University for the year 1997. This was right after some crazy mayhem in my life. Me and your mother started dating during this time. If it wasn't for her, I wouldn't be the man I am today." Al starts thinking about the good and bad memories he had at Seward.

As Allen, his Father, and the rest of the other parents walk around campus they meet the president of Seward University. The Admissions Officer introduces the parents and students to the Dean of the University. "I would like to introduce you guys to President Taylor. President Taylor speaks to the students and their parents. "Hey, welcome to Seward University, first and foremost."

She stops talking as she looks at Al as she says in a curious way, "Al". Al says in a shocking way, "Melanie!" They both stare at one another for a moment and give each other a hug. Allen and Melanie both went to Seward University together and graduated in 1997 together. While holding her hands, Al looks at Melanie and says, "It's been a long time, Mel; I must say you still look the same." She smiles as she looks at Al. "It's been too long Al, you look amazing yourself, is this your son you are with?" Al introduces Allen to Melanie. "Yes, Allen meet Melanie aka President Taylor." Melanie shakes Allen's hand. "It's an honor to meet you Allen, your father is a great old friend of mine. Speaking of which I think Al, you should join me on giving everyone a tour of the campus. You know this place like the back of your hand. Without hesitation Al accepts President's Taylor request. He smiles big as the sun and sounds out loud. "Ladies and gentlemen please follow my lead."

For the next three hours, Allen sees all through Seward University and he sees why his father loves the University. His Dad is smiling ear-to-ear as he showing everyone around campus. While all of this is sweet to Allen, he asks himself is this the right pathway he needs to follow in his life. After the tour is over with, He texts Josh, "The tour is over with now come meet up with me when you get a chance." Josh texts back, "Bet my guy on my way to you." Al and President Taylor approaches Allen. Al asks, "So son how did you enjoy the tour today?" "I had a great time I enjoyed myself. In my opinion I think Seward University is a great college to go to." Al turns his head towards President Taylor. "Well, you look at that Melanie, you might have another Callahan coming on your campus." Allen shrugs his shoulders like Michael Jordan. "You never know what life has in store." "Well either way Allen I'm going to give you my business card it has my personal number on it. If you need any advice or help when it comes to college feel free to reach out to me." "Thank you, I most definitely will."

As Allen is talking to his dad and President Taylor, Josh approaches him. He says, "Excuse me Allen it was so nice meeting you earlier. I hope you decide to join us at Seward University." Allen shakes Josh's hand with a smile and says, "It was an honor meeting you to Josh and you never know I might be a fellow Seward student just like you." Al smiles and says, "See son you are already in the Seward spirit." "My apologizes where are my manners I'm Josh." Josh shakes Al hands. "I'm Allen's Father, you can call me Mr. Al." "Nice to meet you Mr. Al, President Taylor it is an honor seeing you." "I'm glad to see you too Josh. Josh is one of our brightest students here, we are so grateful to have him. Are you ready for Finals coming up?" "I am I can't wait I already know I'm going to pass. Allen, me and a couple of friends of mine are hanging out for the rest of the evening. Do you want to join us? If it's ok with you Mr. Al. Allen looks at his father and is surprised by his response. "It's ok with me go Allen and have fun you deserve it. Just text me and let me know where you be at." Allen is glad that Paul's plan worked. "Ok, what you going to do in the meantime pops?" "I'm going to catch up with President Taylor, I will be ok." "You guys have fun see you later." Allen is glad that his father and President Taylor have a strong prior connection, it worked out better for his plan.

Allen and Josh walk away and get to know one another. Josh asks, "So what do you think about Seward?" Allen says, "It seems like a great college, my father and mother graduated from here. How long you been going here?" "About two years, I'm a sophomore I'm taking up Computer Forensics. To be honest with you, I'm in College to figure out what I want to do with my life. I know by getting a bachelor's degree in Computer Forensics, I will have a high paying job once I graduate. I suggest you figure out what you want to do in life before you graduate from High School." "That's something I been thinking about a lot lately. I believe this trip is going to help me out with that. I forgot to ask you how you know Paul?" "Paul is a fun guy to be around. Me and him met at a Playboi Carti concert last year ever since then we have been friends. I know he told me you guys are in a band together, how long you been doing that?" "Literally for two weeks our band is named The Believers. I'm passionate about music, I love writing and playing the guitar. When I get on stage, I get a great release from everything that's going on in my life. I used to be shy, but now when I get on that stage, I let it rip. When I'm up there I feel free from everything." "I saw the last performance you guys did online, you was fantastic. Your guitar skills and that girl that was singing were freaking lethal." "Appreciated Claudia she is amazing at what she does." "Your two got some great chemistry are your dating?" Allen laughs. "No Claudia is somewhat like a sister to me. She's a beautiful human being one that I am glad to be friends with." "Beautiful girl can't wait to meet her. I got to go to my room to get something then after that I will take you to Paul."

Josh takes Allen to his dorm room where he meets Josh's roommate. Josh says, "Allen, meet my roommate Simon, Simon this is my homeboy, Allen. He's here for the College recruiting tour." Simon daps up Allen and says, "Wassup Allen, Josh told me a bit about you, do you smoke?" Simon pulls out a blunt. Allen says, "Nah bro I don't smoke how long you been at Seward?" "Thanks to my parents, I been here for a year I'm taking up Cyber Security. If it was up to me, I would be in California rapping with my homies. I had a choice to either go to college or find another place to stay at." Allen relates a bit to Simon. "I can understand my father is the same way with me. It seems like parents want to guide all parts of our lives. Why won't they just let us be free and do our own thing. I understand they want the best for us but let us be ourselves."

Simon gives Allen advice that will help change the trajectory of his life. "You know man granted our parents do want the best for us, but at the same time follow your dreams. You live one life, do what you love, for me I got to put my dreams on hold. My parents already invested a good amount of money in my college life. I'm going to at least get my degree and make some connections. Then when I get a job in the IT field, I can use the money I make from it to fund my rap career. You can do the same thing for whatever passion you have. Don't matter what anybody says, follow what's in your heart. Make the best decision that is best for you Allen." Allen can see the realness in Simon's eyes. He decides at this moment he's going to follow his dreams. As he knows in his heart music is his true passion. No matter what anybody has to say about it. Josh comes back in the room and says, "I got what I need are you ready to go Allen?" "Yes, I am, Simon it was an honor meeting you and thank you for the advice." Simon stands up from his chair and shakes Allen's hand. "It was an honor meeting you too Allen, prosper in the right direction my brother."

Josh takes Allen to Paul's Airbnb. As Josh and Allen pull up to the Airbnb. Paul rushes to the vehicle and hugs Allen. He says to him, "My boy how was Seward?" Allen says, "It was great today has shown me to follow what is in your heart. I decided I'm going to fully pursue music." Paul smiles, he is glad that his friend has decided to follow his true passion. "I'm proud of you my brother, just know I'm with you every step of the way. Josh thank you for bringing him here, how's the college life going?" Josh says, "You welcome and it's going that's all I can say. That's why I told Allen to plan out what he wants to do before he graduates. The same goes for you too when you graduate." "I already got my stuff planned out; but for right now we need to practice for our performance."

Paul, Allen, and Josh go inside of the house and are greeted by Joe. As Claudia comes from the back, she smiles as she sees Allen has arrived at the Airbnb. She gives him a hug and says, "Welcome aboard Mr. Superstar how are you feeling?" Allen shows off the bracelet, Shanice made for him and says, "I am in great spirits, tonight is going to be amazing." Claudia can see a change in Allen and loves the new him. "I like this new energy I see from you. Who made the bracelet for you?" "Shanice made it for me." Claudia smiles. "Well look at you already getting gifts after one date. I take it went well." "Yes, it went better than expected, we decided to be boyfriend and girlfriend. And see how things will go. How did your date go with Kevin?" Claudia eyes start sparkling while she reminces about the date. "It was magical talking to him felt like meeting with a long-lost best friend. We both are digging each other, however we still are taking things slow." "I love to hear that." Claudia sees Josh taking glances at her. "Who's your friend?" Allen introduces Josh to Claudia. "Claudia this is Josh; Josh this is Claudia." Josh says, "It is so nice to meet you, you are lovely just like your lovely voice." Claudia responds. "Well since you love my performance you better come see us perform tonight." "Best believe I will watch you spark Ms. Sunlight." Paul runs into the house and says, "Alright peeps let start practicing." The band practices for one hour and then heads to Lakeside Lounge.

While the band is prepared to perform. Al and Melanie are at a restaurant catching up with one another. Melanie says, "I haven't seen you in forever, the last time I saw you was at our 10-year graduation reunion. How's life been?" Al says, "It's been great, I'm still the president of National First Bank in Macon. Me and Imani are still happily married about to celebrate our 21st anniversary in a few months. Trying to raise our two sons in the right direction. I'm hard on both of them, but I just want them to be better than me." "Well in my opinion you doing a great job. I hope to meet your other son one day, you did a fine job raising Allen he's a well-mannered young man." "Allen is different from most kids his age. He's gifted, intelligent and great when it comes to solving issues. Allen Callahan Jr is an amazing talent that is going to make a great impact on this earth with his gifts and talents. I know he thinks I'm hard on him, but I don't want him to go through what I had to go through. I almost ended up losing my life ruined a few friendships and my relationship with you in the process."

Al and Melanie are not only former classmates, but they also used to be in a relationship with one another during their college years. Melanie holds Al's hand. "I'm sorry that I left you during that time, but I'm not going to lie most of us thought you was a lost cause. When you got on drugs, I tried my best to help you with that. When you had your drug overdose that was my final straw. You didn't let that stop you though, you came back better than ever. You are living proof that you can go through a storm in life and still overcome."

Al starts thinking about his wild days at Seward University. "I was a crazy person when I was here, I'm sorry for putting you through all that turmoil. You were great to me; you didn't deserve to go through all the stuff I put you through. Just know Melanie, I will always love and care for you." Melanie has small tears falling from her eyes as she thinks about the time her and Al shared together. "I remember you telling me you were going to be the next Lenny Kravitz, and I was your Lisa Bonet. We had some great times together Al, but Imani was the better woman for you. The way she helped you to recovery and helped you become the man you're. I could've never done that for you. When you came back from rehab and I saw the man you became, I was like that's the man I always wanted. However, it was too late you and Imani started dating during that time. I wish I had a chance with this version of you. Granted just like you, I started a family of my own. However sometimes at night, I think about what could have been between us." They both look at each other as both of them remember the memories they had together. "I know that the love we once had between us can't be rekindled. Just know you will always be in my heart Al."

Even though they have been broken up for over twenty-something years, Melanie has always hoped and prayed that Al stays on the right path. She knows that Al became successful, but the main thing she wonders is did he follow what he was truly passionate about. She leans back in her seat and stares at him. Al can tell something is heavily on Melanie's mind by the way she's looking at him. "I know that look, what's on your mind Mel?" "I'm curious I know you were passionate about music, you never thought about doing Gospel music?" Al is transparent with Melanie on his reason for quitting music. "After I got off drugs, I honestly lost my love for performing music at the same time. Plus, the odds of me to get signed to a major label was very slim. If I would've continued, I probably would be the old man at a bar playing sad tunes all night. In the end, I'm glad I chose my occupation because I have been able to provide for my family and myself." "There is some truth to what you said there, but the passion that you had for music was crazy. In my opinion that something that just don't go away. Who knows maybe you still can?" Al laughs. "They say Kevin Hart is a great comedian, but I think you might have him beat. I do thank you for the nice compliment, but that part of my life has passed me by. I want both of my sons to be better than me. I plan on revealing everything to Allen about my past tomorrow. I really want him to be a better man than me."

Melanie grabs Al's hands and looks at him directly in his eyes. "Well first of, your sons are going to do great things in their lifetime. Second and finally never let your dreams die away. Even though it might seem they have faded away. You should go out and conquer them because you don't want to live life with any what ifs. You are a powerful man, Al; it would be ashamed for you not to showcase all of the great skills you have inside of you." Al smiles as he loves what Melanie said to him. "Ms. Melanie Taylor, you always have a great way with words. Thank you for your words of encouragement." "The same with you to Mr. Al Callahan, so I guess this is where we say goodbye." Al smiles. "More like see you later." "You be well Al, I wish you and Imani nothing but the best and I love you." "I wish you nothing, but prosperity in life, and I love you too Mel." The two former lovers give each other a tight warm hug and go their separate ways.

On the other side of town, Allen is getting prepared to perform with his band, as they are backstage together, Claudia talks to Allen and asks, "Are you ready to bless the stage?" Allen no longer has any timid feelings in his mind and body when it comes to performing on stage. Allen says, "I'm just ready to showcase to everybody what greatness we have in store for them." Claudia looks in Allen eyes and sees the change in him. "I'm proud of you Allen, you starting to turn into who you are truly meant to be. Let's show these people what we are made of."

The whole band is behind the curtain as the host gets ready to announce their name. The host says to the crowd, "Ladies and gentlemen this band hails from Macon I would like to introduce you guys to "The Believers"." The band walks up on the stage.

As Allen walks on the stage, he smiles as he sees Kevin in the crowd, but most of all he sees Shanice. He gets on the mic and says, "Thank you guys for joining us we are The Believers, and we shall bless you with our greatness." Allen grabs his guitar and starts performing the song he and Claudia wrote together called "I Just Want To Be Free". Throughout the performance, Allen sings the song with full passion. The riffs coming from his guitar brings soulful energy into the atmosphere. As in his own life he wants to be free. He wants to be himself and not be judged for it. He wants to be a musician that will inspire people with his music. A resurgence has happened within him. As he knows what he wants in his life, he is going to do everything in his power to achieve it. Allen and The Believers have the crowd in awe as they have them falling in love with them. The band performs three more songs as they have electrified the crowd in Dalton tonight. When the band gets done performing, they get a standing ovation. The host gets back on the mic and says, "Y'all give it up for The Believers!"

As the band goes backstage, Paul yells out loud, "That's how you put on a show!" He puts his arm around Allen's neck and says, "You are the baddest guitarist I know! You was amazing on the stage. I'm proud of you, my brother." Joe congratulates Allen on a job well done. Claudia gives Allen a hug. She says, "I am super proud of you. You finally letting people know who Allen Callahan truly is." Allen says, "Thank you this is only just the beginning." Shanice comes backstage and runs towards Allen and gives him a hug. She says, "Babe you did amazing I loved everything you sung I'm so proud of you. And you did amazing also Claudia." Allen is happy that Shanice came to see him. "You drove all the way here just to see me?" "Of course I wasn't going to miss your performance." Paul and Joe runs towards Allen, Claudia, and Shanice. Paul says, "Guys they calling us back on stage hopefully we win this $500."

All the bands that performed tonight all come back on stage to see who won the open mic and who won the $500. The Host comes on stage and says, "First of, give it up for all the bands on this stage. They did an amazing job on this stage, but unfortunately only one band can win. And you guys voted for which band you like the most online. And the band that has the most votes is." Allen and Paul look at one another nervously hoping the host picks them to win the grand prize. "The Believers! The Believers are the winner of the open mic give it up for them!" The whole band jumps in joy as they win the open mic and win the $500. Allen and Paul, both hug one another and says to one another that they are proud of each other. Claudia hugs Allen and says, "We did it!" Allen smiles as he is getting rewarded for showcasing his gifts. The band goes quickly backstage and split the $500.

After coming backstage, Allen is greeted by Kevin. He hugs Allen and says, "My boy I'm so freaking proud of you. You have officially come out of your shell. You are a freaking rockstar." Allen responds, "Thank you Kevin, for all of your support. I finally decided today to follow my dreams, the ones that I want in my life. I'm finally being the true version of myself." Kevin smiles as he is happy that his friend is finally going after what he wants in life. "I'm happy for you Allen."

As Allen talk to more people, he gets a phone call from his dad. He answers, "Hey dad." Al says, "Hey son just seeing where are you at? It seems a little crowded where you at from what I hear in the background." Allen lies to his father where he is at. "Yeah, Josh has a whole bunch of people in his dorm room right now we all just hanging out. You mind if I spend the night here." Usually, Al would say no in this situation, but he feels his son works hard and deserves a good break. "I don't mind Allen you work super hard you deserve a break. Just have Josh bring you back to the hotel tomorrow morning I love you son." "I love you too Dad."

After getting off the phone with his father, Paul comes toward Allen and says, "Alright Allen, we are about to head to the house are you ready to go?" Allen says, "Yeah man let's go ahead and go." Paul yells out in the bar, "Everybody celebration at our Airbnb!"

As the band heads out the bar, they get stopped by this tall white man in a blue suit and tie. The guy says to them, "Excuse me The Believers can I talk to you guys for a second?" The band walks towards the gentleman, Paul asks, "How can we help you sir?" "I must say you guys did an amazing job. I was wondering who wrote that amazing song that you guys performed. Claudia and Allen step towards the front. Claudia points at her herself and Allen and says, "Me and Allen wrote the song together." "Y'all two wrote a beautiful masterpiece and great singing also. I forgot to introduce myself. My name is Jack Stevens; I'm an A&R Rep at Cloud Records. I have been looking for great songwriters and artists for the label. And I think the

Believers could be a perfect fit. I'm in Georgia for a whole month; I would love to have a meeting with you guys and talk. Here's my card call me if you're interested you guys have an excellent night."

The band are left stunned as they have just had their first meeting with a label executive. Allen asks Paul, "What do you think we should do?" Paul responds, "Let's go to the house and discuss everything." Everyone goes to the house and party the night away. While partying, Paul and Allen go to a private area to talk to each other. Allen asks Paul, "What did you wanted to talk to about?" Paul takes a swig of his drink and says, "I have a made an important decision when it comes to my life and career. I decided I'm going to go to college and take up Business Management at Central Georgia Technical College. I'm still going to be in the band and produce music. I want to become a manager for music artists, but I want to learn the ins and outs of the music industry at the same time." Allen is a bit surprised to hear about his friend's aspirations. "I'm happy for you Paul, I'm not going to lie I'm surprised you are going to college. I'm proud of you, you know I got your back every step of the way." "Appreciated Allen, I really want to hear what you got going on. What dream have you decided to follow?" "I decided to become a full-time musician. It's what I love and that's what I'm going after. I do have plans on going to college and taking up a trade. So, I can have money to help fund our music career. It's just now finding out which college is best for me to go to." Paul is happy to hear Allen say this. "Go for everything you want my guy. How you think your parents are going to take the news of you mainly focusing on your craft?"

Even though Allen has decided to follow his dreams as a musician, he decides to wait to tell his parents about his aspirations. "I'm going to wait to tell them until I get done with the college tours. I like the idea you have of performing in every town I have a college visit at. That will help bring more attention towards us. I have three more college visits I want our band to perform in those cities. Then after that, I will break the news to my parents. In the meanwhile, let's show everybody what we are made of. Everything is a process we must take things slow. We are going to make it together." Allen and Paul dap each other as they have big plans in store for their future.

After talking the guys go back partying with everybody. As everybody is talking, Allen goes up to Shanice and kisses her and says, "Beautiful I am so glad that you are here with me." Shanice responds, "Well I wasn't going to miss the chance to see the great Allen Callahan play in person. I can't wait to see what greatness you display when we have our show together this Friday night." "Well as you can see, I can bring light to anybody's night. As every time I see your face I smile big like a fat kid eating chocolate cake. I'm thinking we should go in a room and talk in private."

Shanice and Allen goes to a bedroom in the Airbnb and start kissing one another. Allen's flesh is telling him to go all the way with Shanice. However, as he is kissing on her body, he can remember his father telling him to stay pure. And the power of creating soul ties with someone. He stops kissing her as he lays down on the pillow to think about some things. Shanice looks at Allen as she is concerned about him. She lays down alongside him to make sure he's alright. "Allen, are you ok?" "I apologize for doing what I just did. I let my emotions take over my thoughts, I'm not with having sex before marriage. I know I can't do it; I can't go against GOD. I hope you don't breakup with me because of this." Shanice isn't mad at Allen for not wanting to have sex. "Silly, I'm not leaving you. We don't have to have sex; that's no issue at all. I was raised the same way to not have sex before marriage. I'm a follower of Christ also, the key thing to make this relationship work is putting GOD number one in our life. Just how we honor GOD with our mind we got to the same thing with our body." Allen is relieved to hear Shanice saying this. Plus, it gives him confirmation that she's the right girl for him. He rubs her forehead as in his heart he is thankful for her being in his life. "This is the first relationship I've ever been in; I don't want to ruin it." "This is my second relationship, one thing I will say is we both aren't perfect. We are going to make mistakes; the key thing is we learn from them and build each other. I like you for who you are, so just staying being you. I'm here for you Allen, I'm not going nowhere." Hearing Shanice says this eases off pressure on Allen. The idea he had in his head of being the perfect boyfriend is erased from his mind now.

Allen decides to tell Shanice what he has planned on doing with his life. "You remember when you asked me about my future?" "I sure do, you have been thinking more about it?" "With the way I feel right now, I want to give my all into music so I can make it big. I truly know now that my purpose in life is to inspire people through music. Tell me what you think about everything I just stated." Allen wonders what Shanice is thinking. "It's great to know that you have recognized your calling in life. Although the dreams and goals we want in life doesn't happen overnight. To achieve them we must go through the process to accomplish them. Babe, you're an amazing musician. I love hearing you sing and play music. I know the whole world is going to see that one day. However, you must make sure you have money to fund your music career. By going to college, you could use a college refund, and a part-time job to help fund everything. Plus, with you going to school you can build a bigger fanbase. And that place you go to, can be your stomping grounds."

Allen knows his purpose, now he must come up with a great strategy to save up money for his music career. "You're correct thank you for your input, I greatly appreciate it. Now I must decide which College I want to attend." "What is the next college you have to visit?" "Georgia State University, Kennesaw State University, and University of Georgia." "Well, when you go to each university you have to see which one has the fanbase that you and your fellow bandmates want to attract. I will say what made me decide to go to UGA was that they made me feel like family when I came to visit. I feel like the best places to go to college are ones that appreciate who you are. And that has programs and people that truly want to help you be the best version of yourself. If you want, I can go with you on these last three college tours. If you're okay with that." "I don't mind at all; it's going to be great having you by my side. I know with that, I want you to meet my parents. I believe they will be happy to meet you." Shanice is happy that Allen wants her to meet his parents. "I will love that let me know when we can meet up." "I will." Allen grabs Shanice's hand. "I have your back just like you have mines." Allen and Shanice kiss one another as they can't wait to see what GOD will do in their lives.

The next morning Allen wakes up as he thinks about everything, he discussed with Shanice last night. He has a detailed plan for what he wants in life now. He says a prayer before starting off his day. "Dear GOD, thank you for this day you have given us. I know that you are using me as a vessel to reach your people. Bring the people around me that I can inspire and teach them your truth. I was thinking of doing everything my way, but I know I need to do it your way. I give it all up to you GOD. Also, I thank you for bringing Shanice into my life. I give you my word that I will protect and always be there for her. I hope that this connection between us develop into something special. Thank you, GOD, for everything that you're doing, and I shall honor you in all of my days. In Jesus name, I pray amen." Allen looks at Shanice as she looks like an angel sleeping. He rubs Shanice's cheekbones and says, "Beautiful angel." He gives Shanice a kiss on the forehead.

She wakes up from her sleep, she opens her eyes and sees Allen beautifully looking at her. With a smile on her face, she softly says, "Hey you, is it time to go back to Macon?" "Yes, it is sleepyhead get on up. It's time to hit the road." Shanice gets up from the bed and puts her arms around Allen. "I enjoyed our time together last night; we had a great conversation. Do you mind if I pray for you?" "Sure, I don't mind take it away."

Shanice says a prayer for Allen. "Dear Heavenly Father, thank you for all you have done in our lives. I thank you for letting Allen recognize his calling in life. I believe and I know with his gifts he's going to get more people closer to you. I promise I will do my part to help him be a great vessel for you." Allen tightly holds Shanice's hands and prays for her. "And I promise to help Shanice with the purpose you have given her in her life. I'm not going nowhere; I'm going to stay by her side through thick and thin. We shall put you first before anything GOD." Allen and Shanice at the same time say, "In Jesus name we pray amen." Allen and Shanice hug one another. Shanice pats him on the back. "We're going to be just fine baby."

The whole band is in the living room. Paul claps his hands as he sees Allen and Shanice walks in. He says, "Well, well if it isn't my favorite couple. Shanice, did you enjoy our performance last night?" Shanice says, "I did of course I was mainly looking at Allen, however all of you were amazing. You guys are going places, and I will be in the front row cheering you on everytime." Paul looks at Allen. "My brother you better keep this woman by your side." Allen smiles and responds, "She knows she stuck with me." Shanice laughs. "Any who have you guys decided about that A&R guy we met last night. Paul responds, "I did my research on him, this dude done helped discover a lot of great artists even Tommy Fames and Nicole Wheeler. I say let's give him a call and set up a meeting right after our next performance. I believe he can do big things for our careers and our lives." "Sounds like a plan for me well I got to get back to my dad before he get the SWAT team looking for me. Babe, could you take me back to my hotel?" "Of course I got you. We will see you guys later, have a safe trip back to Macon."

Shanice takes Allen to his father. On the way there, while enjoying the beautiful sunset he thinks about what the future would be like with her in his life. A smile crosses his face as he sees them riding in the sunset together. Holding each other hands and enjoying life.

Shanice drops Allen off at the hotel. She says to him, "Well cowboy it's that time to depart. Let me just say I am proud of you. Never let anything stop you from showcasing your greatness." Allen says, "I thank you for your love and support." "Always that will never change." Allen hugs Shanice as he is thankful to have her in his life.

As she drives away, Allen's Father is on the balcony of his hotel suite looking at his son. Al yells out to his son, "How was your night sport? Allen responds, "It's one night; I will never forget." "I'm glad you had fun I got all your bags pack so go ahead and get in the car. I got a place I want to show you before we head home."

Allen and his father leaves the hotel. On their way back home, they stop at Homer's Lake, which is twenty minutes away from Seward University. Al gets out of the vehicle and grabs his guitar from the backseat. As he closes the door he smiles as he enjoys the scenery around him. Allen gets out of the car as he can tell his father has something on his mind. He asks, "Dad, are you okay?" Al responds, "I'm okay this place that we are at, I use to come to it every time I had an issue or wanted to get away from everybody, I would come here to find peace. It's a lot you don't know about me so I'm going to tell you about my life in college."

Al reveals everything about his experience in college. He says, "When I was at Seward University, I was in this band called "The Phoenix" with your Uncle Scott (Al's best friend and Allen's Godfather). My dream at that time was to be a musician. In my opinion our group was talented enough to break big in the business. I was a rockstar on campus literally, I was living the lifestyle. I was excelling in school; my music career was popping off. Had a wonderful girlfriend at the time." "What was her name?" "Her name was Melanie Taylor, President Taylor was not only my old classmate, but my ex-girlfriend also. We dated for three years it was a great relationship. As everything was progressing in my life, I developed a drug addiction to Cocaine. I was addicted to it for six months until I had my drug overdose. The doctors thought I wasn't going to make it, but through the grace of GOD I made it through. Your Grandpa Bill and Grandma Jill put me through rehab. That meant a lot to me, they could've easily turned their back on me, but instead they did everything in their power to help me. During that time almost everyone on campus turned their back on me except for two people. Your Uncle Scott and your mother. The love and support that they both gave helped me out tremendously. When I came back to Seward, I became stronger than ever. Became Class

President, my last year in college and graduated with a 3.7 GPA. I know some of this information is surprising to you. It's one of the main reasons why I'm so hard on you and Jalean. I want you guys to be better than me. If I don't say it enough just know that I love you, Allen. What do you think about everything I told you?"

Allen is surprised by his father's past as he always saw his dad as Mr. Goody Two Shoes. "I'm surprised you went through all of that stuff. I'm glad that you made it through and changed your life for the better. I am curious by you having your overdose is that what made you quit music?" "Honestly it did when I had my overdose, I lost my passion of being a musician. Of course, I still play for fun, but I do think at times if I would've never done drugs how would my music career would've panned out. Any whom I am happy with the decision that I made. Just know I am proud of you Allen. Before we leave let's play some music together." The Father and Son duo play on their guitars for thirty minutes before going home.

As they return home, Al and Allen reflect on their trip. Both are happy as they now have a closer bond with each other. As they both walk in the house they are greeted by Imani and Jalean. Imani with a big smile on her face gives Al and Allen a hug and says, "My boys are back home how was the trip?" Jalean asks, "Did you guys bring me anything back?" Al pulls out a jersey from his suitcase and says, "Yes, I did, I bought you a Lamar

Jackson jersey your old man didn't forget about you son. And me and Allen had a great time together. Plus, I was able to make peace with some stuff from my past. Overall, I think we might have another Allen Callahan going to Seward University." Al pats Allen on the back. Allen smiles as he has three more college tours. Imani asks him, "So son what do you think about Seward?" Allen says, "It's a great college, I made some great connections there. It looks like a great college to go to, but pops hold your horses I got three more universities to visit before I make my decision. Shanice wants to accompany me on my final visits. Before that happens, I want to bring her to meet you all." Both Al and Imani are happy about this. Jalean is surprised that his brother finally got a girlfriend. Imani says excitedly, "Yes we will be happy to have her for dinner." Al says, "Let's have her over Thursday night." Allen smiles as he's glad his family is happy to meet his girlfriend.

After catching up with one another, the family eat Sunday Dinner together. After dinner, Imani goes to talk to Al in private in their bedroom. She says, "Well sir did you tell our son everything about your past?" Al says, "I told him everything that happened during my college years. From me being in a rock band, my relationship with Melanie and my drug addiction and how I overcame it. I hope he listened to everything I told him." "Hopefully he took everything you said to heart; however, you still need to tell him everything about your past. He needs to know about your upbringing, but at the same time I know why you haven't told him. You don't like to think about your childhood." Al had a painful and sad childhood; he never told his kids what he endured when he was young. "I know one day I'm going to have to face the music." "Eventually the truth will come out, meanwhile with you guys going to Seward, I know you had to run into Melanie. How was your meetup with her?" "We had dinner together and fully settled past differences. I'm glad me and her finally talked. But I want you to always remember you are the only lady that has a key to my heart. I love you Imani always and forever." "I love you to Al." Al and Imani hug and kiss one another.

While lying in his bed, Allen goes on his social media page and see he has gained 300 followers. He says to himself, "Holy Smoke". The once shy boy is now getting recognition for his gift. How will this affect his school life?"

Chapter 7: Finding That Special Place

It's a beautiful Monday morning; Allen pulls up in his High School's parking lot blasting Future's song "Honest". As he is in a very good mood. Once he arrives at the school, he meets up with Paul in the parking lot. As he sees Allen, he yells out for him. Paul says, "Allen my boy come over here!" Allen walks over to Paul as they dap one another up. Paul brags about the group's success over the last two days. "Bro we are freaking superstars. The group's social media followers have risen to almost two thousand followers. Your boy getting some groupies also. But any who how many more college visits you have?" Allen says, "I have three more and the next one I have is at Georgia State in Atlanta." "Perfect I will schedule a gig for us when you make your visit. I'm going to schedule a meeting for us with the A&R guy we met on Saturday." "That sounds good let's make it happen."

Allen and Paul walk into their school building. All the students look at them in awe as if they were The Backstreet Boys. The once under looked kids in the school are now being looked at as superstars. Allen, who hardly ever got attention from the ladies before, is getting a good amount of attention from the ladies. As multiple of them says to him with a smile on their face, "You are amazing Allen."

Allen goes to his creative writing class. While in class, Ms. Maggie and Allen discuss his valedictorian speech. She asks Allen, "How's everything coming along with your speech Allen?" He says, "It's coming well through the adventures that I'm going through right now in life it's going to help me give a powerful speech to everyone."

After talking to Allen, Ms. Maggie talks about the Dirty Dancing play that Allen and Shanice are starting in. She says to the class, "In other news, we have our Dirty Dancing play this Friday night at 7 PM starting Mr. Allen Callahan and Ms. Shanice Nicholas. Let's give them a round of applause as they will razzle the crowd with their great talents. Allen and Shanice both smile at each other.

As they walk out of class, Allen and Shanice talk to each other. Shanice says, "You're the man on campus right now. You got the whole school talking about you and girls looking at you. Allen laughs and says, "True I do, but you're the only girl that I want to lock eyes with." Allen's comment makes Shanice feels good as she hopes he stays true to himself as he rises as a star. "You know how to put a smile on my face. I hope you don't let all the attention get to you." "I won't, it's funny though I wanted popularity for a long time. Now that I have it, it doesn't mean anything to me. It's sad that people see your greatness, but don't recognize or acknowledge you until a whole bunch of people do."

"That just how some people are, just know I'm going to be with you during the good and the bad." Allen hugs Shanice as he is very thankful for her love and support.

After practice for the "Dirty Dancing" play, Allen heads straight to work. When he arrives there, he is greeted by Blake and Kevin. Kevin says out loud, "Mr. Rockstar can I have your autograph?" Allen laughs and says, "For one of my biggest fans of course." Allen starts laughing and daps the guys up. "So how has it been here since I been away?" "Not really a whole bunch same stuff just a different day. Our boy Blake stepped up during your time away I'm proud of him." Blake says, "Well what can I say I learn from the best." Blake throws his hands up to Allen as he says that statement. "I'm happy for you Blake and I'm also proud of you." "Thank you that means a lot coming from you. Well, I hear them calling my name to help bag groceries. I will catch up with you guys later."

As Blake goes to bag groceries, Kevin and Allen talks about Allen's future. "So, Mr. Allen you are finally going for your dreams as a musician fully. I'm curious how do your parents feel about everything?" "I'm waiting till I get done with my last college tour coming up before I tell them anything. I'm going to live the life that GOD has created for me. I did get closer with my dad during my trip. He opened up to me on his past life. Found out he tried to be a musician himself, but he lived a rockstar lifestyle.

It almost cost him his life. Which makes sense on why he didn't want me or my brother listening to or playing no music that wasn't Christian music. Even though music didn't work out for him, who say it won't work out for me. I shall chase every dream that is meant for me."

Kevin is very proud of Allen. As he is seeing a transformation from a boy to a man. "I'm proud of you, you finally living life for yourself not for anyone else. I saw Shanice was there to cheer you on when I saw you guys in Dalton. It seems like you two are getting closer." Allen slowly brushes his hair with a smirk on his face. "If you would have told me a couple of months ago, I would be with her I would call you a liar. We had a magical time together out there in Dalton." "Little Allen finally got himself a girl. I'm happy for you, my guy." "I know I'm going to do my best to keep her by my side. How is everything going between you and Claudia?" "It's going well we be having a fun time together. And no red flags has risen during our time together. We need to arrange a double date one day." "Most definitely, well let's start working before Jimmy comes out hollering at us."

It's Thursday evening and the cast of the Dirty Dancing play has its final day of rehearsal. Before the rehearsal begins, Principal Davenport speaks to Allen. He slightly pats Allen on the shoulder as he sitting down and says, "Allen I must say I'm proud of the young man you are becoming. Almost every time I see you it's like you stay growing as a person. Always remember to stay true to who you are."

The final rehearsal goes extremely well as the cast is ready to showcase their talents to the crowd tomorrow at 7 PM. Gabrielle, the director of the play says to the cast and crew, "I must say you all have done an excellent job with preparing for this play. Give yourself a round of applause. And I got to give a special shoutout to our leading man Mr. Allen Callahan granted at first it was bumpy, but you stepped up in a big way and made your light shine. Guys let's give Allen a round of applause." Allen gets a round of applause for his great work on the Dirty Dancing play. As he looks to his right, he sees Shanice smiling at him as she is proud of his hard work.

After the rehearsal is officially over with, Allen speaks to Shanice, "Hey babe how are you doing?" Shanice says, "I'm doing great I can't wait for tomorrow to display my acting chops to everybody. And I can't wait to meet your family today." "I can't wait for you to meet them also. Just so you know, my family doesn't know anything about me performing music. Please don't mention anything about it at dinner. In the meantime, I want to take you somewhere before I go to work." This has made Shanice very excited. "Oooh an adventure where are you taking me king?" "Follow my lead."

Allen takes Shanice to this wonderful park downtown that has a beautiful waterfall. He says to her, "So what do you think of the place?" She says, "I love it, the nature is so beautiful." "I have a surprise for you sit on the bench." Allen quickly goes to his car and grabs his guitar. Allen comes back to the bench where Shanice is sitting. As Shanice sees Allen with his guitar she wonders if he is going to sing something for her. "Are you about to perform out here?" "Yes, I am for the beautiful lady that is in my presence. This song is dedicated to the finest gal I know. The name of the song is "Shanice". Allen starts singing the song. "Baby you are my star, when my nights get cold I look to the sky and I vision you, as the vision of your face drift away all negativity I feel in my life, When I'm down below and my body is weak, just hearing your voice it makes me strong again, stay singing your sweet melodies to me as it makes my heart skips a beat, when you hug me I am let free of the sadness and madness this life brings, you the main lady that makes my heart sings, Shanice I love you, Shanice I adore you, Shanice I need you always in my life(2x). Love kissing your lips as it like feeling the drips of the beautiful deep sea, babydoll you my Lois Lane, my cat woman, my fighter as you bring flame to my life, you the brightest light this world has seen, I hope this love between us stay forever as this is something you would only see in a movie scene. Shanice, I love you, Shanice, I adore you, Shanice I need you in my life(2x)." Once Allen gets done playing the song for Shanice tears start flowing down from her eyes. She hugs Allen tightly as the song makes her feel truly loved. "That is the most beautiful thing that somebody has ever wrote for me." "Well, I had to write a lovely masterpiece, for the beautiful masterpiece that is in my life. I love you, Shanice." "I love you to Allen." Shanice hugs and kisses Allen as the song he wrote warms her heart.

A few hours later, Shanice is about to go to Allen's house to meet his parents. Before she goes over, she decides to talk to her parents about him. She comes from downstairs and says to her parents, "How do I look?" Shanice is wearing a brown sundress with white Chuck Taylor shoes on. Shanice's Mother says, "You look amazing and stunning." Shanice's Father says, "You look great babygirl, how do you feel about meeting Allen's Parents tonight?" "I'm anxious to meet them I want to get to know them. I want me and Allen's relationship to last for a long time. If I'm being honest, I want it to last forever." Shanice's Parents look at each other after hearing Shanice say that. "I know I'm young, but when I'm around him I feel protected and loved. He's a follower of Jesus Christ and has a plan for his future. I'm super invested in him, and I know it's vice versa on his side. The main question I have is how do a long relationship lasts?"

Shanice's parents are happy that Shanice is asking this question as it's a very important one. Both of them give their advice. Shanice's father says, "The key thing to make a long-lasting relationship work is to be dating for marriage. When that happens both people are working to have everlasting love with each other. When both people are committed to that journey, they help each other grow. When you see flaws within your partner, you talk about it with each other. And help one another with it, if the person keeps doing something that overstep your boundaries. Then that person isn't for you. Anybody that truly love and respect you will never play about you. Issues will arise the key thing is putting GOD first in the marriage. He will help you both overcome the struggles you face. And help you both be strong partners for each other." Shanice's Father has given her a lot of words of wisdom. Shanice's Mother says, "Well I don't think it's no way I can top that. Your father hit everything on the nail. The main thing I will say is put GOD first in your relationship. If both of you do that and follow his footsteps you will have a relationship that will develop in a long-lasting marriage." Shanice is thankful for the advice her parents have given her. She has plans on utilizing everything they taught her.

It's almost time for Shanice to arrive at the Callahan's residence. Imani just got done cooking dinner as Jalean helps her put the food on the dining room table. While Al and Allen are in the living room having a father and son conversation. Al says, "Son, how are you feeling about tonight?" Allen says, "I'm feeling great I'm excited for you all to meet her. I believe you guys will like her. Do I look nervous?" Al smiles and laughs. "No, I can tell you just a bit anxious it's normal to feel that way. That's proof that you have true feelings for this young lady." As Al and Allen are talking to each other they hear someone ringing the doorbell at the front door. Allen stands up in excitement. "It must be Shanice at the door." Allen runs to the front door like he's Ashton Jeanty. He opens the door and it's Shanice on the other side. They both smile at one another as they are always happy to see each other. She says to him, "Hey you." Allen says, "Hey beautiful you look amazing tonight." Please come inside my family can't wait to meet you." Allen walks Shanice into the living room where she is greeted by Allen's parents and his brother. "Dad, mom, Jalean this is my girlfriend Shanice, Shanice this is my family. Al shakes Shanice's hand and says, "It's an honor to meet you Allen has told me great things about you." Imani hugs Shanice and says, "I'm a hugger I'm so glad to finally meet you. We are so happy to have you here. Jalean says out loud, "You are actually real!" Everyone stares at Jalean, Shanice laughs. "What made you think I wasn't real?" "I never thought Allen would ever have a girlfriend. Then again, GOD do be performing miracles." Al softly slaps his son on the back of the head. Shanice turns around and holds Allen's hands. "You right GOD do perform miracles, but he also creates divine connection with people." Both Al and Imani side eye one another as they see Allen and Shanice holding hands. Al says, "Well me and my beautiful bride cooked an amazing meal, so let's sit down and eat."

As Allen, his family, and Shanice sit down for dinner, Allen's father and mother uses this opportunity to get to know Shanice. And to also see if she's the right fit for their son. Imani asks, "So Shanice, Allen tells us that you are his co-star in the play he's starring in. How are you feeling about tomorrow?" Shanice says, "I'm excited, but also anxious about the play. I have been to about twenty plays; this is the first one I done been in where I will be dancing. This time around people can see my dance moves along with my great acting. And seeing Allen getting a starring role in the play and practicing with him has been great. He's super talented it has been an honor working alongside of him. With the intelligent, talent, and skills he has I know he's going to do amazing things." Allen smiles as Shanice compliments him. Al says, "From the way you speak it seems like you come from a great family. Do you have any siblings?" "I don't I'm the only child; my father and mother raised me to be a Godly woman. And to always stay following his pathway through the good and bad times. Following GOD and putting him first in my life has been a stewardship in my life. I try my best everyday to be the best version of myself I can be." Imani asks, "That's wonderful to hear what you have plan on doing once you graduate?" "I will be going to University of Georgia to take up being a therapist, I want to help inspire and heal people. It's something I'm very passionate about doing."

Al and Imani listen to Shanice and love everything that she is saying. Both of them want to make sure that she is serious about Allen. Imani asks, "When you vision your future do you see Allen in it?" "I do me and Allen have talked about the future of our relationship. We put GOD first in our relationship, and we will be there for each other through the good and bad times. I don't have plans on leaving his side, I want to help bring more light into his life. And help him grow more into the man GOD designed him to be." A small tear falls out of Allen's eye as hearing Shanice professing her love for him makes him feel super powerful. Al looks at Allen and can truly tell that the love is real between he and Shanice. "My son he's just like me he's loves hard. I can tell by the way he looks at you and talks about you he's in love with you. And I can tell it's the same on your side. That young man sitting next to you is a special person. Cherish him and stay showcasing him love." Imani says to Allen, "You do the same on your side to Allen. Shanice is a bright young lady, I'm happy that GOD has brought her in your life. One of the many things that have made me, and your father's marriage work is pouring into each other. Seeing each other's flaws, speaking about them and helping each other improve as people. Both of you have that same mindset never lose sight on that." Allen and Shanice hold each other hands tightly. For the rest of the night, the Callahan's have a fun time hanging out with Shanice. As they see the joy she brings into Allen's life.

The next day, Allen wakes up for school as today is a big day for him. He's excited about the "Dirty Dancing" play the main reason being because he is the main character in it. He's been apart of five plays, previously. However, this one is special not only because he's the main character, but also it will be his last play before he graduates from High School. He has plans on giving a beautiful grand finale to his stage career in High School. As he gets ready to leave for school he is stopped by his parents. Imani says, "Son, are you prepared for your stage performance tonight?" Allen says, "Yes mom I am, you guys are going to love the play. I hope I make you guys proud." Al says, "You have already made us proud Allen. When you go out on that stage tonight just show everyone on the stage who you made of. We love you son, and we support you." These kind words from his father means a lot to Allen. As he has hardly ever seen his father been this sincere and loving about hus acting career. "I love you guys too and best believe I will make you guys proud."

As Allen pulls up to his High School parking lot, Paul is standing outside of his car waiting for him. Paul sees Allen walk out his vehicle he says out loud, "John Mayer bring yourself over here!" Allen walks over to Paul to meet up with him. He says,

"What's good Paul talk to me what you got going on?" "Other than thinking about my future. Got great plans laid out for the band. Man, we are about to blow up in a big way. No matter what happens we forever got each other's back. I setup a meeting with Jack tomorrow after our performance at The Underground in Atlanta. I know Claudia have written some more songs for the group. I want you and her to stay collaborating with each other, but that's it for now. We will talk about everything else tomorrow morning."

Late in the evening, Allen gets prepared for his acting performance as he is prepared to dazzle the crowd. Before Allen goes on the stage he says a prayer to GOD. "Dear Heavenly Father, thank you for giving me this opportunity. Give me and my fellow co-stars the strength to carry out a great performance. tonight, in Jesus name I pray amen. " Allen goes and meet with his fellow co-stars and director of the Dirty Dancing play. Gabrielle says to the cast and crew, "Alright guys go out there and show these people the amazing stars that you are." Before they go on stage, Shanice talks to Allen. She says, "Well Allen I can't wait for people to see the great talent I see before me. You are going to do great." Shanice gives Allen a kiss on the cheek.

The show finally starts as the crowd are amazed by the talents of the cast, especially Allen and Shanice. From the wonderful chemistry between Allen and Shanice, to Allen's wonderful acting and surprisingly good dance moves. As his brother Jalean says to their parents, "I didn't know Allen could dance." Imani says, "Well son your brother is a jack of all trades and one-of-a-kind talent." Al says, "Yep your brother is one of a kind I'm proud of him."

At the end of the play, the whole cast gets a big round of applause. A lot of people in the crowd was impressed by Allen's performance in the play. Allen smiles big as he knows he did a great job in his final stage play in High School.

As the cast is dismissed, Shanice gives Allen a big hug and says, "You did an amazing job out there today. I am so proud of you." Allen says, "I'm proud of you to you were wonderful and the crowd just witnessed a special talent." Allen and Shanice kiss one another. Allen and Shanice is greeted by Allen's parents, and Jalean. Imani hugs him and says, "My son you did an amazing job on that stage today I am so proud of you." Then she gives Shanice a hug. "You did amazing also tonight Shanice and you look marvelous." Al gives Allen a hug also and says, "Son you did amazing, I am blessed to be your father. Amazing job on stage tonight, Shanice." Shanice's parents come up to her and gives a hug. Shanice's Dad says, "Babygirl, you did so amazing tonight. I am very proud of you." Shanice's Mother says, "You did amazing on stage precious." Shanice's Father pats Allen on the shoulder. "My man Allen you did your thing on stage. Don Cheadle don't got nothing on you." Allen smiles and says, "Thank you for Mr. Greg let me introduce you to my family. This is my father Al, my mother Imani, and this is my brother Jalean." Shanice's Father says, "It's so great meeting you guys, I'm thinking since we all are here that we can go to dinner together." Al says, "That will be perfect I would love to get to know you guys."

Allen and Shanice go to dinner with their families. Both of their parents get connected with sharing jokes, and meaningful conversations like they are best friends. While at dinner, Allen gets a call from Claudia. He whispers in Shanice's ear, "I got to take this phone call I will be right back." He goes to the bathroom to talk to Claudia. Allen says, "What's up Claudia is everything ok?" She says, "Yeah everything is good, listen I got this song halfway written out that I want the band to perform. I was wondering if you could write the other half of it possibly tonight. If you can come over my apartment, I will greatly appreciated." Allen loves seeing his family getting close with Shanice, but he must make sure everything is up to par with the band's music. "Me and Shanice are at dinner with our families. Give me about an hour and I will be over there."

After dinner is over with, Allen talks with Shanice after meeting with their parents. He walks her to her car and says, "This was an amazing night we had together. Seeing your parents and my parents connecting is great to see." "This is just the beginning Allen. The connection between us is going to stay growing." "Yes, indeed my love, well I got to meet with Claudia to write a song. Once I get done doing that, I'm going to give you a call." "I will be waiting to hear from you, have a great productive writing session." Shanice gives Allen a hug as he goes to meet up with Claudia.

Allen goes to Claudia's apartment with his guitar to finish writing the song she was writing. He knocks at her door as she quickly let him in. Allen says, "So tell me what the name of the song and the inspiration behind it?" Claudia explains everything about the song to Allen. "The name of the song is called "Destiny" it's all about leaving the past and chasing you dreams and goals in the present. So, you can live in your vision and dreams for the future. I'm going to hop on my keyboard and play you the hook, it's the only part I have written out. Claudia starts playing her keyboard and sings the hook. "I'm letting go, I'm letting GOD take me to my destiny, no more worries about my hardships, all the rough times has pass me by, No turning back to the past. I shall lie in in my destiny." Claudia sings the hook of the song two times. Allen hears the hook that Claudia sings and automatically has a song written in his head. "Give me a pen and some paper I have something perfect for that. Allen writes out the rest of the song within twenty minutes.

After writing the song, Allen and Claudia start singing the song. Allen says, "Alright I'm going to sing the whole song, and you sing the hook of it." Claudia responds, "Bet let do this." Allen plays his guitar, and Claudia plays on her keyboard as the pair sing the song together. Allen sings first. "I'm sorry for what all I have done, want to be the seed that shines bright, trying my best to make things right, asking myself will I ever take flight, I got to put down my ways so GOD can carry me to a better place, no more drinking, no more smoking as it has my heart sinking, I'm destined to fly this little light of mine shall shine, I'm going to live in my destiny before I die, will not let my past mistakes hold me back, let loose of the chains as I am released of the cage I put myself in, won't be no has been I shall be the superstar I was created to be." Claudia sings the hook of the song. "I'm letting go, I'm letting GOD take me to my destiny, no more worries about my hardships, all the rough times has pass me by, No turning back to the past. I shall lie in in my destiny." Claudia sings the hook of the song twice. Allen goes back singing the second verse of the song. "Sun is finally out now I'm headed to my future, goodbyes to the rainfalls because here I am I'm standing tall, been through the thunderstorms it formed me into a better man, it seemed I was going to live in cold nights forever, escaped the painful yesterdays, living in the wonderful todays, as I shall say hello to my beautiful future." Claudia sings the hook of the song two more times. "I'm letting go, I'm letting this life take me to my destiny, no more worries about my past, all the rough times has pass me by, No turning back to the past. I shall lie in in my destiny." Claudia and Allen claps their hands once they get done singing. Claudia says, "That's a freaking hit, I know it's late but if you up for it I say let's go to Joe's house and record this in his studio." Allen responds, "I'm down for it lets go ahead and go over there."

Claudia and Allen goes to Joe's house to record the song. Not only is Joe the drummer of the band, but he also produces and engineer music on the side. Allen and Claudia records the song "Destiny" they wrote for the band. After recording the song, Joe is impressed by what Allen and Claudia created. "You guys have created a masterpiece. This song can be an inspiration to a lot of people. Your got plan on us performing this tomorrow in Atlanta?" Claudia responds, "That's the plan we are going to do our thing in a big way." Allen says, "Yes indeed, I'm curious Joe I hope I don't offend you when I ask you this, but how was you able to afford this house and everything?"

Joe tells Allen how he got to his house. "It's very simple I hustled for it. Music is my main passion, but I'm a Systems Administrator, that's what I do for a living. That is what helped pay for the house you are sitting in. I still hope to do music full time. I honestly believe by being in this band we can take over the music industry. I will give both of you this advice. I'm twenty-eight years old; I have been in two other bands. In life, everything is a process. Sometimes it takes a minute for dreams to come into fruition. But enjoy the journey of the process, it's just like J. Cole said there is beauty in the struggle. While you wait for your moment to break big. I will say get a job that pays well so it can help support your dreams. Your two are amazing never give up you guys shall live in the destiny that is destined for you." Allen says, "We appreciate you Joe that means a lot coming from you." Claudia says, "For real look at you on your Dr. Phil stuff. Who would have ever thought." "You welcome I should charge your for that therapy session. Any who you guys might as well spend the night here it's super late." "Sounds like a plan I can sleep in here and Claudia can sleep in the guest bedroom. I'm leaving out early in the morning to pick up Shanice to go to Atlanta." "Sounds good to me goodnight."

It's early Saturday morning, Allen and Shanice is headed to Atlanta for Allen's college tour at Georgia State University. Shanice drives Allen's vehicle, so he can rest on there way up there. She asks Allen, "What time do you and the band are supposed to practice?" Allen says, "Around 4 PM, Paul texted me the address of the Airbnb. It's 8 AM, the college tour don't start till 12 PM. We have a lot of time to just hangout and view the great sights of the ATL." "Since that's the case let go on the beltline and enjoy ourselves." On the drive there, they have a good time from freestyling with each other, cracking jokes, singing songs together, and taking pictures of one another. They arrive at the beltline and go for a long walk. Then they go to Piedmont Park and lay on the grass and think about their future. Shanice lays her head on Allen's chest and looks at the sun shining on them. She says to him, "No matter where we go in life, GOD will shine our light on us. Through the highs and lows he will be there for us." Allen looks at Shanice and says, "Have anybody told you how wonderful you are?" Shanice smiles and says, "No instead GOD blessed me with a great man." Allen and Shanice, both give each other a hug.

Before going to Georgia State, Allen and Shanice go to a Mexican Restaurant. While sitting down and eating, an older black gentleman stares in Allen's direction. Allen notices the older man as he looks at him, he starts starring back at him. The older man resembles him quite a bit. Shanice looks at Allen starring at the man and says, "Allen are you ok? You look like you are staring at a ghost?" The older gentleman walks over to where Allen and Shanice is sitting at. 'Who's this man walking over here Allen?" The man says to Allen, "Excuse me young man, my apologizes for staring at you. You look just like my son. Is Al Callahan your father?" "Yes, it is." The older man face bulges up in a big smile. "I knew we were family when I first saw you. I'm Alvin Callahan,

I'm your grandfather." Allen is shocked and surprised as this is his first time meeting his biological paternal grandfather.

Chapter 8: Unexpected Suprises

Allen is shocked and surprised that he is meeting his grandfather for the first time. His grandfather Alvin is happy to see him as when he looks at Allen, it reminds him of Al. Shanice looks on as she can see the resemblance between Alvin and Allen. He's interested in talking to his grandfather as his father never talks about his childhood. Alvin asks, "What's your name son?" Allen says, "My name is Allen Callahan." "He kept the family tradition going, you look just like your father when he was younger. How old are you?" "I'm 18." A tear falls out of Alvin's eye as he hear Allen says 18. A part of him is saddened that he missed his grandson's upbringing. "It's crazy that we meet like this, but GOD work in mysterious ways. Where are my manners who is this lovely lady, you are sitting with?" "This is my girlfriend, Shanice." Shanice shakes Alvin's hand and says, "It's an honor and pleasure to meet you sir." "The pleasure is all mines. Allen did your parents accompany you on this trip?" "No sir me and Shanice came up by ourselves to visit Georgia State University. I'm on a college tour trying to find out which college will be best for me to attend." "Well, the best advice I can give you is go to a college that will benefit you, but also one that aligns with your purpose."

As Allen and Alvin are connecting, an older woman walks up on them. The older lady walks up to Alvin and says, "There you go Alvin, I was wondering where you went. What you doing messing with these young kids for?" "When you look at this young man, who do he remind you of?" The lady looks closely at him and slightly leans back. "He looks just like your son Al." "That's because he's Al's son Allen." The lady is shocked and surprised. "OMG do you mind if I give you a hug?" "I don't mind at all." The older lady hugs Allen and is so happy to meet him. "I'm sorry I know you're wondering who's this lady hugging up on me. My name is Marjorie; I'm your grandfather's wife. Where is your father and mother?" "They both are back in Macon, I'm just down here for one day for a college tour." "Ok we have a scholar in the house. And who is the beautiful young lady sitting next to you?" "This is my girlfriend, Shanice." "It's so nice meeting you Shanice. We're in town for a day ourselves." "Really where do you guys stay at?" Alvin says, "We stay in Dallas, Ga but I am originally from Macon, GA. Let me give you my phone number, I want to stay connected with you. If that's ok with you?" "We can definitely do that let's exchange numbers." Allen exchanges phone numbers with his grandfather. Alvin firmly holds his grandson's hand. "I know you don't know me, but I love you. We are blood, we are family, you can call me anytime. Tell your father I said hey and I love him."

After Alvin and Marjorie walks out of the restaurant, Shanice wants to make sure Allen is okay. She says, "Wow that was like an episode of General Hospital right there. How are you feeling after seeing your biological grandfather for the first time?" "I'm shocked and surprised, I want to get to know him. However, before I proceed any further, I need to talk to my dad about this. It's almost time for the tour we've to go."

Allen and Shanice arrives at Georgia Southern University. As the young lovebirds walk around campus Shanice says, "This is one big campus I would say, this could be a good school for you to attend college and do music at the same time. We need to find out if they do any open mics here. And need to know where most of the student's hangout at." Allen says, "Let's discover and find out." Allen walks around the campus as he loves the scenery and atmosphere. He talks with students on campus and make connections with them. He finds out there isn't no open mic at Georgia Southern. As Allen and Shanice stay touring around campus and tells people about The Believers performance at Nicolette's Bar. They make a few connections as a few people are excited about the performance tonight. After talking to some people, they go to the Bridgepoint, it's the hangout spot on campus. They are hanging out with students on campus. One of them asks Allen to play a song. A young lady says, "Excuse me Allen, can you play me a song?" Allen smirks and says, "I might can do a little something." Allen gets his guitar out of his vehicle and starts playing and singing Tom Petty's "Free Fallin". People are automatically drawn to Allen's vocal style and his great guitar skills. As he sings the song a crowd of people draw closer to him as they are amazed by his talent. People pulls out their phones and records him as if they are witnessing a young prodigy. He has people singing alongside him. After he gets done singing the crowd gives him a standing ovation. Shanice points at Allen and yells out, "That's my man!" Allen takes in the crowd energy as he knows he has a special gift.

After the college tour at Georgia State, Allen and Shanice head to the Airbnb where the rest of the band is at. As they walk in the kitchen, they see Joe and Paul eating at the kitchen table. Allen smells the good food and asks, "Who cooked?" Claudia comes from the backyard and says, "Me I made you guys a plate eat up so we can practice."

After everyone get done eating, they start practicing for their performance tonight. As practice begins, Allen instructs the band how everything is going to go. He says, "Alright guys we going to perform three songs tonight. Put your heart and soul out there on stage tonight. This is our biggest performance yet. Let's show everybody who the hell we are." This motivates the band as it makes them less nervous about the performance. Claudia is amazed and proud of Allen and says, "You have officially grown some balls little grasshopper. Let's start from the top." The Believers practice for their performance for an hour. The Band sounds great and astounding. After practice is over with, Paul says, "That was amazing now let show Atlanta what we are made of."

After an hour backstage, the band is announced to perform on stage. Shanice prays with the band before they hop on stage. She says, "Dear Jesus Christ thank you for this lovely day you brought us. I pray that tonight that these awesome groups bring power on the stage, that will truly bless the crowd tonight. In Jesus name, I pray amen." All the members of the band says amen. Allen gives Shanice a kiss before going on stage. The host of the event says to the crowd, "Ladies and gentlemen give it up for "The Believers".

The Band comes on stage as there are 175 people in the crowd and Jack Stevens is in the crowd also. Allen gets on the mic and talks to the crowd. He says, "Atlanta, GA first of thank you for having us. We are The Believers and best believe we will bless you with our greatness." Allen turns around and yells. "Band on my count 1,2,3!" The first song the band does a cover of Creed's "My Own Prison". The way Allen sings the song so raw and his guitar playing automatically makes a great impact on the crowd. As they are extremely moved by his voice as it hits their soul. The next song the band plays is their original song "I Just Want to be Free". The crowd falls in love with the song as some are touched by the lyrics in the song. The last song the band plays is the song

"Destiny". This is the song that Allen and Claudia wrote last night, and Joe produced. Claudia gets on the mic and says, "We all live one life, follow what you feel in your mind, heart, and spirit so you can live in your destiny. We love you Atlanta, let's ride out band." The band plays the new song "Destiny". As Allen and Claudia sings the song, the crowd moves back and forth as they start singing the lyrics along with the band. As Claudia sings the hook of the song the whole bar sings it with her. As the song ends the crowd gives them a round of applause. And Jack is even more impressed by the band after watching their performance. The host comes back on stage and says, "Y'all give it up for The Believers!"

The band walks off stage and goes backstage and they are built with excitement. Paul high fives all the members of the band and says, "That's how you put on a show!" Shanice hugs Allen and says, "You did an amazing job tonight." The owner of Nicolette's Lounge approaches the band. She says, "You guys did amazing out there. I would love you guys to come back to my bar and perform. Here's your payment thank you and can't wait to see you guys prosper in music." Ms. Nicolette gives the band $500.

The band comes backstage and goes to the front of the bar. Quickly new fans of theirs come up towards them to hang out with them and take photos with them. The band is creating a solid fanbase in Atlanta, GA. After the band has gotten done signing autographs, taken photos, and hanging with their fans they go to Jack. He claps his hands at them as he was truly amazed by their performance. Jack says, "You guys did an amazing job I'm looking at future legends. I made reservations for us at Batel's about 20 minutes away. We can eat and have a meeting about you guy's future." Allen says, "Sounds good to me come on guys let's go."

The Band alongside Shanice, and Jack meet up at Batel's Restaurant as Jack has a private room for them to sit in. The band is amazed by the room as they feel like true superstars. The room is like something you would see in a magazine as it has chandeliers, six tables and a bar.

The crew and Jack start eating and start talking about business at the same time. Jack says to the crew, "Your are some freaking rockstars. People love hearing you perform, but overall, I think people love your authenticity the most. I have been following you guys closely you got about 3,000 followers on your social media. I know I can work on upping that up for you guys. I know you guys have some performances coming up. I have found a great way to get you guys signed to my label. You guys know Larry Nash and Danielle, don't you?" Larry Nash and Danielle are two multi-platinum selling artists. All the band members yells out of course. "Well, we want them to do a collaboration together. I want Allen and Claudia to write the song and Paul, I know you are the producer of the group, I would love for you to produce the song. This will help get you guys on mainstream as writers and artists. I want all your artistry to be showcased so tell me what you think?" The band is excited for the opportunity as Larry Nash and Danielle are big time artists. Paul says, "We are down to do something special for Larry and Danielle. The two big questions I have is how much will we be getting paid for creating the song? And will we be receiving royalties?" If Larry and Danielle like the song, then Allen and Claudia will be paid $5,000 each. Paul, you will be paid $2,000 for producing the song. And Joe, you can be our engineer and will be paid $2,000 also. And there will be royalties involved. I will have a contract written out for you guys." Allen asks, "When can we start working on the song?" "As soon as you want, I want the song written by next Saturday and then on Saturday you guys fly to Memphis, Tennessee. First class flight, record the song with Larry and Danielle at the luxury Kings studio, then at 8 PM you guys perform at Missy's Bar as you will be headlining. What do you think?" The Band doesn't hesitate to give Jack an answer as they are thankful for the opportunity. Allen says, "We are down for next Saturday I cannot wait!" Jack stands up from his chair with excitement. "Cheers to the future success of The Believers." The band and Jack raise their glasses as they celebrate the future of The Believers.

Back at Callahan's residence, Al gets a phone call that leaves him in shock. Al is laying down in bed as he gets a phone call from his former bandmate Scott. He answers, "Hey Scott, it's been a while how are you doing?" Scott says, "I'm doing well my brother. Listen, I was on TikTok earlier today and I saw this kid doing a cover of "Free Fallin". And I looked closely I see that the kid is Allen. Found out also he's the lead singer of a band called The Believers. How come you never told me he could sing and play guitar like his old man?" Al thinks Scott is playing a joke on him. As he always tried to steer his son away from being a musician. "You messing with me ain't no way that's my kid you talking about. Now my son can play the guitar, but he's not a musician. He's going to do bigger things than that." "Let me send you the video so you can see if it's him or not."

Scott sends Al the video and other videos of Allen performing. He looks at the video and is in shock to see that the person singing in the video is indeed his son. Now that Al knows about Allen performing music how will he confront his son about this?

Chapter 9: Stepping Up

Al has finally discovered that Allen is in a band and is performing music in lounges across Georgia. He's mad and upset that Allen lied to him and Imani. Most of all he's saddened that his son followed the same footsteps he did. Imani wakes up in the middle of the night as she sees Al sitting at the front of the band. She can tell by his posture something is wrong. Imani asks, "Babe, are you okay?" Al takes a sip of water in a glass. He says, "I just found out our son is in a band and has been performing in lounges across the state of Georgia." Imani is surprised to hear this. "I know you aren't talking about Allen." Al shows Imani a video of her son performing. Imani looks at the video and sees Allen performing in it. She covers her mouth. "OMG it's really him. He knows not to do this without our permission."

Imani is also upset that Allen has been lying to both her and Al. However, as she continues watching the video, she sees a newly transformed version of her son. He's no longer shy or timid, he's a confident young man who is having fun doing what he loves. She's very proud of him. She understands why Al feels the way he does. Instead of the both of them judging their son's choices. She feels it's important that they be there to support and guide Allen in the right direction. She softly hugs Al from the back. "Two things I noticed when I watch the video. One our little boy isn't little anymore. He's a boy that has grown into an excellent man. Second, he plays music just like his father. Seeing him play reminds me of how you were back in the day. I know when you watch him, he reminds you of himself. And you scared what happened to you, might happen to him. I think what we should do is find out how serious Allen is about music. When he comes back tomorrow let's sit him down and see what he wants in his life. His vision for his life is probably different from the one we visioned for him. The key thing is we help him along the journey he's reaching for." Al takes in what his wife has just stated. His whole vision was for Allen to go to college and get a good job. However, he never once considered what Allen truly wanted in his life. He decides at this moment he wants to fully support his son towards his goals and dreams. Al tightly hugs his wife. "We shall support our sons no matter which season they enter in their lives. We will sit down with him tomorrow."

After their meeting with Jack, the band throws a small party at their Airbnb. A good number of people who was at their performance earlier tonight is at the party. While everyone is partying, Allen and Shanice are in a separate room talking about everything that has transpired today. Allen says, "Today has been one hell of a day." Shanice says, "Yes it has almost been like a movie. So, what did you think about everything Jack stated in the meeting?" "It sounds promising, but I want to make sure that we own all our music. We just got to be very smart and strategic with our plans. Would you like to come to Memphis with me?" "I would love to, but I promised my mom I would help her out at the flower shop next weekend. I will be there with you in spirit." Shanice touches Allen's rib cage. "Always follow what you feel in here. It will never lead you down the wrong path." Allen, hugs Shanice. "Thank you for being there for me. And showing me unconditional support and love." "I know you will do the same for me." Allen kisses Shanice as they dance to Monica's "Why I Love You So Much" as it's playing very loud throughout the house.

The next morning, as the guys pack their bags in their car, Paul talks to Allen just for a few minutes. Paul and Allen walk along the driveway of the Airbnb. He says, "These dreams of ours are finally turning into reality. With everything that has transpired I'm going to put my all into this. We can become legends and create amazing wealth for our family. I just want to make sure you are all in with me also." Allen assures Paul he is with him for the long haul. He says, "We are in this together my brother." Paul and Allen dap one another up as they plan on doing legendary stuff together. As Allen and Shanice drive back to Macon, Allen have his head out of the window as the sun shines gracefully on him. As he vision himself years from now, being a musician, songwriter, married with kids and having a big house. He shall enjoy his happiness for now. As he is in a rude of awakening when he gets home.

He arrives back at his house excited as he know there is a lot in store for his future. Allen walks into the house filled with joy until he sees his parents sitting in the living room with his father having a firm mean look on his face. Allen knows he's in some type of trouble. Al stands up from the couch and pulls up a video of Allen singing on his phone and says in a firm voice, "When was you going to tell us you was in a band? Imani softly says, "We are your parents we should've known about this. Why didn't you feel comfortable telling us your secret?" Allen knew sooner or later his parents would find out. He wasn't hoping it would be this soon. Now he must face the music. He says, "I know you both wouldn't accepted me being in a band. This is something that I love to do. If I could play guitar and sing every second of the day I would. This isn't just a hobby for me, it's a passion I feel alive everytime I step on stage. I apologize for lying to both of you, I was wrong about doing that. I hope that you both forgive me, but I can't, and I won't quit playing music." Allen is anticipating a harsh reaction from his parents as both of them are looking at one another. His father gets up from the couch and walks up to him. "Me and your mother forgive you son. We love you with all our heart, we want to support you. The main question we have is do you see yourself playing music for a living?" Allen is transparent with his father. "I do pops I want to do this for a living. In my heart and spirit, I know music is my calling." Al smiles. "Well with that being said, we need to have a conversation about your future. Go ahead and unpack your clothes and eat dinner. Then afterwards you, me, and your mother are going to talk about your music career. And how we can help you out." Imani is happy to see Al putting his feelings aside and considering their son's feelings first. Allen is surprised and relieved that his parents support his dreams and aspirations.

After getting unpacked and eating Allen sits down with his parents to have a meaningful conversation with them. Allen tells his parents everything about his music journey. Imani asks, "How long have you been in the band?" "For about two months, Paul invited me to be a guitarist at first. Then he felt like my skills as a vocalist could help the group. So, then I became co-lead vocalist of the band. We have been doing great we have been performing at different venues almost every weekend. The genre of music we perform is R&B and Rock. And just yesterday we got our first contract offer." Al quickly interjects he wants to make sure his son hasn't signed anything. "Did you sign anything?" "No" Allen's parents are in a sigh of relief. "Who the contract offer is from?" "It's from Jack Stevens he's an A&R rep for Cloud Records. Me and the guys checked him out he's legit." "Well ma dukes is about to see if this Jack guy is solid." Al and Imani look up Jack Stevens online, they want to make sure their son isn't dealing with a con artist. Imani says, "He and Cloud Records seems like legit people." Al asks Allen, "What type of deal are they offering you?" "They are offering me and my bandmate Claudia $5,000 each to write a song for their biggest artists." "$5,000 isn't a bad payment for a new songwriter. What percentage of royalties would you be getting?" "I don't know I guess we will find that out once we go to Memphis this Saturday." Al and Imani at the same time says, "Memphis!"

Al continues. "What you mean when we go to Memphis?" "We must write the song and have it made by Saturday. Once we go to Memphis, we meet with Jack, Larry Nash, and Danielle to see if they like the song. If they like the record, it will be recorded on that same day." Al has some worries about this deal it sounds too good to be true. "A part of me feels like this Jack guy, got you guys going up there to build your excitement to sign you guys to his label. Then if you guys were to do that you wouldn't own majority of your music. I watched your videos it truly reminds me of myself. You put your heart and soul into this craft, don't sign that away. It's important that you own your stuff. I'm coming to Memphis with you; I'm going to make sure you don't end up in a bad deal. You have a lot of talented artists that signed over their rights to their music and get nothing in return from it. I'm not going to let that happen to you." Allen is thankful and happy to have his parents as allies by his side on his journey. "Thank you pops." "I gotcha your back man that will never change. We have a lot to talk about, instead of you going to school tomorrow you are hanging out with me. And I want to meet your bandmates tomorrow also." Allen smiles as he glad his father has a change of heart on his view of him being in a band outside of church.

Allen decides to tell his dad about meeting his grandfather for the first time. "Pops there is something else I need to reveal to you also." Al and Imani lean back on the sofa as they wonder what Allen is about to reveal. "While me and Shanice were eating lunch yesterday, a gentleman approached us. He said I looked like someone he knew, he asked me my name, once I told him my name his face frozed. Then he asked me, is your father Al Callahan I told him yes, then he told me then that makes him my grandfather." Al and Imani are surprised to hear this. Al says, "Was the man you talked name was Alvin Callahan?" "Yes, it was." Al sighs in disbelief as he is shocked. "Then that was indeed your grandfather, was he happy to see you?" "He was and he said looking at me reminded him of you back in your younger days. I met his wife Marjorie, and he gave me his phone number. He wanted me to tell you that he loves you."

With Allen meeting Alvin, Al decides to tell Allen the full story of his upbringing. He says, "I love you Allen, I never wanted you or Jalean to experience the hardships I had to go through.

That's the main reason why I have been so hard on you. I apologize if I ever made you feel like you never was doing your best. I can honestly admit that you give your all in everything you do. I'm blessed and proud that you are my son. Your mother made me realize, I can be the father for you, that I needed when I was your age. Don't get me wrong, Bill made a huge impact on my life. However, I didn't have him by my side when I was pursuing my own dream of being a musician. If I did or I would've allowed him to be by my side things might've gone different. Music was the safe haven of my life.

Growing up as a kid in Dallas, GA, my mom would always play the piano we had in the house. She taught me how to play and write music. I became addicted to every great melody and beat I heard. I wrote to it and played to it; my mother saw my talent and bought me a guitar when I was twelve. Everything was good, up until I was thirteen. Your grandfather came up to the school with tears in his eyes and picked me up. He didn't tell me what was going on, but I could tell something was off. When we got home, he broke the news to me that my mother passed away in a car accident earlier that day. My whole life changed forever. The aftermath of her death was hard on me and your grandfather. I became heavier into playing music, as my father removed everything in the house that reminded him of my mother. He became an alcoholic, if I wasn't getting good grades in school he would beat on me. Whenever he saw me playing the guitar or piano he would always tell me I wouldn't be nothing."

Al starts crying as he reminisces about the dark times he experienced with his dad. Imani rubs him on the back. "I'm sorry it hurted me that the main person that I saw as superman would turn into a villain in a second. Eventually I got tired of it, when I was 16 me and him got into a fight and I won. He was mad and kicked me out of the house. He sent me to Macon to stay with your Grandpa Bill and Grandma Jill right afterwards. They showed me love and showed what a healthy family looks like. Ever since then, Alvin has been dead to me. I haven't spoken to him in almost thirty years."

Hearing all of this makes Allen respect his father more. He knew a bit about his father's upbringing, but he didn't know the full depths of it. Hearing how his father treated him and him overcoming his drug addiction he's proud to have Al as his father. "If it's means anything I'm proud to have you as my father. I love you and I thank you everything you have done for me." Al starts tearing up and gives his son a hug. "Thank you, son that means a lot to me." "Mom, did you know about all of this?"

Imani says, "I did I'm glad he finally talked to you about his childhood." Imani tells Allen how she and Al got together. "When me and your father first met, I didn't like him. He was a smart guy, but he was somewhat a pain in the butt at times. Then doing our junior year of class, our Professional Management professor decided it was a good idea to pair us together for a project. I thought why in the hell they teamed me with him. Although when he and I was working on the project together, I got to truly know the flaws I saw inside of him I recognized where some of it came from when I asked him about his childhood. I came from a different background; I was born in a Christian household, had great parents and siblings. During that time, I felt in my soul that I can be a great influence on him. We starting hanging out and became close friends. I knew he was on drugs I used to pray for him night and day. And did a few bible studies with him. When I got a chance to know who he truly was I became attracted and admired by him. When I found out about his drug overdose, I was devasted. I rushed to his bedside to be there for him. I prayed Romans 12:2 to him every day. "Do not conform to the pattern of this world but be transformed by the renewing of your mind. Then you will be able to test and approve what God's will is his good, pleasing and perfect will." I hoped that his life would be transformed when he woke up."

Al says, "I made a vow that day that I will live my life for my Jesus Christ. When I got out of the hospital, I automatically had to deal with the consequences of my actions. Melanie left a note on my apartment door to let me know she was done with me. I was upset and saddened, but I understood why, I put her through a lot in the three years of us dating each other. Then, due to my drug overdose, me and Scott lost out on our opportunity on being signed by a label. We decided to disband The Phoenix due to that. With both of us being drug addicts and me almost dying we decided it would be best to leave the music scene. To make sure I stayed on a straight path, I had AA meetings, and your mother became my account ability partner. We rounded up becoming best friends. We would meet every week to do bible study together, go to church together, work on our schoolwork together, and help solve out each other's life issues. Within six months of my overdose, I wanted more than just a friendship with Imani I wanted a relationship. We started dating even though we both came from different backgrounds what mattered to me was we were two people that were there for each other during the good and bad times." Al looks at Imani and says, "I'm blessed to have her as my wife and the mother of my kids." Imani says, "And I'm blessed to have you as my husband and the father of my kids."

Al says to Allen, "When you was born, my goal was to provide a better life for you than I had growing up. Plus, I never wanted you to go through the issues I went through. I'm proud of the man you've become, me and your mom is always here to support you. And we know that the future is bright for you son."

Al and Imani gives their son a hug as they will always be by his side.

It's late at night; Imani sees Al on their balcony looking at the stars in the sky. She knows a lot is on his mind after their conversation with Allen. She goes outside on the balcony to makes sure he's ok. Imani hugs him from the back and asks, "Are you ok baby?" Al thinks about his relationship with his father. He says, "I'm thinking about my father, I'm asking myself should I actually meet with him after everything he did." "I think you should it's time that you make full peace with your past. You have never told your father how he made you feel growing up. You need to let go of the pain you have inside of you. You are great at hiding it, but I know it's still there. I believe GOD allowed Alvin and Allen to run across each other for you two to reconcile. Life is short, I have already lost both of my parents, and you have already lost your mom, Jill, and Bill. He's the only grandparent that the kids have left. Maybe GOD has changed his heart but pray to GOD about the situation and ask him to lead you in the right direction with this decision." Al hugs Imani and kisses her. "The best day of my life was when I made you, my wife. Thank you for the love and care you have shown me. I love you with all my heart." "I love you to, we are in this together."

It's a bright sunny early Monday morning; Al's main objective today is to make sure Allen has a great strategic plan for his future. Before he gets his day started, he says a prayer to GOD. "Dear Heavenly Father thank you for this day you have given us. Stay watching over my wife and kids. First, I pray that me and Allen can come up with a plan today to make sure his future is set in the right path. He's a great kid; I'm going to make sure he doesn't fall into the same traps that I did. I know I have been strict and maybe even overbearing when it comes to him. I must remind myself; he's your son also. You will protect him from anything or anybody that is not meant to be in his space. He's a man now I got to put him in your hands. I raised him to be a great man that will follow the pathway you have created for him. I believe he will do amazing things in his lifetime. You appointed me to be his earthly father, I promise you I will always support him. And then with my relationship with my own father it's time I spoke my truth to him. All the hurt and anger, I still have inside of me I want to let go of it all. I have been having this anger caged inside of me for the last 30 years. It's time I found full peace and if our relationship can be reignited from this that would be great. But only if he has truly changed as a person. I pray that his health is well, the same for his wife also. And I hope that he has accepted you in his life. In Jesus name, I pray amen."

Allen gets up for the day as he wonders what his father has in store for him. After eating breakfast, it's time for Al and Allen to have some father and son quality time together. Al asks

Allen, "What time are you meeting with your bandmates?" Allen says, "I'm meeting them at 4 PM." "Great that gives us time to go to Atlanta. Get your guitar we are leaving in ten minutes." While Al and Allen ride to Atlanta they sing some R&B music together and rap with each other.

After riding for two hours, Al and Allen arrives at a café in Atlanta. Al wants to sit Allen down to discuss making long-term money. "One of the things I want to talk you about today is making money. With you deciding to be a musician you have got to make money to finance your career. And until you make it big you have got to have a steady income coming in. How much money do you have in your account right now?" "I have about $3,000 saved in my savings account right now. I know we are not going to become well-established overnight, that's take work. I do got plan on attending college, I know by me getting a great job in my major I could make a lot of money." "What major do you have plan on taking up?" "Cyber Security it would be easy for me to learn the trade and plus Cyber Security Analysts make a good amount of money." "That's very smart in my opinion instead of you going to a four-year college you need to go to a trade school. Look into going to Central Georgia Technical College, you can take up Cyber Security there you will be done within two years. And get a job once you graduate, possibly making $100,000 a year. By doing that you will always be financially stable." Allen like his father's idea, however he had his mind set on going to a State University due to the fan base he can create there. "I like the idea, but I was thinking about going to a state university. More students which equals more people that will be interested in the band." "I peep your point what I'm about to ask you ties into what I'm about to say. Shanice, she has plan on attending University of Georgia, correct?" "Yes, she do." Al breaks down a marketing strategy he used in college. "When I was in The Phoenix, I would have Melanie market all the band's performances on campus. She was the most popular and smartest girl on campus anytime she spoke about anything people listened. Just by her talking to people and making posters and passing them out helped bring a lot of attention towards our way. With Shanice, she can help do the same thing for you and the rest of The Believers but even bigger. She is a beautiful, intelligent young lady people are automatically going to be drawn on what she speaks about. You get her to create a street team in Athens to market you and the band. Then I got your godfather coming up here to help us market in Atlanta. Speaking of the man himself here comes the myth, the legend Scott Walker!"

Al and Scott hug one another. It's been about two years since they last seen each other due to their busy lifestyles. Al has always seen Scott as a brother due to their close friendship in college. No matter how far away the two best friends are they will always have each other's back. Scott says, "It's been too long my brother you still look the same. I know this isn't little Allen sitting here give your uncle a hug." Allen hugs Scott, Scott is Allen's Godfather. "It's great to see you Uncle Scott it's been a minute." "Yes, it has you have grown I feel like Danny Devito standing next to you." Everyone at the table laughs. Al says, "So the way I found out about you performing around the state were through this man." Scott puts his hands up in the air. "Guilty as charged I saw this video of you performing "Free Fallin" it's was a beautiful performance, you had people drawn in. It reminded me of how Al use to move the crowd back in the day. When I looked at your face and the name, I told myself I believe this is my nephew I'm listening to. I texted your father about it, and he confirmed it was you. I checked your band's music on Soundcloud and other social media platforms y'all are dope. Old man Al texted me stating I might can be of assistance in helping you and your band market your music." Al says, "Yes sir, I know you host an open mic up here every Saturday. I have listened to the band myself, I think it would be great if they be a feature at your open mic." "I'm down for that; my open mic is called Melodies and Flow it's one of the biggest open mics in town. I have been doing it for ten years; a few big names have got their start at it. I love your talent, so I would love for you and the band to perform. I can have you guys as the featured performer for our next showcase next Saturday. And since you family I will pay your band $1,000 to perform. And then usually it's about 150 people that comes, trust me you are going to have a lot of people that wants to get to know you. So, what do you think about everything I just stated?" "I love it I know everyone in the band would be down for it." "That's perfect let me know when you talk to them. In the meantime, since you boys are in town let's go to the beltline for some entertainment." Al starts laughing as he knows what Scott got up his sleeve.

The guys arrive at the beltline as they are getting out of the vehicle, Al says to Allen, "Get your guitar from the back son, we are about to have a jam session." Allen is excited about this as he quickly gets his guitar. Both Al and Scott sit on a brown bench on The Beltline. They reminisce about their time performing together. Scott says, "We made a lot of money performing out here." "Yes, we did I remember we did something like this."

Al starts singing an original song that was popular among fans of "The Phoenix" called Broken. "Feel that my heart is broken, my life seems hopeless I don't know where to run to, dancing with the white lines to keep me between the cards I been dealt with, I feel that the end is near I'm trying my best to hold on, wish I can hear momma's voice just to hear her say everything will be alright, I wish I can take a flight to heaven to just hug her tight with all my might, so the hate in my heart can be replaced with peace, but instead at night I hug my pillow tight wishing about them great nights as a young boy, because now as a young man I'm broken, I'm down on my luck, I got no bucks in my pockets, I'm depressed I don't know how to express, wish I could repossess the past to feel the depths of warm love that moved beautifully within my blood vessels like a river, now I'm left crying with full water of tears hoping for a better tomorrow so my sorrows can be swept away." Scott sings the hook of the song. "I'm broken seeking for better, writing this letter to let off my pain, hope I sustain to fly like an eagle so I can live in my dream." Al sings the second verse of the song. "Daddy was my superman, but turned into the devil had to escape the hell he created, wish the nails and knife wounds I feel from my back and feet can be release, so I can be replenish into someone freshly made and new, I wanted to be renewed like Jesus on the cross come back from the brokenness I'm enduring and walk into that great pathway that has been created for me, because I'm broken seeking for better, writing this letter to let off my pain, hope I sustain to fly like an eagle so I can live in my dream."

As Al stops singing about thirty people are around him and the guys and they give him a standing ovation. A lot of people were moved by the words he and Scott sung and the tunes and melodies of his guitar play. He stands up on the bench with his guitar around his neck to talk to the crowd. "Thank you, ladies and gentlemen, my name is Al Callahan. That song you just heard is called "Broken". I wrote that song while being high off crack. I was a young man that had a lot of hate and anger in his heart. Due to that it blocked me from the mission GOD had me on. I used drugs to fill the void I was feeling, it took me almost dying from a drug overdose for me to transform my life. I'm telling you today the storm that you're in right now won't last forever. Seek GOD and his kingdom and spread your wings and fly. You are someone that is going to make it and be a testimony to many people. That brings me to my son Allen as his song "Destiny" signifies that. Son showcase who you are to everyone."

Allen is happy that his father is a fan of his music and that he is standing alongside him. He starts singing the song as his dad and Scott looks proudly at him. The people that are standing around take photos and videos of his performance. They are moved by Allen as his music brings inspiration and transformation into people's souls. After performing, he gets a standing ovation from everyone. People rush up to him to take photos with him and gets his autograph. Scott puts his hand on Al's shoulder and says, "He's just like his father." Al smiles proudly as he see his son living out his dream.

Before the guys go back home, they say goodbye to Scott. Allen says, "It was nice seeing you Uncle Scott thank you for your advice. And I hope to perform at your Open Mic Next Saturday." Scott responds, "It's no problem we're family, if you ever need anything don't hesitate to reach out to me. Love you nephew." Scott gives Allen a hug.

After Allen steps away, Al and Scott talk to each other. "You and Imani raised a fine young man, Al; you should be proud of yourself. The father you needed when you were younger, you became that for your kids. You made it happen Al." "Thank you that means a lot coming from you. Speaking of dads, I know Allen met my father for the first time." Scott has a shocked look on his face. "You finally reunited with your dad after all these years?" "I haven't he saw Allen at a restaurant, when he saw him, it reminded him of me. So, he went and talked to Allen and discovered that it was his grandson he was talking to. He gave him his phone number and told him to tell me he loved me." Scott hears this and keeps it very transparent with Al. "You know I buried my father last year, now granted me and him never had the best relationship with each other. But when I found out he had stage 4 cancer, I made it my mission to make amends with him. It took me forty-some years to let off the pain I felt against him. And he was sorry for neglecting me at a young age. Both of us was able to find closure before he passed. Life is short if we can make amends with someone it's best we make that happen." What Scott just stated has Al thinking about reuniting with his father. "You always know what to say Scott." Scott smiles and laughs. "I'm always going to be honest with you; I always want the best for you brother. Despite all you went through, you became successful and created an amazing family. I'm proud and blessed to call you a friend of mine. I love you man it's time for you to have full closure in your life you deserve that." "I appreciated man if you need anything don't hesitate to reach out to me." The two friends hug one another, no matter where they are at in life they will always have each other's back.

The guys arrive back in Macon they go straight to Paul's house. All the band members of the band are in the front yard when Al and Allen show up. Paul sees Allen's father 2022 White Chevy Silverado pulls up in his driveway. With Allen's dad showing up at their band practice, Paul has a gut feeling that he knows about Allen being in a band. When the father and son duo exits the truck Paul says, "Mr. Callahan it's such a pleasure to have you here. How have you been doing?" Al says, "I have been doing great just helping Allen with his music career." Paul and the rest of the band now know the cat is officially out of the bag. "I'm not here to sabotage anything you guys got going on. Music is my son's passion, and he truly cares about this group. I'm always going to support him, and due to the love he has for you guys, I'm always going to support this band also." All the bandmembers are glad they have Allen's Father support. Paul says, "Thank you for supporting us Mr. Al, it truly means a lot to all of us." "No problem with that being said I want to talk about the business overview for your group. Do you guys have time to talk?" Joe says, "We do." "Perfect let's talk business."

Al sits with all the band members of The Believers to talk about their future. "I know Allen told me you guys got plan on meeting with Jack Stevens in Memphis this Saturday. He told me the contract details that has been offered to you guys for writing a song for two major artists on his label. And that can lead to you guys signing a major distribution deal. I was wondering have you guys thought about being fully independent and creating your own label?" This idea has never crossed the band's mind until now. Claudia says, "We never have it is important for us to own our music. Do you know how we can do that?" "Yes, I do, you create an LLC for your own record label. I can walk you through the steps to make that happen." Joe says, "That sounds great but if we were to sign with Cloud Records we would be instantly known." "You're correct, but in the process, they will own a major percentage of your work. All of you put your heart and soul into this. Don't give away a heavy percentage of that to just gain fame and notoriety. By creating your own label all of you will be creating generational wealth for your family." Everyone understands and loves what Al is saying. Paul says, "I'm glad you are giving us great insight on this Mr. Al. I believe all of us want to go in an independent direction. However, what about Memphis?" "Still write the song and fly down there on Saturday.

I'm going to be there with you guys; the amount of money they are offering you guys sounds decent. The biggest thing is what percentage of royalties will you get for the song." "That something I honestly wasn't think of, we haven't signed anything with him. We will find out on Saturday before any ink is on paper, but do we all vote to create our own label to distribute our music?" All the band members vote yes. Claudia says, "In my opinion I think Paul and Allen need to be the CEOs of the record label. Both of your are the most business-minded out of all of us. And we can call the record label Believing and Faith Records." Allen says, "I'm down for it, Paul are you down?" "I most definitely am my brother." Allen and Paul dap each other up. Al says, "With that being said, I'm going to get my laptop out of the truck and create the LLC with your parents Paul."

The band prepares to write a hit song for Cloud Records. Paul says to the band, "We got to write a killer hit for Larry Nash and Danielle. Allen, Claudia, what type of song was your thinking about writing for them?" Allen says, "Definitely a love song, me and Claudia talked last night. This song is going to be one that plenty of people will get married to. We shall create history together with this song." Paul loves the idea as he hopes that this song bring huge opportunities towards everyone's way. "Well in that case let's get down to business." For an hour, Allen and Claudia work together to piece together an amazing song. They listen to the beat Paul made for the song. Finally, after an hour they finished writing the song. Paul comes towards Allen and Claudia and says, "So what do you guys got?" Allen says, "The name of the song we have written is called "Meant to Be". Claudia says, "Sit back and take a listen."

Claudia plays the guitar and starts singing, "When I first saw you, I knew you was the one for me, The man I need the man that will empower me, the man that will make me believe in my dreams, as my soul lights up when you are around me, as you are my fire the only one I desire, know we are a match made in two, I'm glad my eye caught you as I truly know." Claudia and Allen sing the hook of the song together. "This love of ours is meant to be, baby you my heart, my source, my one and only, you the one I can't live without as we shall be together for always and forever." Claudia stops singing as Allen plays his guitar as he continues singing, "Baby, I knew you was the one for me, you my sun in the sky, you brighten me up, when I'm down and out you pick me up, you love me at my worst, you love me at my best, you ride for me, I ride for you, Life was hell before you came, Now I'm thanking the heavens above for sending their angel to me." Claudia and Allen sing the hook of the song. "This love of ours is meant to be, baby you my heart, my source, my one and only, you the one I can't live without as we shall be together for always and forever." After the hook, Claudia sings, "Even through the storms we shall stay united never no disconnection as this is a divine connection baby." Allen cuts in and starts singing, "My lady, my baby, my ride or die, we will never leave each other's side, you are forever mine, I'm forever yours, my love, my girl, you are my world." Claudia and Allen sing the hook of the song one last time. "This love of ours is meant to be, baby you my heart, my source, my one and only, you the one I can't live without as we shall be together for always and forever."

After singing the song, Paul and Joe gives Claudia and Allen a round of applause. Paul with small tears in his eyes says, "That was amazing that's a hit right there for sure."

Later, that night after bible study, Dennis is cleaning his church. He starts singing Mary Mary's "Can't Give Up Now" as he singing, he hears a voice behind him that's singing alongside him. He looks behind him and sees that the person behind him singing is Al. Dennis says to him, "You still got that voice on you Al. Is everything ok you usually don't come here on Monday's?" Al came to get some advice from Dennis pertaining to his father. He asks, "Came to ask you for some advice?" "Lay it on me." "Allen ran into my father unexpectedly, while he was in Atlanta weekend it was the first time they ever met. Of course he asked about me and told Allen to tell me he loves me. Out of anyone on this earth, you know what all me and him went through. I have been asking myself should I meetup with him." Dennis knows this is a big decision for Al. "Let's sit down and talk."

The two of them sit on the front row of the pew to have a meaningful conversation. "I remember all of the turmoil you and your dad went through. He put you through a lot of stuff you didn't deserve. I know it's been almost thirty years since your last talked. During that time have you ever wondered what led him to be the way he was." "I feel like it was my mother's death, I know he was heartbroken when she died. To fill that pain he had inside he drunk alcohol literally everyday. I did the same thing with drugs. I look back on me and his relationship it makes me wonder if my father had something deeply rooted in him from his childhood that he didn't make peace with just like me." "The key question for you is have you made peace with everything from your childhood?" Al starts tearing up. "I haven't all I wanted was his love and care. When we got in our big fight I made a promise to never see him again. At the same time, I know it wasn't just a coincidence that he and Allen met. It's time we meet up and talk about everything it's been too long. I hope we can make amends if not I can honestly say I gave it my all. What is the best advice you can give me going into meeting up with him?" "Let GOD speak through you but listen to your father's story. Understand why he became the man that you hated for so many years. By him seeing Allen, I believe it more than likely had him reflecting on how he could've did things differently. With that being said, I think it's the perfect time for the both of you to talk. Let me pray for you brother."

Dennis says a prayer for Al. "Dear Heavenly Father, thank you for this day you have given us. We are grateful that Alvin was able to meet his grandson for the first time last week. We hope that he has made peace on what has had been holding him back for years. But also, that he is free from a man filled with hate, to a man that has been transformed. I hope that when he and Al meet, that there be peace and understanding between the both of them. I hope both of them find closure in things that have been haunting them in their lives. And hopefully this could be the beginning of a fresh new start for them. I say all of this in your name in Jesus Christ we pray amen." "Amen, I greatly appreciated Dennis I needed that." "No problem you know I always got your back. How's everything with Allen and Jalean?"

"Jalean is doing great he just got promoted to the 8TH grade. And got accepted to be a part of the beta club at his school. Then with Allen, he decided his passion in life is playing music, I discovered this a couple of days ago, at first I was upset because I don't want him to go down the same path I went on. But Imani made me realize that I need to be by his side while he is living his purpose. It's not what I visioned for him, but it's the vision that Jesus Christ put in his mind. I'm proud of him, me and Imani raised two outstanding gentlemen."

Dennis has something he must admit to Al. "You are my brother so I must admit something to you." Al is curious on what Dennis has to admit to him. "I been knew about Allen performing music. I promised him I wouldn't tell you, I have been keeping tabs to make sure he is straight. If I would've told you, I know you would've had a fit. My apologizes for not telling you." Al leans back on the church pew and pats Dennis on the back. "It's ok brother I know your heart was in the right place. If you felt my son was in any danger I know you would've told me. And you right, I would've had a fit if you've told me. Now that I know I'm going to support him and help him out. I look back at my life, I done came a long way from that crazy teenager I once was." "Yes, you have just remember to always put GOD first. I'm proud of you Al. I know pops and mom were proud of you when they were alive. And they are smiling down from heaven seeing the way that you're leading your family." "Thank you, Dennis, for all the love and support you have shown over the years. And I know they are proud of what you have done with the church. I'm blessed to have you as a brother." The two brothers give each other a hug.

After his conversation with Pastor Dennis, Al sits in his vehicle and pulls out his phone to call his father. Before calling he says to himself, "Jesus Christ I hope this goes well." Al calls his father; his heart is beating fast as he awaits an answer. Finally, someone answers the phone. The person on the other end says, "Hello this is Alvin, who do I have to pleasure on speaking to." Al slowly sighs and says, "This is Al it's been a long-time pops." Alvin is surprised and happy that his son called him. Emotions are running high on both sides of the phone right now. Alvin has tears coming from his eyes as he emotionally says, "My son man it's been so long since I heard your voice how you been doing?" "I been doing great listen it's about time that me and you talk, but it needs to be face to face. I was wondering what will be the best day to meet up." "This Friday would be perfect would you be able to come down?" "Yes I will l be down there by 11 AM, we will talk then you have yourself a great night." Al quickly hangs up the phone before his father can respond back. Al is happy and proud of himself that he is close with making peace with his past. The key question now is will this meeting help bring closure to both Al and Alvin?

Chapter 10: Generations

It's Tuesday Morning, it's Senior Ditch Day at Terry High School. Allen surprises Shanice with flowers at her house. She answers the door and he starts sings Jodeci's "Forever My Lady" as he stands in her doorway with flowers in his hands. She puts her hands on her face, she is in awe of this wonderful kind gesture. Shanice says, "This is so beautiful thank you babe." She gives Allen a kiss and a hug. He says, "You welcome I want to do something for you. You supported me these last two weekends, the least I want to do is show you how I greatly appreciate you. I got the day off today from work, I want to take you somewhere today. Get dressed up we are about to go on a great adventure." Shanice smiles as she jumps in the air and quickly run upstairs to put something on. Allen puts his sunglasses on as today is going to be a magical day.

The two young lovebirds go on a two-hour drive to Charleston, SC. On the way there they capture the beautiful spring weather, singing songs together, and cracking jokes together. Shanice lays her head on Allen's chest and hold his hand while he is driving. In her heart and mind, she knows Allen will protect her and always be there for her. Finally, after a long drive, the two arrives at a beautiful setting with a lot of trees and a swamp that you can sit at all day and look at. Allen takes his sunglasses off and asks, "Does this place looks familiar to you?"

Shanice hops out of the vehicle she's automatically drawn to the place. She quickly recognizes the place. She says, "OMG! This is where Noah took Allie to in The Notebook." "Yes, it is this is the legendary Cypress Gardens. I know that the Notebook is your favorite movie and novel, I wanted to surprise you with a full day at the Gardens." This means a lot to Shanice, despite his busy schedule, Allen made it his mission to spend quality time with her. And take her to a place that she holds near to her heart. This showcases no matter how busy his life might be, Allen will always make it a mission to spend quality time with his lady.

The two of them walk around and enjoys the beautiful scenery around them. They take pictures of themselves at various spots, and eat honeysuckle off a tree. Finally, they get on a rowboat together that oversees the swamp. Shanice lays on Allen's chest as he is rowing the boat. Feeling each other's warm touch brings comfort and peace to the both of them. "So how's your mental baby?" Allen is confused by the question. "What do you mean?" "How are you feeling mentally? Just seeing how's everything is going in your life?" "Well, my parents finally found out about me being in a band." Shanice turns around and looks at Allen. "What was their reaction?" "It was surprising I thought they were going to kick me out of the house. Instead, they really wanted to know if music were truly a passion of mine. Once I told them it was, they fully supported my decision. Ever since, my father has been helping me a lot with my music career. Thanks to him, me and the band got an opportunity to perform in Atlanta again next weekend. And with his advice we are about to start our own label. It's important that we own everything that we create. I want to create generational wealth for my family." "I love it you guys need to create merch for the band. Like have the band name on front of the shirt and then have lyrics from your song on the back of them." "I like that if only we knew of a designer?" Shanice clears her throat. She says in a sarcastic voice, "Well I know this girl who has a printer in her parents garage that she uses to help make merchandise for her mother's flower shop. And who will love to help her boyfriend to achieve everything GOD wants him to accomplish." Shanice gives Allen a kiss, Allen loves Shanice's vision. "I love it let me talk it over with the band. Also, even though we are going fully independent we still have plan on going to Memphis this Saturday. We believe this song we wrote for Larry Nash and Danielle will put us on the map. I just hope Jack will understand our decision on not signing to the label." "That's something to pray about but also pray that Jack has a full sincere heart with you guys. Either way I will still be your biggest fan." "That's fascinating either way I leave with a blessing. I know also after talking with my father I'm heavily considering attending Central Georgia Technical College." Shanice is surprised by this. "Why? Going to a state university will help create more people be invested in the band's music." "I'm thinking about our future, I hope to make it big in music. By going to Central I will graduate quickly and automatically get a job in the IT field. I have to make sure that we are financially stable for our future."

Shanice softly asks, "We?" Allen stops rowing the boat and touches Shanice's chin and looks directly at her. "Yes we I want you in my future, I'm not afraid to admit you're the only girl I want in my life. I just don't want a moment with you, I want forever. I know this relationship is still somewhat new, but I'm here to stay. I want us to help each other grow through the good and bad. No matter how hard it gets I know we will make it through." Hearing Allen say this signifies in Shanice's heart that Allen truly cares and loves her. "Allen Callahan, I love you with my whole heart. I never felt this amount of warmth and peace until I started getting to know you. It's something I can't explain it's like I'm living in a fairytale." She touches Allen's face and softly brushes his hair. "Through thick and thin, I'm here to stay. With you going to Central I am in full support of that. It doesn't matter what I say or anybody else you follow what you feel in your spirit. And I will always be in your corner supporting you no matter if it's 100 or 1,000 miles away." "I love you Shanice, I'm blessed to have you alongside me. You are not only the girl I dreamed of, but the girl I truly needed. Together, we're going to create an amazing future together." Allen and Shanice kiss one another as the beautiful sunset oversees them.

It's Thursday morning, Allen and Paul walk into school together as they are automatically treated like celebrities. It's like watching Justin Bieber walking in the hallways. Girls are all over the guys getting their autograph and photos as they are truly getting recognized for their greatness. As the guys try to walk through the halls they get called to the principal's office.

The guys walk into the principal's office as Principal Davenport says to them, "Well, well, well if it isn't Babyface Jr and little Quincy Jones over here. Have a seat my celebrities." Allen and Paul are curious about what Principal Davenport wants to talk to them about. Allen says, "Thanks for having us in your office Mr. Davenport. How can we help you out?" Principal Davenport has an amazing proposition for Allen and Paul. "Well, I heard about the band you two are in and watched some performances you guys had. Your are spectacular and amazing, Prom is one week away. And I would love for The Believers to be our performers for the event. What do you guys think about that?" Allen and Paul are excited about this opportunity as they quickly accept the offer. Principal Davenport claps his hands in excitement. "Perfect I will get Ms. Cheryl to contact you guys on payment details for the event. Thank you, guys, for coming in and have a blessed day."

After school is over with, Allen goes to work as he works alongside Blake on his shift. The two haven't seen each other in a minute as they reconnect with one another as they are both stocking groceries. Blake says, "Mr. Superstar it's been a minute how you been doing?" Allen smile and says, "I don't know about me being me a superstar, but I'm doing great. School is almost over with; within two weeks we will be graduates. What are your plans after you graduate?" "Well, I decided to go to Middle Georgia State University for teaching. I want to be a PE teacher and eventually open my own gym business. I want to teach people about the importance of working out and physical health." Allen is happy that he and Blake was able to put their differences aside and became friends. He is also happy to see Blake has changed his ways and is focused on helping people. "I'm proud of you Blake it's great to see your growth. Never lose sight on who you are." Blake is also happy that he became friends with Allen as Allen has been a positive figure in his life. "I appreciated Allen same here it's great to see your growth. I know you are heavily invested in being a musician, but do you have plan on attending college?" "I do I got plan on attending Central Georgia Technical College. My major is going to be Cyber Security; I got to go up there tomorrow morning to sign up for classes. My calling is to be a musician, however at the same time I got to make sure I have money to support my dreams. Either way I'm know I'm going to be okay, when we fully follow GOD's pathway and live by truth everything else will come into fruition. We also have to stay believing in ourselves, working hard for that goal we want to achieve, and always trusting the process along our journey in life." "You are the most intelligent person I know, those were great gems you just dropped. I know you are going to be a superstar, just don't forget about me when you make it big." Allen laughs. "I won't my brother."

After family dinner, Imani sees Al talking to himself outside on their balcony. She knows he is going to see his father face-to-face for the first time in thirty years. From the way he's moving and been acting these past two days, she can tell he is nervous about the meeting. She goes outside to make sure he is okay. When he sees her coming towards him, he starts trying to act calm and collect. He quickly leans back on the balcony and says, "Hey babe how are you doing?" Imani says, "I'm doing well, I'm here to see how you are doing. You are walking around out here like you have to testify against a mob boss. How are you feeling about tomorrow?" Al can put on a front of everyone that everything is fine, and people will buy it except for his wife. "I'm nervous Imani, a part of me hope this meeting help resolve our differences. And we could possibly form a close bond. To have a close relationship with him, would mean a lot to me. The other part of me is scared he's still the same man he always been. With him meeting Allen, I know it's important for our kids to know their grandfather. Plus tomorrow isn't guaranteed I want both of us to speak our peace before it's too late." Imani softly rubs Al's shoulders as he looks directly at her. She smiles and says, "Everything is going to be just fine. You are not that same troubled young man you were when you last seen him. You are a man that overcame the hardships he faced and became a great husband and father. People in our community respect and adore the man that you are. Seeing your growth over these years has been amazing to see. I thank GOD everyday that he chose me to be your wife. And I know when you come back to this house tomorrow evening, you are going to be more powerful as you would have made full peace with your past. And our family will transcend in more brighter light due to you doing this." Al starts crying after hearing everything Imani just stated. "I thank GOD for you, you are the best thing that ever happened to me. Tomorrow, I make peace with everything that has been holding back. In return, the Callahan family will be stronger. Thank you for putting up with me all of these years, I love you my mi amor." "I love you too baby." Al and Imani hug one another.

It's a bright early sunny Friday morning, Before Al leaves out to meet up with his dad, he and Imani prays together. Imani leads the prayer. She prays, "Dear Heavenly Father, thank you for this day you have given us. We come to you today as Al goes to meet up with his father. I pray that the both of them find peace today in their conversation. That they are truly let go of the hurt and pain that the both of them have carried over the years. I'm thankful to have Al as my life companion and him being the father of my kids. Stay building and molding him sure he has done an amazing job, however I want to see him use all of the talents you have blessed him with. Give him strength where he is weak at, so he can soar into the dreams you have created for him. In Jesus name, we pray amen." "Thank you babe." Al hugs Imani. "Well it's time I hit the road, I will see you and the kids later on tonight, I love you." "I love you to baby." Al kisses Imani as he heads out of the door.

Imani goes with Allen as he signs up for college. She says to him, "So how are you feeling? This is a big thing that you are about to do." Allen says, "I feel good I done prayed about this in private with GOD, I know I'm making the right decision. Even though I'm fully focus on music, it's nothing wrong with getting knowledge in other fields and making money at the same time. Again I do apologize for lying to you and Dad." Imani smiles. "You know in a way I'm glad you did hide about you being in a band to us. If we would've found out about it when you first started, we would've shut that down in a heartbeat. But when I watch your father looking at your videos, I see the excitement and joy in his eyes. By you knowing and accepting your calling into being a musician, it made your father want to make sure you were fully equipped with everything you need to be successful. And it has made him want to make full peace with his past. I haven't seen him this happy in a very long time. Stay spreading what GOD has put inside of you as it really is helping people." Allen sits back and think of the impact he is making. He hopes that GOD stay using him as a vessel to help people be the best version of themselves.

After driving for three hours, Al arrives in Dallas, Georgia his hometown. Once he enters town memories starts running through his head of all the good and bad memories he experienced as a kid. Before heading to his father's home, he heads to his mother's grave. Despite not talking to his dad in twenty-five years, he always visit his mother's grave at least once a year. He enters the cemetery with flowers in his hand, once he gets to her grave he puts the flowers in a concrete vase next to her gravestone. He softly brushes her gravestone with his hand as he talks to her. Al says, "Hey mom it's been a minute since I been out here. Trust and believe, I haven't forgotten about you. I wish you were to see your grandkids. Allen is about to graduate from High School. Time goes by fast it seems like it was just yesterday I was teaching him how to walk and talk. He's a phenomenal young man, I'm proud that GOD blessed me to be his earthly father. I smile bright as the sun knowing the good works he is going to do in his lifetime. And Jalean is growing like a grasshopper, he will be entering his final year of middle school next year. An A-Honor Roll Student, a great soccer player, a member of the Beta club, and one of the funniest people I know. Even though you not here in the physical, I know you always around us in spirit. I know you probably have been saddened by me and pops relationship. I want things to be fully resolved between us. Me and him both aren't getting any younger, it's time we hash things out as men. As I plan on talking to him today, I hope that everything is laid out on the table. And we can start a healthy father and son relationship. I love you mom stay watching over me and the family. Al kisses his mother's gravestone as he heads to his father's house.

Al arrives at his father's house, it's a big house with about 10 acres. The house has a long driveway, it takes about 30 seconds to get to the front of the house. Finally, he is in the front yard where a beautiful garden is displayed up front, a beautiful furnished porch, with four vehicles in the yard. As he parks his truck, an elderly black woman with black hair comes outside to greet him. The woman stands on the front porch as she awaits for Al to get out of his truck. Before getting out of his vehicle, Al says to himself, "GOD help me and father say what is needed to be said in our conversation today amen." He gets out of his vehicle and goes to meet the lady on the porch. As he is walking onto the porch he says to her, "Hey hope you're well, my name is Al Callahan, I'm Alvin Callahan's son." The lady smiles as Al greets himself to her, she says, "I know exactly who you are, I been wanting to meet you for a long time. My name is Marjorie, I'm

Alvin's wife. Is it ok if I give you a hug?" "I don't mind it's totally ok." Marjorie gives Al a soft warm hug like she is hugging her long-lost son. Tears start flowing from her eyes. "It's so great to see you here, you don't know how much this visit is going to mean to your father. He's been wanting to meetup with you for a long time. I know this meeting means a lot to you also. Before I take you to him I want to make are you ok to meet with him." "I am I have done a lot of praying and meditating on this, I'm ready it's been a long time coming." Marjorie looks at Al and sees he is calm and collect. She smiles and says, "Well with that being said let me take you to your father."

Al walks inside of his father's house as it's pretty big on the inside. He walks through the living room he sees pictures of his father and Marjorie and her children, then he sees a picture of him and his father together when he was a little kid. Seeing the photo surprises him because even though they haven't talked in decades his dad still keeps a part of him near him. As he walks in the kitchen, he sees a guy out of the window cutting wood in the backyard. He looks at the guy and quickly recognizes it's his father. His father looks very different than he did thirty years ago. He's more muscular and is in better shape now.

Marjorie walks Al out on the back porch, while Alvin is still chopping wood in the backyard. She yells out loud, "Honey you have company?" Alvin looks up and sees Al. All types of emotions is running through his head right now, the last time he seen his son he was a young boy. Now when he looks at him, he sees a man who looks like he got himself together. He smiles and says, "It's been a long-time son, you look wonderful. If you don't mind, can you help me put this wood in the cages behind me." "I sure can." Al helps his father out with the wood. "This is a beautiful home you have here, how long have you and Ms. Marjorie been staying here?" "We have been staying here for about ten years. When me and Marg got married, we wanted a place that was peaceful to us. When we first visited this property, we both decided this would be our home. I still have the family home, I rent it out to single moms to live in. Just so you know, if something was to ever happen to me you would be the official owner of that house. It's the first house I bought, I always want to keep it in the family. Me and you have a lot of things we need to say to each other. I want you to speak your peace son. Tell me or ask me anything that you feel need to be said."

Apart of Al wants to lash out and yell at his dad, however he knows that's not the right way to have this conversation. It would probably lead to another huge argument. Instead, he thinks about what Dennis said to him in the church. What led Alvin to become the man his own son despised? "Growing up as a kid I admired the man you were. You were like superman to me, but when mom passed away you turned into someone I hated. How did you go from a loving father to an abusive father?" Alvin is transparent with his son. "Honestly it dates back to my childhood let me tell you about my upbringing so you can have a full understanding. I was the only child that my mother and father had. I was born and raised in Macon, Ga. I had a great childhood at first, I was the only young kid on my street that had a Dad and Mom in the household. Me and my father were close. Everything was good until I was eight years old, my daddy left the family to marry this white woman he met at his job. I never ever saw him again after that. That left, me and my mother together. Before my father left, me and my mom honestly didn't have the best relationship. She never said I love you or attended to me when I needed her. She was a stay-at-home mom that drunk all day and watched TV. But when my pops left the family, it became 100 times worse. Due to me looking just like my dad, she couldn't stand to look at me. If I didn't do anything right which seemed liked all the time she would beat me with a switch from a tree. That lasted all the way up until I was sixteen, one day I didn't do the dishes she was about to hit me with a frying pan. I blocked from her hitting me and I knocked her out. Due to that, I got kicked out of the house and became homeless. I took a greyhound bus from Macon to Dallas. I never saw my mom again, I didn't get a chance to tell my parents how they made me feel. I had anger and a lot of torment in me, to fill that void I felt inside my heart I turned to alcohol and drugs. Then I met your mother, she was the best thing that ever happened to me."

Alvin smiles as he thinks about Al's mother. "Ruth, she was truly a breath of fresh air. We both came from struggling families, just like my mom was abusing me, her father was abusing her, her mom passed away while giving birth to her. When she found out I was homeless, she would sneak me in to stay inside her father's basement. For six months, we saved up money to rent out an apartment. Eventually, we got the apartment within eight months. The start of our relationship was great, for the first time in my life I got a sense on what happiness was. Then when we were eighteen she got pregnant with you. That's when challenges started entering our relationship, because as you know having a child takes a lot of work. I wanted to make sure you had everything you needed, it was a lot of pressure on the both of us, we stressed about bills all the time. However, when you were born, it was the best day of our lives. Holding you in my arms were the most amazing feeling I have ever felt. Your mother was smiling ear to ear holding you in her arms, and singing hymms to you. She loved you with all of her heart Al. When you growing up as a young boy, I worked three jobs to put food on the table for us. Reason why I would come home super late. I wanted your mom to be a stay-at-home mom; I look back on that I wish I never would've did that. Ruth was talented in a lot of things; she never got a chance to tap into what she was meant to be in life. I remember she taught you how to play the piano and guitar. She would play the piano and we would sing songs together. The greatest thing that brought her joy in life was seeing you happy. We created great memories together. One morning, I asked her to pick up a paycheck for me from a lawn care job I did for someone. I could've got it myself, but I was tired she went ahead and got it for me. On the way back to the house, a police chase happened the person they were pursuing rounded it up hitting her, instantly killing her. I blamed myself for her death for a long time.

The night of her death, I bought a bottle of gin and a small bag of coke. I rounded up having a twenty-year addiction to drugs and alcohol. When it came to you, I knew I wasn't going to be a great parent like your mom was. My main objective was for you to be perfect. Which was super unfair to you, I wanted you to be the best. When I felt you didn't do your best, I would beat on you. Most of the time when I was doing it, I was either high or drunk. Still when I would beat you I thought that would help you be a better person. The same thing my mother did to me. But I turned you into me, you turned from this smart intelligent kid, to this young boy who would smoke weed all day and skip school. Then I would always see you playing your guitar, I would think to myself he's wasting his life away. That last time I tried to beat you,

you fought back and you beat me. After the fight, I knew I was wrong in the situation and that I had a lot of issues going on. I made a decision to call Bill, to have you stay with him and his family in Macon. Apart of me wanted you stay, but then I felt like you was better off without me. You would have a better life without me being around. I was a mess Al, I had no love to give to no one even myself back then. When Bill told me he would take you in, I knew you were in good hands. He was the man that you needed to be around to help showcase who you needed to be.

Over the years, I stayed keeping tabs on you. When I found out about your drug overdose, I wanted to be there by your side, but I was partaking in the same stuff. I prayed that you overcame those battles you faced. And I see you have; I looked you up online a few years back you have a beautiful wife and kids. The lifestyle that most African Americans dream of you was able to create that for your family." Al starts weeping as a part of him wished he would've attributed more to his son's life. "I'm sorry for all the pain I put you through. You didn't deserve none of it, I have been ashamed of myself on how I treated you. I don't deserve to be your father, but I'm hoping I can be involved in your life. I'm not the same man I was back then. I'm full changed man that is a follower of Christ now. I hope and pray you forgive me please son, Please I'm sorry! I love you and I want you apart of my life."

All of these years, if he was given the opportunity Al visioned himself lashing out against his father about the stuff he put him through. Instead, just hearing his father apologizing to him, showing sincerity, and explaining on what led him down a bad pathway, is what Al truly needed to find peace and to forgive his father. With tears flowing from his eyes Al says, "That's all I wanted to hear from you over the years, that you was sorry for your actions. It's going to take some time, but I want to develop a strong relationship with you. As long as we both are breathing we can make things right, I love you pops." "I love you to son." Al and Alvin hug one another. After almost thirty years, father and son are reunited and stronger together.

Al and Alvin goes inside of the house so Al can be better acquainted with his stepmother. And to learn how his father transformed into the man he is today. "So pops when did everything transformed in your life?" "One day in 2005, I tried to do some yard work while at the family house. When I went to lift something, I rounded up having a stroke. Luckily, my neighbor found me within minutes and called the ambulance. I was in a coma for about five hours. Through the grace of GOD I survived, I was told by doctors I had passed away twice on the way to the hospital. And that I was blessed to be here, my addiction to drugs and alcohol had finally called up to me. In my mind, I knew I had to be here for a reason. I reached out to Bill to get some help, he helped me enter a six-month rehabilitation center in Chattanooga, Tennessee. Of course, while being in there, I got a full detox. Also, for the first time in my life, I faced all of the pain I felt as a young man. I rounded up forgiving my parents for everything that put me through and forgiving myself for what happened to your mother.

When I got out of the program, I wanted a fresh start. I had a lot of money saved in my whole life insurance policy, I decided to use part of it and travel. While visiting the Grand Canyon, I met this beautiful bundle of joy sitting before you while there. After you mom died, I didn't looked into another woman's direction. But with Marg it was like my heart was calling me to get to know her." Margarie says, "I saw him from a far and I was like he's a handsome guy. I didn't think he would approach me, but when he did we automatically clicked. We shared a lot of things in common; I had just lost my husband the year prior before meeting Alvin. It was my first vacation since his death I had to learn how to live life without him. When Alvin found out about my husband's death he asked have I made peace with it." Al asks, "Did you make with it?" "I did my husband Roger was on hospice before he passed. The two biggest blessings in that was we were able to talk about everything that needed to be said. And he no longer had to worry about any pain or suffering. When one of our loved ones die, sometimes we are quick to get upset with

GOD and maybe even in ourselves. What I learned from my husband's death is when our loved one die is to carry on their memory and legacy. They wouldn't want us being sad or mad, they would want us to be happy and enjoy our lives. Otherwise, if we don't, we will be wasting our whole life away."

Alvin says, "When Marg told me that, it made me realize I wasted twelve years of my life, I didn't want to waste no more time. We automatically became close during the trip, I found out that she stayed in Atlanta. Once we came back from Arizona, we never let the connection die between us. With us staying fifty minutes from another, we visited each other every weekend and talked everyday. She helped me turn my life over to GOD, we would go to her church together every Sunday, and have bible study together at my house every Wednesday. We were close friends until one day while spending time with her I told myself I never don't want her to leave my side. I asked her would she like to date me." "And I told him yes, I myself was growing romantic feelings for Alvin. I didn't know how to express them, but when he told me how he felt it made me feel relieved because I was feeling the same way. My kids had already met him and they loved him so that made things easy. We dated for about two years and then he proposed to me. And we got married on Mother's Day in 2009. I'm grateful and blessed to have him in my life. Seeing the transformation in him has been beautiful to see. He leads Bible studies every Wednesday with the men at our church. We have our own worship time together on Mondays, we read the Bible together every day. He's a great leader and a great man."

"So, when you were was getting to know him did he talk about me?" "He did at first just very little, but then one night while we were getting to know one another we talked about our big regrets. His was not being a great father to you, for years he has been wanting to reach out to you, but he was scared you would turn him away." "Like I stated when we were outside together, I always kept tabs on you. I have the newspaper article when you became president of National First Bank back in 2011. It made me proud, despite what you went through you made a name for yourself. And I'm glad that we get to be by your side now on your journey."

Hearing all of this showcases Alvin's transformation from an abused father to a Man of GOD. One of the interesting parts of hearing his dad speak was that the both of them found GOD in almost the same fashion. "I thank GOD that I came out here, when I hear your story of finding Christ it reminded me of my story. My wife was the first friend I had that taught me about GOD's word. When I woke up from my coma from my drug overdose, she was holding my hand and was by my side. She helped me grow stronger and become a believer in Christ Jesus. Another reason why I came up here is because of my son, Allen who you both met. Recently, I just found out he wants to be a musician for a living. When I found out he was performing across the state at first, thoughts in my head was running rapidly on how can I prevent this from happening. As I didn't want him to get sucked into the evils of the world like I did. However, my wife reminded me that we have to support our children in their dreams, in less they doing something that will bring destruction to people. When I was pursuing music, I didn't have my earthly father, I didn't listen to anything Bill was telling me, nor listened to my heavenly father due to that I endured a lot of pain and suffering during those times. The man that I needed back then is the man I'm going to be for my son. When he told me he met you, I knew that was a divine meeting created by GOD. I knew in order for me to be the best father for both of my sons, I had to make peace with you. So, this generational curse of pain and anger in the men of our family don't carry over to the next generation. We had our good and bad moments pops, but as I look into your eyes as a man I can honestly say I forgive you and I love you." Alvin hugs his son as tears fall from both of their eyes. Tears fall from Marjorie eyes as she looks up in the ceiling and says, "Thank you GOD."

For the next couple of hours, Al spends time with his father and stepmother. As he and his father haven't laughed and joked together in thirty years. Finally, after hanging out with his father and stepmom all day, it's time for Al to head back home. Alvin and Marjorie walks him to his truck. Al says, "This has been a great day, I'm glad I came out here." Alvin says, "We glad that you did also, you and your family are welcomed here anytime." Marjorie says, "Next time you come, you should bring them." "Well, it's funny you say that Allen is having a performance in Atlanta next Saturday. Me, my wife, and my other son Jalean got plans on coming up here to support him. With Dallas and Atlanta being just fifty minutes apart, I would love to invite you guys to come to his performance."

Alvin loves hearing this as it creates a better idea in his head. "I will do you one better, how about your come down here next Friday night and spend the night here the whole weekend. That way you guys won't have to drive far for the performance. And it gives us time to bond more." Al loves the idea and plan. "I'm down for that, I know my wife and kids will love that. Thank you both for this day." Marjorie says, "We are extremely thankful for this day also. It was an honor meeting you Al and I can't wait to see you around here more. Tell your family we said hello and if you ever need anything don't hesitate to call us, we love you" Al gives his dad and stepmom a hug. Alvin and Marjorie watches Al as he drives off, Marjorie is leaning on Alvin's shoulder as he says, "GOD is truly a miracle worker and way maker." While driving Al says, "Lord Jesus, I love you thank you."

After rehearsing for tomorrow's performance, Allen and Paul has a conversation with each other. Paul says, "It seems like your father turned over a new leaf, I'm surprised he's really trying to help us further our music career." Allen says, "I am also, but I'm happy about it. Me and him have a closer relationship thanks to that. I know me and him were talking about our future he recommended that I go to a technical college instead of going to a State University. With that being said, I got plan on attending Central Georgia Technical College this fall and taking up Cyber Security as my major. Just in case this dream of ours take a minute to accomplish I will be in a field that will help make me a lot of money." "It's funny you say that my parents was telling me the same thing, I also have plan on attending Central Georgia this summer to take up Business Management. Look at this, we're going to be going to college together." Allen is excited by this news as just like in High School he will have his best friend by his side in College. "This is perfect together we can promote the band's name on campus, possibly even throw events there. But most of all, with everything that we are doing we will be there for each other every step of the way." "Yes, indeed my brother." Allen and Paul dap one another up.

Al returns home after visiting his father, as he enters the house Jalean joyfully runs up to him. He says, "Daddy look at my report card." Al looks at his son's report card and smiles as he sees his son had an A+ average in his classes. It's not the grade average, that makes Al happy, what makes him happy is seeing the joy and how proud his son is of himself. It's precious moments like this that makes Al feel proud and blessed to be a father. He says, "I'm proud of you son, we're going celebrate your huge accomplishments next week. This is just the beginning the main thing I will say is always believe in yourself and know your worth. Now, where is your mother?" "She and Allen are in the kitchen cooking together.

Al sees Imani and Allen cooking together as he walks into the kitchen. "Look at GOD performing miracles today, we got Mr. Allen Callahan cooking in the kitchen I thought I would never see the day." Allen smiles and says, "Well with me getting close to be a grown up I need to learn how to cook. Plus, momma is cooking her special Chicken Alfredo tonight, so I definitely got to learn her special recipe." Imani says, "I don't know babe I think Allen can give you a run for your money." Al starts laughing and hugs Imani while she's cooking. "Oh baby, you're the best comedian I know." Al gives Imani a kiss on the cheek.

After Allen and his mother finished cooking Chicken Alfredo and Texas Toast. The Callahan family eats dinner together. They sit down at the dining room table as Allen blesses the food. "Dear GOD, thank you for this day you have given us. I'm blessed and thankful for the parents and brother you blessed me with. I hope and pray that you stay strengthen our family and that we stay getting closer with each other. And that the love that we showcase to each other can be a pillar of what a Godly family should look like. In Jesus name, we pray amen." Al says, "Amen! First a musician now pastor, Allen you're a jack of all trades." Allen puts his hands up in the air. "I try my best pops."

Imani looks directly at Al as she wants to know how everything went with his father. "How was your day honey?" Al opens up to his family on how his day went. "Today was a good day, I met with my dad for the first time in almost thirty years." Allen is surprised to hear this, while Jalean says, "But Grandpa Bill has been dead for two years." "Grandpa Bill was my adoptive father; Alvin Callahan is my biological father." "So, I guess by him meeting me in Atlanta made you want to meet up with him." "Kind of, it was a sign of GOD that I needed to make amends with him before it was too late. I learned a lot today talking to my dad, found out it's been a generational curse in our family that I never knew anything about. That helped me realize why he treated me so badly when I was a kid, which is something I needed to know. He was forgiving and apologetic towards everything he put me through. All of the pain and hurt I had in my heart today for thirty years was officially buried today. And now my father and I are back on speaking terms. This is the happiest I've ever been in my life; I'm so blessed to have you all in my life." Imani smiles as she prayed that Al would find peace today. "I'm happy for you babe." Jalean asks, "When will we be able to meet our grandfather?" "You will be able to meet your grandfather and step grandmother next Saturday they invited us to stay with them for the whole weekend. Would that be something you guys would love to do?" Everyone at the table yells out, "Absolutely!"

Imani says, "I can't wait to meet your father and stepmom next week. Speaking of trips Allen how are you feeling about tomorrow?" "With the guidance pops gave me and my bandmates we are prepared for tomorrow. We don't know what the outcome will be, but I know in my spirit and heart that we will be ok no matter what happens. Plus having dad by my side tomorrow will give us comfort." "Well, I'm grateful to be there with you guys tomorrow. No matter what happens, keep your head high. And this go to you and Jalean no matter where you go in life showcase your full greatness to the world." Imani puts her glass of Lemonade in the air. "Cheers to the greatness and legacy of the Callahan family."

Chapter 11: Me and My Guitar in Memphis

It's Saturday Morning, Al and Allen gets ready to go to Memphis, Tennessee. Imani takes the both of them to the airport, on the way there she says to them, "I believe today is going to be a day of discovery for the both of you. Sometimes things happen in life in order for us to walk in our full potential." Al and Allen look at another as they know today is going to be a day to remember. The guys arrive at the airport to meet up with the rest of the bandmates. They greet each other in the middle of the airport. Paul says to everybody, "How's everyone feeling today?" Allen says, "I'm fully prepared for today, no matter what happens today we stay keeping our head up as we are a force to be reckoned with." Al loves hearing his son's words of affirmation, it showcases Allen's abilities to be a leader. The band is confident and are prepared for Memphis.

After flying in the air for an hour, The Believers along with Al arrives in Memphis. once they have arrived, they drop off their luggage at the hotel and go straight to the legendary Luxury Studios. Before going into the studio, Al gives the band a pep talk. He says, "Before going in there just know the time we walk in there, they are going to show us things to excite us. However, when it comes to business you have to see the difference when someone is offering you an opportunity or taking advantage of you skills and talents." Paul says, "We are with everything that you are saying Mr.

Al. The main question I have is when do we talk about royalties with Jack?" "You want to play it smart, first play the song for Larry Nash and Danielle. Once you get their reaction then talk to Jack about the contract and royalties." "Sounds like a plan let's go inside and make it happen. Everybody walks inside as they are greeted by Jack's assistant once they enter the building. As she shows the band around. They are amazed by the famous portraits of famous artists being in the same studio they are walking in.

As they walk into the studio booth, they see Jack sitting in the middle of the studio with Larry Nash and Danielle. The band are in awe of meeting them. While Al has a trick up his sleeve to help the band out. Jack sees The Believers walking in the studio booth as he is happy to see them. He says to them, "Well look who it is the biggest band out right now The Believers. Paul, Allen, Claudia, Joe, and Eddie this two-time Grammy award winner Larry Nash and this multi-platinum artist Danielle." I have already told Larry and Danielle about you guys they love your music as much as you love theirs. And they can't wait to hear the track you guys wrote and produced for them."

Jack is curious about who Al is, he walks up to him with a smile on his face. "I'm sorry excuse my manners Jack Stevens A&R Rep for Cloud Records." Al shakes Jack's hand and says, "Al Callahan, I'm Allen's Father." Jack usually doesn't deal with parents when he is trying to sign artists. Seeing and meeting Al has caught him blindsided, but he keeps focus on the task at hand. "It's great meeting you Mr. Callahan, Allen he is a phenomenal artist and songwriter. You should most definitely be proud of him." "Me and his mother are always proud of his accomplishments; I'm blessed to be his father. So, Mr. Jack, how long have you been an A&R rep?" "For about fifteen years, my main thing is getting great talents showcased so that can make a massive impact in the music industry. Whom massive impact, what about massive money also?" "Oh, yes of course that, got to make sure we making that money." From the tone of Jack's statement, Al can tell something is fishy with this deal he's offering the band.

Paul says to Jack, "Mr. Jack, do you mind if I go ahead and play the song we wrote for the two great talents behind you?" "Please be our guest, Paul." Paul plays the song that Allen and Claudia wrote for the duo as he also helped produce the song. The band looks at Larry and Danielle as they hope they love the song. The band see them bobbing their head as they hope that this means that they love the song. After the song ends, Larry says, "Well I got one thing to say." The band looks at one another as they wonder what Larry is about to say. "When can we start recording the song?" Allen says, "Let's go ahead and get started right now."

For the next hour, Larry Nash and Danielle record the song "Meant to Be" Allen and Claudia wrote for them. The band take pictures as they are stunned and shell shocked that they are in a studio working with famous musicians. The band bonds with Larry Nash and Danielle. Before the studio session ends, Allen says to Larry Nash and Danielle, "I want to say thank you guys for recording this song. I'm still in shock; I can't believe a song I co-wrote is being sung by Larry Nash and Danielle." Claudia says, "For real it's feel like I'm in a dream." Danielle smiles and says, "Me and Larry are glad to be singing on you guys' song. When I look at both of you, Allen and Claudia you remind me of me and Larry. You guys can be legendary singers, writers, and producers. Stay working with one another you two can create legendary magic that can impact a generation for a lifetime." Larry says, "I agree with Danielle you two have a great connection don't let it die out." Allen and Claudia look at one another for a second as in both of their minds they know they are going to be a dynamic duo. Jack says, "I told Larry and Danielle about you guys' performance they will be in attendance tonight. Sound check at the venue is at 7 PM. In the meantime, you guys go ahead and enjoy good old Memphis, Tennessee."

Right before Jack is about to step out the door, Al stops him. "Hold a second this song is going to be a smash hit, the kids told me how much they are getting paid. I'm curious what percentage are they getting in royalties?" The million-dollar question has been asked everyone is looking at Jack for an answer. He surprisingly is transparent with his answer. "Well, our goal was to just give them a payment and that's it. This is a once in a lifetime opportunity that they are living in. Not too many people get to be in a studio with grammy award winners and multi-platinum artists. They can capitalize off this and makes five times the amount they will be making off this song."

All the band members of The Believers is surprised to hear this as they just found out they were about to be used. "Kids take this as a lesson don't take everyone to be your friend. You were going to make possible hundreds of thousands to millions off this song from years to come and not the give the people that created the song their shared percentage in it." Larry Nash says, "Jack you got to make this right. Daniellé says, Yes indeed Jack you got to do something." Al asks Jack, "Do you have kids?" Jack answers, "Yes I have two." "Wouldn't you want your kids to get a return on something they put their heart into. That's what The Believers did, and they deserve to make money off this song they created from years to decades from now. I'm thinking the whole group gets 40% with it being split individually. Which leaves everyone with 10% in royalties for the band, Cloud Records get 40%, and your two artists split 20% together. Now to me that's sound like a fair deal. Believers what do you think about this deal?" Everyone in the band loves the deal, Larry Nash and Danielle loves the idea also.

Jack wants to talk to Al outside one-on-one outside. "Do you mind if we talk outside real quick?" "Sure thing." Both men go outside of the room to discuss business. "Listen as a father I understand you want the best for your son. However, I done already created a marketing plan for this group. I admit I was wrong for not including royalties in the agreement, but I still want to work with them." Hearing Jack's point of view and knowing what each person in the group needs, gives Al a great idea. "You know Paul and Allen are about to graduate from High School within two weeks, Claudia is already one year removed from High School and is living on her own, Joe is a husband and father that is trying to provide for his family. I think with all their individual talents they can benefit your company and themselves in the process." Jack likes the idea that just been presented to him. "I like what I hear all of them got skills that can help us out. In return, it would create another stream of income for them outside of the band, I love it. Let me work on some stuff with my team and I will have new paperwork printed out by their performance tonight." "That's sounds like a plan."

Jack excitedly walks into the studio booth. "Me and Mr. Callahan has come up with a great plan long term for you guys." The band is curious about what plan has been created. Joe asks, "What plan you got for us?" "I want to sign all of you individually, for your songwriting, production, and engineering skills only. I believe this can be beneficial for all of us. You create hits for us; you get paid a good amount of money for each song you help create. You will have a bigger percentage of royalties by doing everything individually. Due to the band not signing with Cloud Records, the label wouldn't promote you as a band. However, I will most definitely promote you guys on my social media every time you put out a song or an album. I believe in you guys, I know you are going to go far. What do you think of everything I just stated?" Everyone in the band loves the idea. Claudia says, "We love the idea just shows us the numbers and we go from there." "Sounds like a plan I will have the paperwork printed out for you guys tonight. I will see you all at 7."

After the meeting in the studio, the group goes to a restaurant downtown to talk. Claudia asks Al, "Mr. Al how did you know to propose your proposition to Jack?" Al says, "When it comes to business you going to have people that are going to use you for their benefit, however when that happens you got to see what they can bring to the table that will benefit you also. Plus, for him to fly you guys out to Tennessee and pay for everything shows he sees a lot of value in you all." Paul says, "You ever thought about being our manager?" Al starts laughing. "No that is not for me, look at me as your advisor. Paul, I think you're a great manager, you just got to remember as much as you create music, you have to study the business behind it also. Speaking of which, I have a surprise for you guys." Al pulls out an envelope and hands it over to Allen. "Son, do you mind opening that envelope for me? And read what's inside of it." Allen opens the letter and smiles like he just won the lottery. "These are certificating's and documents of LLC for our own record label." The band crowds around Allen as they are excited to see the papers. Eddie says, "This is amazing thank you so much Mr. Al." "You welcome and Paul's Mom has trademarked the label's name. It will more than likely be owned by you guys within 1-2 years. Joe says, "For real I don't know how we can re-pay you for this." "It's simple showcase your full greatness to the whole world. That's all I ask for in return and I will always be there to support you guys." Allen sits back as he is glad to see his father supporting him and his fellow bandmates.

It's almost showtime for The Believers as they are about to have their biggest performance yet at the legendary Missy's Lounge. The band does soundcheck for thirty minutes to prepare for their performance. After soundcheck the band goes backstage as they talk to Jack. He says to the band, "Your sounded amazing up there listen we got some heavy hitters in the crowd. I want you to give it all you got on stage tonight. A lot of people don't get this opportunity, but the five of you got it show everyone who you guys are out there tonight."

A few opening acts perform at the bar before "The Believers" get on stage to perform. Right before the band gets on stage, Allen prays for everyone. He says, "Everyone let's pray before we go on stage." All the members of the band bow their heads for prayer. "Dear Heavenly Father thank you for everything you have done for us. Thank you for giving us our God-given gifts as we use them to bring inspiration to people. We shall give inspiration and prosperity to the crowd tonight. In Jesus name I pray amen." Everyone says amen. Allen says, "Alright let's go out there and do our thing." Jack goes onstage to introduce the band. He says to the crowd, "Memphis how are we living?" The crowd yells back good. "That's what I'm talking about! I want you to give a warm welcome to our final performers tonight all the way from Macon, GA y'all give it up for The Believers!"

The band goes on stage as there are 200 patrons in the crowd waiting to hear them perform. Al is in the crowd also as this will be his first time seeing The Believers perform live. He has Shanice facetiming him, so she can watch Allen perform. The band does a rendition of "Proud Mary" by Ike and Tina Turner for their first song of the night. Claudia and Allen's chemistry wows the crowd as they get energetic by the band's musical talents. The second song of the night, the band performs is one of their original songs "I Want to be Free" as Allen's voice moves the crowd. For some of the patrons it was like listening to Eddie Vedder sing. As you can hear Allen's passion as he sings the song. After performing "I Want to be Free", Allen does a solo performance of Ben E. King "Stand By Me". As if people didn't know who Allen Callahan was before they know now. Al looks proudly at his son as he sees how Allen is positively impacting the crowd.

After his solo performance the crowd gives Allen a standing ovation. He gets on the mic and says, "Memphis I love you; we got one final song for you. No matter what comes your way in life stay following the pathway towards your destiny." The Believers performs their song "Destiny". Allen and Claudia voices bring a soulful and powerful vibe to the crowd. With the guys playing the instruments in the back, the performance bring chills and even some tears towards some people's eyes. Allen ends the performance with a one-minute guitar riff. Afterwards the crowd give them a standing ovation as all of the patrons believe in The Believers. Jack comes on stage and says to the crowd, "Y'all give it up for The Believers."

After performing, the band goes backstage as Claudia gives Allen a hug and says, "You're the man I'm so proud of you." Paul and Joe hug Allen as they are proud of him. Paul says to him, "That's how you put on a show! You are a freaking legend in the making." After the show, numerous people come backstage to get photos with the band and get their autographs. Well known musicians including Larry Nash and Danielle take photos with the band and post them on their social media. Allen and the rest of the group is on cloud nine as they are being recognized for the true superstars they are. Jack comes backstage and congratulates the group on their performance. He says, "You guys did a phenomenal job up there I'm proud of all of you. I have the paperwork printed out; I made reservations at Sherman's Restaurant downtown. Would love for you all to join me to eat a delicious meal and talk some business." Paul says, "We will do that after we socialize with our fans."

After taking photos, signing autographs, and exchanging conversations. The Believers along with Al go and meet up with Jack to go over the paperwork he drew up for them. Jack raises his glass of wine and says, "Cheers to the great future success of The Believers." Everyone at the table says cheers along with Jack. "As we grub in, look at the contract that is in front of you. Carefully look at it and let me know what you think." Everyone does their due diligence and looks at the contract. Allen, who is sitting alongside his father has him look at the contract with him. He asks, "Dad, what do you think of this contract?" Al says, "Well you are being offered a $100,000 salary for four years with 10% royalty to be a songwriter for the label. To most people this sounds like a good deal, but you must ask yourself is this the best deal for you?" Allen takes a minute and visualizes his future if he signs this contract. He thinks to himself he would be giving a big percentage of his work to Cloud Records. However, the money he will make off the songs he write can help fund his music career, help him give back and set up generational wealth for his family. Plus, with what each member is contribution to Cloud Records, it will help bring more recognition to the group and their own record label. With seeing this deal as being something that will change his life for the better good, Allen signs the contract and everyone else at the table sign their contract also. Jack smiles and says, "Well it brings me great honor to have you guys at Cloud Records. Now it's time to make history together." With Allen signing this contract how will his future be impacted?"

Chapter 12: A New Season

Allen has just made one of the biggest decisions of his life by signing a songwriters deal with Cloud Records. If he uses the money wisely that he will receive from his contract, he will be set for life. Just a couple of months ago, Allen was a young kid who didn't know where he wanted to go in life. Now he is walking in his calling and just gained a financial blessing from it. He's super excited right now as he returns to his hotel room and facetimes the main person he visions to be by his side in his future.

Allen facetimes Shanice to tell her the great news. Shanice answers the phone as she is excited to hear from Allen. She wants to know how his day has gone. She says, "Hey there superstar, I know you been all over the place today." Allen sightly laugh with joy and says, "It's been a day I will never forget. Larry Nash and Danielle loved the song I co-wrote with Claudia, due to that my dad was able to structure a deal for all of us to individually help contribute musically to Cloud Records." "Wait so that mean you guys did sign to the record label?" "Not as a band, we signed individually as creatives. Me and Claudia signed on as songwriters, Paul signed as a producer, and Joe signed on as a producer and engineer. The contract I signed will last four years and it's going to generate a lot of money for our future. Also, what we just did will help bring a lot of attraction towards the band.

If you had told me this would happen a couple of months ago, I would call you a liar. Everything that I'm experiencing in my life right now showcases how GOD gives us preparation before he blesses us in life. And I'm extremely thankful for everything he has done for me. Not just the last couple of months, but also in my entire life." Shanice is happy and proud of the man he has become. "I remember observing you when we first started going to school together. I marveled at how intelligent and smart you were. Then seeing you growing out your shyness and walking into your purpose has been a great sight to see. GOD is using you as a vessel to reach people through your music. And I'm proud on how you have grown and like we always tell each other no matter what we are going to be ok."

Shanice's statement gives Allen's spirit warmth and makes him shed a tear. He's happy that she sees his true identity and who he is as a person. She sees him crying on the phone and asks, "Why are you crying babe?" "I'm thankful that you see me for who I am. And that you love and respect me for who I am. That makes me know I'm valued, and it brings comfort to my soul. Thank you for your love and I promise you; you will not regret it." "I know I won't I love you, Allen." "I love you to baby." The two young lovebirds give each other a kiss through the phone.

Al is laying down on his bed in his hotel room as he smiles while staring at the ceiling. Seeing his son living out his dreams makes him happy. When Al became a father, his biggest goal was to make sure his kids had a better upbringing than he did. He's proud that Allen became the man that he needed to be while on his adventure towards his goals and dreams.

Al talks to GOD while laying down. He says, "Lord you are one funny and amazing man. By Allen stepping into the destiny you created for him, has made me take a second look in my life and adjust things. What you're doing in his life has and is changing our family history for greater good. Thank you for Imani, I was going to force Allen to give up on being a musician, but instead she showed me a different perspective. By that happening me and Allen are closer, it made me look at what was broken in me, and I was able to get healing from childhood trauma. I'm a better husband and father thanks to all of this. Thank you for preventing me from passing down a generational curse to my sons." Even though he hides his feelings at times, Al cries tears of joy. "I love you GOD thank you for your mercy and love you have for us. Me and my family shall always stay following the footsteps you have made for us."

The next morning, the whole crew flies back to Macon. While on the flight back, Allen talks to his father. He asks, "Pops with everything that is going on in my life what would be the biggest advice you can give me?" Al says, "Always stay putting GOD first, stay focus, don't lose sight on who you are, and don't lose sight on your vision. Your special son a lot of young men are going to be looking up to you, be a good example for them. I'm proud of you kiddo, when we get back home get some rest."

After returning home, Al and Allen are greeted by Imani and Jalean. Jalean asks the both of them, "How was Memphis?" Al says, "It was a great time, we did a lot of sightseeing. While the band didn't sign with the label, Allen did come back home with a huge surprise for you guys. Son, show your mom and brother what you did last night." Allen pulls out the songwriter's contract that he signed with Cloud Records. Imani and Jalean look at the paper together, both of them gets excited as they are reading it. Even though everything looks good on paper, Imani wants to make sure Allen didn't feel pressured into signing the contract. She asks, "This is great son, the amount of money you are going to make is going to help you and your future family out for a long time. The question I have for you is did you use your due diligence before you signed? And were you at peace when you signed the contract?" Allen doesn't have any regrets signing the contract, he's comfortable with the decision he made. He says, "I used Godly wisdom before signing it and I asked pops advice before signing. I'm ok and happy with the decision I made." "I'm happy for you son and this is just the beginning for you." Imani gives Allen a hug. Jalean says, "Proud of you big bro." Al asks, "Has anyone ate dinner yet?" "No, I was just about to cook." "Don't worry about that, today I want to celebrate our sons. Both have done some amazing things recently and they deserve to be celebrated for it. I'm taking everyone out for dinner." The whole family is excited about this as they quickly head out the door.

It's the end of the night, as they both are about to go to bed, Imani beautifully stares at Al. He chuckles and says, "Why are you staring at me like a piece of steak?" Imani says, "I'm just in awe of the man that you are. The way that you have been bonding with Allen and taking the steps to finally make amends with your father, it has been amazing to see. I'm proud of you Al, by you letting go of all the pride and anger you had inside of you, not only have you been transformed but our family has been also. This house is filled with more warmth and love. And our sons won't have to carry the burdens that you had to carry." Al would love to take full credit for all of this, but it's two people that led him to follow the right path. "Thank you, babe, but it's all thanks to GOD and Allen that this has happened. He lit a fire under our son to step out his shyness and to follow his calling. Observing Allen these past weeks has been inspiring to see, when he plays his guitar and sings, it creates this soulful and positive vibe in the atmosphere. He truly touching people's souls, every word that comes out his mouth has meaning. Seeing him living out his dream has made me want to find my calling in life also. I know I have an amazing job that has made me a lot of money. However I know GOD has something bigger for me, I just got to talk more with him and stay following him to see what that is." "Praise GOD, I love you baby." Imani hugs her husband tightly as she is proud of the man he is and is happy to see what GOD has in store for him.

It's Tuesday Evening, Allen is at work stocking groceries with Kevin. While stocking groceries a customer notices him. The young man taps Allen on the shoulder and asks, "Excuse me are you Allen Callahan from The Believers." Allen responds, "Yes sir, the one and only." The young man gets excited. "Oh, snap Chrissy yo! You got to come over here, Allen Callahan is next to me." Chrissy yells back, "I know you lying!" She rushes over to him and sees Allen and yells in excitement. "OMG! It's really you can I give you a hug?" "Sure thing." Chrissy gives Allen a hug and takes a photo with him also. "I'm sorry if it seems like I'm acting crazy, but we're huge fans of yours. We saw your performance in Atlanta it was electrifying and inspiring. Recently I got fired from my job, I was in deep depression because of it. My hubby Mark wanted to take me to Atlanta, to get out of the house. We went to The Underground and saw you. Your song "Destiny" touched me, more than you know. I literally started crying as it's something I needed to hear. I downloaded the song to my phone after it was released on streaming services. You're saving lives with what you're doing, that's not me hyping you up. Please keep doing what you are doing and speak what is stored inside of you. I can't wait to see what the future has for you. Thank you for being you."

The interaction Allen just had with the customers showcases why GOD has him on the journey that he is on. Kevin is proud to see the growth and recognition that Allen is getting. He says, "Man that was a beautiful sight to see, I'm proud of you my brother. Just a couple of months ago, you was this timid kid who was trying to figure out what he wanted to do with his life. Now you a boy who grew into a man with confidence, that has stepped in the destiny that has been created for him. And you're impacting people with the gifts that has been instilled in you. You are living in your purpose brother; that's something I'm not even doing in my life. I'm honored to personally know you and call you a friend of mine." "Thank you, bro, that means a lot coming from you. I'm just following GOD's footsteps that's all I'm doing."

"Keep doing that my brother. How do you feel about Prom coming up?" "I'm excited about it, me and Shanice got matching color outfits. We can't wait to showcase to the school our dance moves. I hope she wins Prom Queen; she deserves it. I know most people vote based on popularity, but my girl is one of the smartest people I know. I hope they see her for who she truly is. If not, that's ok because she has people that love her and see her true worth and value." "It's good that you're a very supportive boyfriend, but I don't hear a lot of talk about you hoping to win

Prom King." When Allen first signed up to be Prom King, he wanted to win to feel validated by his peers. Now that don't honestly matter to him, because he truly knows the only validation that truly matters is the one from GOD and the man he sees when he looks in the mirror. "Honestly bro, I'm not worried about it, I'm just excited to go to support my lady and for me and my band to rock out the stage. There are going to be some beautiful memories created on Friday night." "I'm happy for you, one thing I will say is the way that you're going in your life right now, you are not going to be here for long. My brother is going to be rich!" "Yes, Sir Rich in the Holy Spirit."

It's a beautiful sunny Friday evening, Allen and Shanice are taking prom pictures together at Callahan's Residence. The lovely couple are dressed to impressed as Allen is wearing a light brown tailor-made suit and tie, light brown pants, and black dressed shoes. While Shanice has on a light brown dress with brown high heels. Both of their parents look at them proudly as they love seeing the love that Allen and Shanice have for each other. Shanice's Mother say to Imani, "They are so cute together." Imani responds, "They are when you look at them you see true love." Shanice's Father says to Al, "Looking at them reminds me when I went to prom." Al says, "I didn't go to prom when I was in High School. That's something I wish I would've done, seeing my son going to prom almost bring tears to his eyes." Shanice's Father pats him on the back. "You raised him to be a great man. I'm honored and blessed that he is dating my daughter. I know he will treat her like the queen that she is. And I feel safe knowing she's in his care." "It's vice versa with me and my wife also. Shanice has been a great influence on our son, she' is an amazing young lady. How do you think they will react to our surprise?" Shanice's Father smiles. "I don't know, but we are about to find out."

Al sends a text message to someone. After he does that, he speaks to the kids. "Alright lovebirds me and Greg has a surprise for you guys. Look down the street and tell me what you see." Allen and Shanice look down the street and are surprised at what they see. Shanice says, "Oh my GOD! You got us a Limousine what!" Shanice jumps in joy and hugs her dad and Allen's dad. "Thank you, daddy and my other daddy, I love you both." Allen is shocked and surprised that his father got him a limo for prom. Al smiles and asks, "Young king what do you think?" Allen says, "You went all out for us thank you pops." Allen hugs his father, Imani and Jalean sees this and take a photo of this beautiful exchange. After hugging his son, he looks into Allen's eyes, "You're a king son you deserve to be celebrated. I know you have a performance tonight but have a fun time on the dance floor with your queen. And you are free to use the limo until 2 AM. I know you will use it wisely." "Thank you, dad."

Allen and Shanice ride in the limo as they take photos with each other inside of it. Then they both let the windows down as they have people looking at them like they're the president of the United States. They wave at everyone who is looking at them. Seeing them together is like watching a mid-2000's Disney Channel romance movie except with true reality. Paul calls Allen to see when he will arrive to the school. Allen answers, "What's up Paul, how are you feeling about tonight?" Paul says, "Me and the band are feeling great we was wondering what time you are going to arrive?" Allen looks out the windows and see that he is pulling into the school's parking lot as he is on the phone. "I'm pulling up right now look out front."

As the limo pulls up to the school's gymnasium, people automatically crowd around it as they are wondering who is inside of it. Allen looks at Shanice and says, "You ready baby?" She says, "I shall follow your lead captain." Allen kisses Shanice and grabs her hand as they go inside. Paul and the rest of The Believers see Allen and Shanice get out of the limo and say together, "Superstars!" Paul says, "Oh snap! My boy out here looking like a million bucks." People automatically take photos of Allen and Shanice like they are at The Academy Awards.

After taking photos, Allen goes to meet with his bandmates. He daps up Paul and everyone else. He says to them, "What's going on everyone, y'all look sharp tonight." Paul says,

"I'm trying to get like you boss. You and Shanice are a glamorous couple. Got the limo out tonight, you stunting hard like you're Ric Flair in 1985." "Our pops went all out for us. I'm thankful for it, the night hasn't even officially started yet, but I have already created meaningful memories." Claudia says, "Well tonight we are going to light up the stage together. Joe says, "Full greatness is being showcased tonight." Paul puts his hand in the middle of everyone. "Everyone put your hands in with me." Everyone put their hands in with Paul's hand. "Tonight, we will showcase the gifts that GOD has blessed us with. On my count, 1,2,3, The Believers!"

Prom has begun as the students at Terry High School have a fun time as they start dancing. Monica's "Angel of Mine" starts playing as Allen and Shanice dance to the song. Years of dreaming and hoping, he finally got his angel of mine. At first, it was just about him getting his dream girl, but instead he got so much more than that. He got a woman that sees him, believes in him, loves him, but most of all she's a woman of GOD. He smiles brightly at her; he is truly blessed to have her in his life.

It's time to announce who will be the Prom King and Prom Queen of 2025 at Terry High School. Allen says to Shanice, "How are you feeling about this?" Shanice says, "No matter what happens I'm just happy to be here with you. That's all that counts either way we leave here together that's a win for me." Allen gives Shanice a kiss on the forehead. Principal Davenport comes up on the stage and announce the winners. He says to the crowd, "Class of 2020 and 2021 how are we feeling tonight?" The students yells out good. "That's what I love to hear. Well, it's time to announce this year's Prom King and Prom Queen. This Year's Prom Queen is Ms. Shanice Rodgers!" The crowd gives Shanice a standing ovation as it was highly anticipated that she would be Prom Queen. Allen takes photos and videos of her on stage. He is proud of her accomplishments.

Now everyone wonders who the Prom King will be. Allen looks on as he wonders if he will win the award. "And this years Prom King is Mr. Allen Callahan!" The crowd erupt in cheers as Allen wins Prom King. As in the last three months, Allen went from an Underdog who was overlooked by his peers to the most popular person in the school. Blake daps up Allen and says, "Congratulations Allen you deserved to be Prom King." Shanice hugs and kisses Allen as he hop on stage to get his crown. Principal Davenport puts the crown on Allen's head. Allen and Shanice goes to the front of the stage with their crowns on their heads. Principal Davenport says to everyone, "Ladies and Gentlemen give it up for your Prom King and Prom Queen!" The crowd gives Allen and Shanice one last standing ovation. "King and Queen take your royal dance." Allen and Shanice dance together to their favorite song Ed Sheeran's "Thinking Out Loud". As the love they have for each other is on full display.

After Allen and Shanice get done dancing it's time for The Believers to hop on stage. Principal Davenport introduces the band to the crowd. The crowd rushes up close to the stage to see The Believers perform. Principal Davenport says excitedly, "Ladies and Gentlemen I want you guys to give a warm welcome to The Believers!"

As soon as the band hops on stage they go straight into performance mode. The band performs a cover of Nickelback's "How You Remind Me" which puts the crowd in a good mood. The second song the band performs is "This is Me" by Demi Lavato and Joe Jonas. As the chemistry between Allen and Claudia moves the crowd. The third song the band performs is their song "I Want to be Free". Allen vocal range hits the crowd soul like lightning. The band perform one last song they perform their song "Destiny". Allen wanted to perform this song as it means a lot to him. As he didn't know how he would accomplish his dreams, deep down in his heart he knew one day he would and he did it. Allen takes off his sports jacket for the guitar solo of the song. As with his guitar solo, he shows so much power. People take pictures and videos of Allen's guitar solo as they are witnessing greatness. It's like seeing Prince perform "I Would Die for U" at the end of Purple Rain. After the band gets done performing, they get a wonderful standing ovation. Allen gets on the mic and says, "We're the Believers thank you for having us and always stay believing in yourself we love you!" Allen's greatness has been felt and shown tonight at Terry High School.

After the prom is over with, Allen and Shanice goes back to the limo. They have three hours left to use the limo, their limo driver asks Allen, "Mr. Callahan, where do you want me to take you and Ms. Rodgers to?" Allen leans back in the backseat as he honestly doesn't know where to go since it's late at night. He looks over to Shanice and asks, "Babe I'm sorry I didn't come up with a plan for us to hang out together after prom. Dang it I'm sorry about this." Shanice softly grabs Allen's hand and says, "It's ok baby you not perfect you not going to know or remember everything. Remember you're not in this relationship by yourself; we both are going to forget stuff. The key thing is when that happen, we both come together and create a plan. This relationship is between you and me, it's 50/50. I gotcha and I got an idea on how we can spend these next three hours together." Allen is curious about what Shanice's idea is. "Excuse me sir, can you drive us to Rodgers Flower Shop it's downtown. Me and Mr. Callahan are going to hang out there for the rest of the night." "You ask and you shall receive I will take you guys there Ms. Rodgers." Shanice lays on Allen's chest and softly says, "When I'm with you I know everything will always be ok."

Allen and Shanice arrive at Shanice's mother's flower shop. She has the key to the shop in her purse. Shanice says to the driver, "We will be out of here by 1:30." Allen and Shanice walk inside the flower shop, Shanice takes Allen to her mother's office. When they go in there, she gets some notebooks and gives Allen one. Allen asks, "What is this for?" "With both of us dating with the intent of marriage, I think it's important that we write down our goals and dreams. And then write down what we hoped the future holds for us." Allen loves the idea that Shanice has. "I love it let's get to writing." For the next hour, the two of them joke around and write down the goals they have for themselves. After writing everything down, Shanice plays Toni Braxton's "The Little Things" on her mom's radio. "My mom was playing this song earlier in the day. And it made me think of you, I feel like sometimes in relationships we think we must throw these massive surprises and events to impress our partner, but that's not the case, it's just the little things that truly matters. That's what I love about you; it's the little things you do, they bring me comfort and makes me feel loved. I love you Mr. Allen Callahan." "I love you to Ms. Shanice Rodgers, P.S. just know I have intent to turning your last name to Callahan one day." Shanice smiles and laughs. "Well, I most definitely can't wait till that day my love." She gives Allen a kiss as they both slowly dance to the beautiful song that is being played in the background.

After hanging out, for the last two and a half hours it's time for Allen and Shanice to head back home. As the limo arrives at Shanice's house, Allen walks her to her front door. He says, "What an eventful night we had, this is just the beginning of many meaningful nights together. We are going to have a lot of more like these in the future." Allen kisses Shanice. Shanice says, "Yes, indeed my king, we are going to be by each other's side no matter the storm or weather. I love you text me when you get home and get some rest for tomorrow." "Will do and I love you too." After Allen returns home, he texts Shanice that he got back home safe.

Before going to sleep for the night, he says a prayer to GOD, "Dear GOD, thank you, thank you for this amazing day you have given me and my loved ones, this has been a remarkable day." Allen starts tearing up. "I never thought Shanice would become mine, but not only the girl I wanted, but the girl I needed. I thank you for letting her being in my life and I promise to protect her and show her unconditional love. I love her with all my heart, and I hope that the love between us will inspire people to see what a true Godly relationship looks like. In Jesus name, I pray amen."

It's an early Saturday Morning; Al prepares for his wife and children to join him to meetup with his father and stepmother. He's in the kitchen and fixes himself a cup of coffee before everyone in the house wakes up. He prays to GOD about the family's trip to Atlanta. Al says, "Dear Jesus Christ, my messiah thank you for another day you have blessed us with. My wife and Jalean will be meeting my father and his wife for the first time. The last meeting I had with my dad was great; it gave signs that me and him can build a healthy relationship with each other. I hope that this weekend together will start a new beginning in the Callahan family. And stay empowering Allen and Jalean with your wisdom, they both are doing a great job following your commands father. Thank you, GOD, for everything, in Jesus' name I pray amen."

The rest of the family gets up and gets dressed to head to Dallas. Allen sleeps on his way there as he's tired from last night. Plus, he must get ready for his performance later on this evening with The Believers. Jalean has his headphones on and watches a movie. Al asks Imani, "How are you feeling about today?" Imani says, "I'm excited I can't wait to meet your family. I hope that we can form a bond with them and establish a healthy relationship. If it means anything babe, I believe everything will be fine don't stress."

After driving for two hours and thirty minutes, Al and his family arrives at his father's house. Alvin and Margarie are standing on the front porch waiting to greet Al and the rest of his family. Imani looks at Alvin and automatically notices the resemblance between him and Al. "Babe you and your father look just like each other. His wife is a beautiful lady also." Jalean asks,

"I know they are supposed to be our grandparents, but do we call them grandma and grandpa?" Al says, "It's totally up to you whatever makes you feel comfortable." Allen says, "Well let's go and meet up with them."

Al, Imani, and the kids get out of their vehicle as they meet with Alvin and Marjorie. Alvin says, "Well look who it is the one and only Al Callahan." He comes down from the front porch and gives his son a hug." "I'm so glad to have you back here. Who is this special lady you have next to you?" "This beautiful queen next to me is my beautiful wife Imani." "Alvin smiles at Imani as a part of him holds back tears. He does his best to try to hide how he feels, but instead the tears starts flowing out. "This is a day I have been dreaming for a long time. Do you mind if I give you a hug?" Imani happily says, "I don't mind come on over here pops." Alvin tightly hugs Imani like she is his long-lost daughter. "It's an honor to finally meet you. I'm thankful GOD put you in my son's life. I know GOD used you as a vessel to help Al be the man he is today. Let me introduce you to the lady of my life. This is my beautiful wife, Marjorie. Marjorie says, "I'm a hugger is it ok if I give you a hug also?" "I don't mind at all we are family."

Imani says to Alvin and Margrie, "I know this means a lot to Al, but this means a lot to us also. This is a special moment for me, just feeling the love from the both of you, I know this is going to be a meaningful event for everyone here. These two handsome gentlemen behind us is our wonderful sons. I believe both of you have already met Allen, he's our oldest. He will be graduating from High School this Friday coming up." Alvin says, "I most definitely remember meeting this young king. How are you doing?" "I'm doing well, I can't wait for my performance tonight. Will you guys be there?" "Yes, we will, once your father told me about it, I made sure to put it on my calendar. We will be there to cheer you on son." "I love it, and this is our youngest son Jalean, he just got promoted to the eighth grade. And is apart of the Beta club and soccer team at his school. Just like Allen, he is a young genius also." "What's going my guy, how are you doing?" "I'm doing great you have a beautiful house." "Thank you, Jalean, I greatly appreciate it." "Is it ok if I can you call grandad? I feel like it's weird to call you Mr. Callahan." Alvin smiles and laughs. "I don't mind at all son." Margrie says to Imani, "Imani, do you mind if I show you around the house as Alvin spends time with Al and the kids?" "Sure, I don't mind you fellas have fun."

Alvin takes Al and his grandchildren to his back patio to get to know them better. Alvin says to Al and his grandkids, "So how has you guys' week been?" Al says, "It's been great working, but also making sure everything went well for Allen. Last night, he and his girlfriend were named Prom King and Prom Queen of their High School." "Wow man you are like a superstar. Do you have any photos from last night?" Allen says, "Yes sir, I sure do."

Allen shows his grandfather photos he took for Prom. Alvin smiles as he look at his grandson's photos. The last photo he looks at is Al and Allen taking a photo together with both of them smiling. He stares at it for a second and starts crying.

Al gets concerned as he puts his hand on Alvin's back. He says, "Pops are you ok?" "I am what you see right now is tears of joy. No man in our family got a chance to experience this. Going to Prom and having their father by their side to support them. Al, you are breaking generational curses in our family. Me, you, or your grandfather never got a full glimpse of what true fatherly love was. By the grace of GOD, your sons are getting that experience now. Son, I'm proud of the man, leader, husband and father you have become. You are setting a great example for these two young men on what it takes to lead a Godly household. I wish when I was younger, I was the same type of father as you were your kids. I'm proud of you, son, and I know I'm not deserving of the title, but I'm proud to be your father. Allen, what time do you have to be at your performance?" "We have mic check at 5 PM." "Perfect that gives me time to show you around town and show you your roots. You guys mind riding with your old man." Al says, "Not at all we follow your lead."

Alvin takes the boys to the family house that Al grew up in. This is Al's first time being back here since he got in a fight with his father thirty years ago. At first, when he looks at the house, memories of him and his father fighting start rushing through his head. Then, he sees this beautiful brown butterfly on a red rose in the front yard. Looking at the butterfly reminds him of his mom. As he reminisces about the good memories he shared with his parents. Allen looks at his father and is concerned, as it looks he is in a different space in his head right now. He asks, "Dad, are you alright?" Al responds, "Yes son I'm ok, looking at the house has me thinking about my childhood. And reminiscing about the good times I shared with my mom and dad here. Pops can we go inside?" Alvin says, "Yes we can follow me." Alvin gives the boys a tour of the house. He tells the history of the house and their family history also. Allen and Jalean are shocked to hear some of this information. They didn't know that they came from a broken family, this makes them respect and appreciate their father more. Most people wouldn't have survived what Al went through, but through GOD's grace he was able to overcome.

When the boys go to the garage, Al sees the piano that his mom used to play when he was a kid. When he looks at it, he can hear his mom singing beautiful tunes and playing the keys like she's Stevie Wonder. He says, "I can't believe you still have this after all of these years." Alvin says, "Well, it's a funny story behind it, I sold this piano back in 2000, but one day back in 2016 I was at a music store and I saw this beautiful brown piano I automatically felt attached to it. As I looked closely, I noticed it was your mother's piano. I went ahead and re-bought it that day. When I think about her sometimes, I come out here and play a little a bit it reminds me of the times me and her had together. There is a not a day that goes by, that I don't think about her. Have the boys ever been to her grave?" "Only once, they do know about her and knows what she looks like." "Let's go out there together right now."

The boys arrives at Al's mother's grave. Alvin sits down at his widow's gravestone and softly brushes it. He starts singing The Jacksons "Good Times". By hearing his grandfather singing, Allen can tell the music gens runs deep in his family. Alvin says, "Baby our son and grandsons are here to see you." Alvin starts telling Allen and Jalean about their grandmother. "Ruth Callahan, she was a beautiful, caring woman. The first woman I ever met in my life that showed me love. One of the smartest women I knew she could break down problems like it was nothing. She was a nurse; she loved to take care of people and heal them. Would help out anyone she could, one of the best cooks to ever touched this planet. Her homemade Pecan pie, and Chicken Marconi casserole, were to die for. Most of all she was a caring mother, she loved Al with all her heart. She would sing lullabies to him as a baby; he would just fall asleep in her arms. Truly taking time up with him and showcasing true motherly love. I was truly blessed to have had her in my life and for her to be my wife."

Al gets down on his knees and pats him on the back. "We were both blessed to have had her in our lives. Your Grandma Ruth, I know she's proud of all of us with everything we have accomplished. Mom, me and daddy are back reunited, and we are going to stay connected. You showcased to me how to show love to my kids and so many more lessons and skills. Just know, I cherish, value, and use everything you taught me till this day I love you momma. Thank you for everything and we are going to stay making you proud." Al kisses his mother's grave as the kids sees how much their grandmother meant to their father and grandfather. Before Al gets up from the ground, a brown butterfly sits on his shoulder, while the wind beautifully passes through the cemetery. With seeing the butterfly and feeling the wind, this shows the guys that Ruth is with them right now and everywhere they go in life.

After leaving Ruth's grave, Alvin takes the guys to a restaurant. While there, he bonds with them more and have meaningful conversations with them. For Allen and Jalean, they are just now getting to know their grandfather, but the more that they talk to him they feel more comfortable speaking to him. As it feels like he has been a part of their life for a long time. Al takes pictures of his sons bonding with their grandfather. Alvin never thought this moment that he's living in right now would happen. He's happy to have his family back together.

It's almost that time for The Believers to perform at The Melodies and Flow Open Mic, that is hosted by Al's best friend Scott. Allen, his family, and the band arrive an hour early. When they arrive, they are surprised by what they see. Allen walks in the venue and he sees Shanice selling The Believers merch. There are shirts, T-shirts, pants, shorts, and hats with The Believers name on it. While she is wearing a hat that says, "Allen Callahan." Allen is surprised and amazed by the merch that he sees has been created for the band, but also the love and support that his girlfriend is giving him. He says, "Baby, you did all of this yourself?" Shanice says, "I wish I could take all the credit, but me Claudia, and Kevin created all this together. What you guys are creating right now is a whole movement. We wanted to make sure that it was showcased with the clothing that we designed. What do you think of everything?" "I love it all for real, you did your thing." Claudia coughs. "You did your thing to Claudia. I will say bae the main thing I love is this hat you got on. You must be a huge fan of this Allen Callahan?" "Oh yes, I am I'm his biggest fan, I love all of his songs. If only if I could get a kiss from him." Allen whispers in Shanice's ear. "Your wish is my command." He gives Shanice a kiss on the lips. Alvin and Al looks on as they see Allen and Shanice's interaction. Alvin says to Al, "Our young lad is in love, I don't know that much about Shanice, but she seems like a good woman for him. Especially to do all of this for him." Al says, "She's a great young lady, I do believe one day she will be my daughter-in-law. From her actions, I can tell she has unconditional love for Allen."

As everyone is getting prepared and seated for the open mic, Scott comes out from the back to greet Al and his family. He says to Al, "My brother it's so great to have you here. I can't wait to see what The Believers have in store for us. I already see Lexi (Scott's wife) talking to Imani. And my son is hanging out with Jalean, it's great to see everyone together." "Yes, indeed I'm happy that everyone is reuniting. Speaking of that, I want to introduce you to someone. Dad, this is one of my closet friends, Scott. Me and him went to college together, we have been brothers ever since." Alvin shakes Scott's hand. "It's an honor to meet you Mr. Callahan. Your son is the most talented and smartest person I know. Being a friend of his, has impacted my life for greater good."

As Scott says that a surprise visitor shows up to the open mic. A guy taps Allen on the shoulder and says, "What's up young king." Allen turns around and sees his Uncle Dennis has come to see him perform. "Uncle Dennis!" Al hears Allen yells out Dennis's name and turns around. He is surprised to see that Dennis drove all the way up to Atlanta to see Allen. He walks over to Dennis and Allen to join the conversation. Al says to Dennis, "Well look who the wind blew in." Al and Dennis smile and hug one another. Dennis says, "I had to come through ever since I saw him live, I've been a fan. He's doing GOD's work through his music. I have been listening to your songs Allen they are very encouraging and inspiring. You are going to help transform lives with the talent that GOD has gifted you with. I'm proud of the young man you have become." "Thank you, Uncle Dennis, I wish Grandpa Bill and Grandma Jill was here to see this." "Well, I know they are smiling down from heaven looking down at us right now. I see Mr. Alvin is in the building also, man this is a beautiful moment right here. GOD is so good everything is coming together for greater good in our lives."

The open mic is about to start; there is already about 130 people in the building. Scott gets on the mic as he has a surprise for everyone in the audience. "Peace and Blessings everyone, I hope everyone is having a marvelous Saturday evening. We have an epic show for you guys tonight, but before we get started, I want to highlight a special guest in the crowd tonight. My good friend and brother Al Callahan is in the house tonight, I want your to give it up for him." Everyone in the crowd claps it up for Al. "You know back in the day; me and Al had our own band together called "The Phoenix". We created some electrifying music together, with this being his first time here at Melodies and

Flow, I would love to perform one of our original songs if he's up for it." Al starts smirking as he had a feeling Scott might do something like this. The crowd cheers him on, his father says to him, "Go on up there son and show these people who you are."

Al gets up from his seat as the crowd gets excited. This is his father, stepmother, and kids first time watching him perform. Scott whispers in his ear. "What song do you want to play?" With everyone he loves and cherish coming together for his son, he decides to perform a song that he and Scott wrote together called "Happy Days". He says to Scott, "Let's do Happy Days." Scott says, "Let's rock and roll like old times."

The keyboard player starts playing a low melody, as Scott plays his acoustic guitar while Al sings. "Thinking about those days when I will reap what I sow, asking myself when will I grow, will I develop into that seed that develops into someone beautiful, I don't know, but I'm doing my best to follow these flows of life, I want to be the star on the screen that you see on TV, just need someone to believe in me, receive my greatness and help me multiply this gift of mine, tired of living on broken roads, I want to live in a big old house with a white-fitted fence, with a beautiful wife and kids, and make it into a home, all the hard times of rain in my life turn into sunshine." Scott sings the hook of the song. "I want to live in Happy Days, lord please make my day, just want to lay somewhere where I'm happy and free, Lord please let me see that day." After the hook Al goes into the second verse of the song. " I been broken, at momma's grave telling her I'm tired, she speaks back to me and tell me son you're a superstar, you have to believe, so you can achieve, you fight for what you want in life, so you can take flight in your field of dreams, you are destined to be great don't give in because you don't want to be on your death bed saying it's too late for me." Al sings the hook of the song one more time. "I want to live in Happy Days, Lord please make my day, just want to lay somewhere where I'm happy and free, Lord please let me see that that day."

After the guys gets done singing, everyone gives them a standing ovation. Both Al and Scott take a bow before the crowd. The most beautiful thing about the song is everything that Al wrote rounded up coming true for him.

After Al and Scott get done performing, the open mic officially starts. A lot of great performers of all types of genres come on stage back-to-back to showcase their full artistry to everyone in the crowd. Each performance has created a beautiful and positive energy in the building.

Now it is time for The Believers to perform. The band walk up on stage with full confidence as they are fully prepared. The first song they perform is the song they wrote for Larry Nash and Danielle "Meant to Be". Since the song was just released yesterday and is already getting heavy traction on the radio and streaming services. Allen and Claudia both passionately sing this song as they think about the loves of their life. The energy that they are spreading from the stage has people moving side to side, people clapping their hands, couples dancing with one another. Al and Imani are dancing together to their son's song. After the song is over with, they transition into "I Just Want to Be Free". Allen's vocals during this performance are extremely powerful and gut-wrenching. As you can feel the words representing the blood vessels in his soul directly talking to you. The same thing with his guitar as the sounds echoes massive power, and impactful energy into the crowd. The band perform one last song which is "Destiny".

Before performing the song, Allen gives the crowd an impactful message. He says, "Before we get into this last song, I want to say this. Love who you are, know that you are someone special. All of us on this planet are destined for greatness no matter what background we come from. What GOD has created for all of us is meant to come to fruition. If we just follow his pathway we will live in our destiny, let's rock out band." The band performs "Destiny" the words that Allen and Claudia are singing are giving people in the crowd hope and inspiration. Some people even start crying and waving their hands as the band perform. Once the band stop performing, they receive a beautiful standing ovation. Allen's family look at him proudly as he is a symbol of beacon of hope.

After the performance and the open mic, people come up to the band taking photos with them and getting their autograph. All their merch is sold out within fifteen minutes. People are all over Allen like a magnet. Scott looks at Allen and says to Al, "He's just like his daddy." Al responds, "No he ten times better than me. He's a one-of-a-kind talent, thank you for doing this for him and the kids." "It's no issue at all; we're family we forever got each other back. It's good to see you and your old man being reunited. I'm proud of you and I'm happy for you. I know with everything going on it closes a dark chapter in your life and opens up a fresh new one for you and your family."

The band alongside Shanice go outside to see how much money they made tonight. Paul says, "I just got our payment from Scott, two hundred fifty dollars for everyone. Shanice, how much did we make selling merchandise?" She says, "Well we sold out everything, but we made around $500." Everyone jumps in joy. Paul yells out, "Let's go! Team this is only just the beginning we are about to do some amazing things." Alvin comes outside to speak to the group. He says, "Man I must say y'all were amazing up there on stage tonight. Grandson, you made me proud tonight keep going, everything that you're doing is going to pay off for you. That's go for all of you, me and my wife have got plans on cooking some homemade gumbo and frying some catfish if y'all free we would love for you all to join us for dinner. Joe says, "Say less we are hungry we will be there."

After the open mic, everyone meets up at Alvin and Marjorie's house. Alvin sits back as he is happy to have friends of his son and grandson at his table. He decides to make a toast. Alvin grabs his fork and hits it towards his glass of lemonade. He says, "Attention everyone, I want to make a toast." Everyone at the table centers their attention towards him. "This day has been one of the best days of my life. Meeting the beautiful family that my son created. Getting to know each and every one of them today has brought me so much joy. And having their friends here at the table is a beautiful sight to see. One thing I know is life is short, we must tell people how we feel before something happens. The main thing I want to leave with you guys is this, love and support one another. The generosity and care that you showcase to your fellow brother and sister can positively impact their entire lives. When you want a positive life, you have to be positive and spread positivity also. Cheers to love, happiness, but most of all GOD's happiness for all of us at this table." Everyone at the table yells out cheers.

It's Sunday Morning, The Callahan Family goes to Alvin and Marjorie's church. While there Al and the rest of the Callahan family get a chance to meet Marjorie's kids. She smiles and says,

"This has been a day I have been waiting for, for a long time. Al these are my kids Cody, Nate, and Sandra. Kids this is Al, he's your stepbrother." Everyone starts smiling as the whole family is finally coming together as one. Cody says to Al, "We have been waiting to meet you for a long time, welcome home my brother." All of Margrie kids gives Al a hug. Everyone starts tearing up, Margrie says to Al, "Our prayers have come true, praise GOD."

The family enjoys the word of GOD and worship service together. The pastor preaches about Joseph and his trust in GOD. But also, how to use our dreams to guide people towards their God-given purpose. The pastor says, "You know sometimes in families we have this thing called generational curses. When that happens GOD molds and build one person in that family to break it. When that person fully walks into the destiny that GOD has created for them, a transition happens in their family. When that happens, it generates curiosity in the family members' minds. Like how they did this or how did they achieve this? The answer to that question is very simple it's because they decided to follow GOD's pathway. When you believe in him, yourself, and start taking action a new beginning starts in your life and around the people that you love. Never be afraid to walk in his pathway, even if the valleys are high just know there is so much greater on the other side." This message resonates with Allen and his family. His grandfather puts his hand on his shoulder and says, "Thank you

Allen, if it wasn't for you, I wouldn't be reunited with my son. You not only helped rebuild our relationship, but you helped rebuild this family for greater good. You are special son; I love you with all of my heart." Allen says, "I love you to poppa." Allen and his grandfather hug one another.

After church, the whole Callahan family have Sunday dinner together. Al bonds with his brothers and sisters. Allen and Jalean bond with their cousins. Margrie says, "I have to get a picture of all of us together one second." Margrie takes a photo of the whole family together. As a family that was broken has been restored.

After creating beautiful memories with their family, it's time for Al, Imani, and the kids to head back to Macon. Al says, "This weekend has meant a lot to me. Thank you pops and Margrie for opening your home to us." Marjorie says, "All of your are family any home of ours is yours also." Alvin says, "Indeed it is, never forget that we love all of you. You are welcomed back here anytime. And we will be in town this Friday for your graduation, Allen. We love you guys, have a safe trip back to Macon and text me when you guys make it back home safe." Imani says, "We will we love you all."

Chapter 13: The Final Adventure

It's Wednesday evening, Allen has completed his last shift at Rick's Grocery Store. With him getting a $100,000 salary for four years from Cloud Records and going to college, he decided it would be best for him to quit his job at the grocery store. Allen walks in the break room as the whole team gets him a cake and a lot of cards. In celebration of him moving on to a greater journey in his life. Mr. Jimmy says to Allen as he shakes his hand, "Allen it's been an honor having you work for us for the past two years. I'm proud of you stay prospering in life, don't stop. Ashley hugs Allen and says, "Congratulations don't you go Hollywood on me." Allen says, "I would never, thank you for being a great friend of mine." Kevin comes into the room as he and Allen hug one another. He says, "My boy you made it. I'm proud of you, I knew you would be something and now look at you. Don't look back stay shining that light that's inside of you." "I always will bro thank you for everything." Kevin and Allen dap one another up. Allen pats Blake on the shoulder who is standing next to him. He is taking Allen's position as he is going to Middle Georgia State University nearby. Allen stands in the middle of the break room and gives thanks to everybody. "I know for sure Blake is going to do a great job in my place. I love every one of you and thank you all for the great memories." Everybody in the room claps for Allen. Ashley says, "Blowout the candles on your cake and make a wish." Allen close his eyes and visions his future. "Let everyone in the world see my greatness." He blows the candles as he hope his wish comes true.

It's Thursday afternoon, Allen goes to meet with Ms. Maggie, his literature teacher, to go over his valedictorian speech. After reading Allen's speech she says, "Well Mr. Callahan I love this speech mainly because everything you stated in this speech you have done and going to continue to do to be successful in life. I'm proud of you always stay spreading the knowledge you have learned and gained to the universe." "Thank you, Ms. Maggie, the words that are written on paper shall come into fruition."

The time has arrived! It's finally graduation day for the Class of 2025 at Terry High School. Allen wakes up as he is super excited for today. When he gets out of bed, he starts dancing and singing. Jalean joins him as they dance together. The Callahan eats breakfast together as everyone is dressed up. Al says, "Well son today is a big day for you. How are you feeling?" Allen says, "I'm excited today starts a new beginning in my life. These twelve years have been an amazing journey. I can't wait to see what GOD has in store for me."

Allen arrives at the school he meets up with Shanice. Both of them will be giving speeches in front of everyone before graduation starts. Shanice hugs Allen and gives him a kiss. She says to him, "We made it happen! How you feeling?" Allen says, "I'm feeling great it's crazy on how everything transpired our senior year. How do you feel about giving your speech?" "A tad bit nervous, but I believe everything will go well. How do you feel about your speech?" "I feel great about it; I hope that it inspires someone today." Paul runs up to Allen and hugs him. He says to Allen, "We did it bro!" Allen says, "We made it happen bro! Today starts a new beginning for our future."

Graduation starts as parents are extremely proud to see their kids graduating today. Allen's parents, brother, grandfather, step grandmother, and his bandmates are in the crowd to cheer him on. After Shanice gives her salutatorian speech, it's time for Allen to gives his Valedictorian speech. When Allen steps to the podium almost every student in the school chants his name like he is The Rock. It's an amazing sight to see, just three months ago he was getting laughed at by his peers in the same gym. Now he is getting recognition and being celebrated by them.

Allen gives a powerful speech to his fellow classmates. He says, "Greetings my fellow classmates, well it's time to say goodbye to this chapter of our lives as we go to the next. What is the best advice I can give you?" Allen reflects on everything he has gone through these past months and how it humbled him into the man he needed to be. "The best advice I can give you is go for everything that GOD has laid on your heart to do. In life, we get hit in our heart and soul to go for our dreams. Sometimes we get scared to go for it, or we think to ourselves it's impossible for us to accomplish it. I'm here today to tell you that you can. Anything that we envision for ourselves can come to pass. It's like driving to Downtown Atlanta, on your way to your destination, you are going to encounter some bumps and some stops. However, if you stay going though eventually you will reach your destination. We must have that same concept with our goals and dreams. Never quit, never give up, give it all that you got for what you want in your life. We are all great stars that shall shine bright. My name is Allen Callahan, and I wish each and every one of you nothing but success in life." Everyone in the building gives Allen a standing ovation.

Finally, it's Allen's turn to receive his diploma. His father, mother, brother, Claudia, Joe, his grandfather, and step grandmother are in attendance to see him graduate. Principal Davenport calls Allen's name to receive his High School Diploma. "Allen Callahan!" Allen's family cheers in excitement. Imani yells out, "That's my boy! Momma is proud of you!" Al points at his son with tears in his eyes and says, "That's my son! That's my boy!" After receiving his diploma, Allen sits down in his seat as he knows great things are in store for him.

After graduation, Allen's parents throw him a graduation party at their house. Family and friends of Allen are at the house celebrating his accomplishments. While talking to people, he receives a phone call from Jack. He answers the phone and says, "Hey Jack, how are you doing?" Jack says, "I'm doing amazing my guy. I know you are on cloud-nine right now with you just graduating. I got some amazing news for you, Larry Nash and Danielle "Meant to Be" has reached number 1 on the Billboard Hot 100." Allen is stunned by the news; he pinches himself to make sure he is not dreaming. "Jack, you joking with me?" "No, my young brother you have your first number 1 congratulations. Due to this I already have a couple of artists that want to work with you. Be prepared to have a lot of people knocking on your door, Mr. Callahan. Congratulations and I can't wait to see what the future has in store for you."

Al and Imani look proudly at their son as they are proud of the man he has become. Imani says to Al, "We did it Al our first born is officially a high school graduate. Seeing him transform from a shy boy to a young man filled with confidence has been amazing to see." Al says, "You are right our little boy isn't a little boy anymore. He's a man that is making his dreams come true he's an inspiration to many people including myself. I'm going to go talk to him for a minute.

After Allen, Paul, and Shanice gets done taking a photo together. Al walks over to Allen to talks to him. "Congratulations to all of you guys, I know great things are in your future. Do you mind if I have a word with my son?" Shanice says, "By all means you guys go ahead and chat." Once Shanice and Paul walk away, Al talks with his son. "Allen Callahan Jr, the brightest young man I know. I'm proud of the man you have become, I'm blessed to be your father. When you were born, my main hope for you were that you be a better man than me. They say that kids learn from their parents, but in my case I'm glad to be learning from you son. Watching you has shown me that when you truly walk into your calling, your life isn't just transformed but your family's life is also. The main thing I want to say to you is this, stay focus on what GOD is calling on you to do and never forget who you are. I love you son and I'm proud of you." Allen says, "Thank you dad and I love you too." Both father and son hug one another.

After everyone leaves after celebrating, Allen goes into his room and writes in his journal. He writes, "What an adventure this life of mine has been these last couple of months. Just three months ago, I was looked at as a nobody to my peers, now I'm respected and loved by them. I realize now the reason that happened is because I finally learned to respect and love who I am. When that happened, a full transformation happened in my life. I walked into my calling of being a musician and songwriter, GOD blessed me with the woman that I needed in my life. In addition to that, I was able to help rebuild my father and grandfather's relationship. I am Allen Callahan, a smart intelligent young man that has a great mindset. I'm going to do great things and make a huge impact. My purpose in life is to bring inspiration to the world, with the words that I speak and write from my spirit. I can honestly say, I love the person that I see when I look in the mirror. I'm thankful to Jesus Christ for what all he has done in my life. I know that by continuing walking in his pathway the future is going to be bright for me."

It's five years later August of 2025, the whole Callahan family are together in downtown Macon at the grand opening of The Callahan Community Center. The Community Center was developed by Allen and his father. The purpose of the center is to provide services for people who needs therapy, people who wants to record music, people to obtain their GED and learn different trades, but mostly a place where the people in the community can come to, to get the better knowledge they need in their life. Almost the whole town is at the grand opening for the center.

The Mayor of Macon, GA speaks to the everyone in the crowd, "Greetings my fellow citizens of Macon, GA. Today is a remarkable and legendary day in our city. Today starts a brand-new beginning as this beautiful building behind me will be a place where our people can come to, to get everything they need to be successful in life. When Al and his son Allen came to me about opening The Callahan Community Center and the purpose behind it, I knew right away this would be a place that will help transform lives. I'm honored and blessed that GOD gave these two men the idea to create something that will change a lot of people lives. Without further or due let me introduce you guys to Allen and Al Callahan. Everyone in the crowd gives the father and son duo a round of applause.

Allen lets his father speaks first. Al says to everyone, "It's an honor and privilege being in front of you all today. Me and my son are blessed to have our family with us here today. They were the inspiration behind us developing the community center. The Callahan family roots started here in Macon, GA. Even though our foundation started here, it was spoiled and toxic for a very long time. Due to that, it created a lot of issues in our family specifically the men. However, one day my son Allen decided to listen to what GOD was calling him to be. He decided to walk into the destiny that our father in heaven created for him. By doing that, it helped transformed our family life forever. As it created opportunities for me to look back at my past and make peace with issues I had deeply rooted in me. And I was able to rebuild my relationship with my father and find my own purpose in life. We want everyone in the world to experience what we did; we want you to find out who you truly are, we want you to find your purpose, we want you to make peace with what holding you back, and we want you and your family to be walking in a righteous path. That's our purpose for this center, son come on up here."

The citizens of Macon gives Allen a standing ovation as he walks to the podium. He says, "First and Foremost, praise GOD for the mercy and grace he shows us. I stand here today extremely proud of my family. As my father stated, we were a broken family, however we are now restored. This center is to help some transform lives. And to help build more positivity within everyone in our town. The Callahan Community Center is a building filled with hope, faith, but most of all the power of GOD. Thank you all for being here and I hope that you all enjoy this beautiful center thank you." Everyone gives Allen a round of applause. The whole Callahan family takes a picture with the mayor in front of the building. Then afterwards, Jalean cuts the ribbon for the grand opening of the center.

Over the last five years, The Callahan's family has changed for the better. After graduating High School, Allen went to Central Georgia Technical College where he obtain an associate degree in Cyber Security. While doing that, he and The Believers have become a well-known band around the whole globe. As they have three albums, they have won numerous of awards and have had two number one songs on Billboard. He also wrote numerous hit songs for Cloud Records with seven of them reaching number 1 on Billboard. Once his contract with Cloud Records ended, he and Claudia started their own songwriters record label called "Rising Songbirds". To help aspiring songwriters write songs for major artists in the music industry. Just like his professional life, his personal life has blossomed also. After dating for four years, Allen and Shanice got married on May 20th, 2024. They share a beautiful house together in the suburbs of Macon. And are expecting their first child together later this year. Shanice graduated from University of Georgia with a bachelor's degree in psychology. She's now a licensed therapist and opened her first office last month.

Al retired from his job at the bank two years ago. Just like his son, he walked into his purpose of being a musician. He released a gospel album titled "The Comeback" under The Believers label which reached number 1 on the gospel charts. In addition to that, he and his father Alvin wrote a book together called "Breaking Generational Curses" which focuses on breaking generational curses in families. The book became a New York Times Bestseller. With Imani by his side he knows travel the world as a motivational speaker, singer, and author.

Jalean is doing great things in his life also. As he recently graduated from High School, just like his big brother, he was valedictorian of his graduating class. His purpose in life is to help people sustain great health in their lives. He has plans on becoming a doctor. Starting this fall, he will be attending Augusta University as he will be majoring in Biology.

While walking inside the community center with Marjorie, Alvin says to himself, "Look at what GOD did in our lives." Alvin and Marjorie talk to Allen, Imani and the kids everyday. Alvin wrote a full memoir of his life titled "The Troubled Man" which also became a New York Times Bestseller earlier this year. He's now a life coach that coaches' men who have anger and substance abuse issues.

Paul daps Allen up as he is extremely proud of his friend. He says to him, "My brother you are always levitating in every craft that you partake in. I'm proud of you bro." Allen says, "Thank you bro we really turned our dreams into reality." Paul is now the biggest music producer in the music game. As he has won numerous awards and has multiple hit songs under his belt. Just like Allen, he went to college at Central Georgia and obtain an associate's degree in business management. As he oversees operations for The Believers label. Joe and Eddie are also at the grand opening to support Allen.

Kevin along with Claudia by his side congratulates Allen on the center. He says to him, "My brother, you doing it big, big timer." Allen smiles. "Like we use to tell it each other back in the day, forever levitating like an elevator." With seeing Allen finding his purpose, it made Kevin want to find his purpose in life. He went back to church and accepted GOD as his Lord and savior. He found his purpose and that is helping the youth. He went back to school and got a bachelor's degree in teaching. He's now a 6TH grade Math teacher at Macon Middle School and is attending University of Georgia online to obtain his master's degree.

Claudia gives Allen a hug and says, "I'm proud of you, my brother." Claudia and Allen are the most well-known songwriters tandem right now in the music industry. With running a label with Allen, and being a member of The Believers, Claudia has a busy fulfilling life. Her personal life is prospering as she and Kevin are engaged to get married. And they just closed on their first house.

Blake goes up to Allen and gives him a hug. He says, "Thank you my brother for everything you have done." After graduating from High School, Blake went to college at Middle Georgia State University and got a bachelor's degree in teaching. And is a 10Th grade Social Studies teacher at Macon High School. He also has his own workout group and is in the works of opening his own gym. And thanks to the help of Allen's father and grandfather he was able to rebuild his relationship with his dad.

Many people from Allen's life comes up to him and congratulates him and his father for opening up the community center. He and Shanice takes a moment to take in all they have achieved in the past five years. Shanice says, "Babe we have done so much in these past years and impacted so many lives." Allen says, "And it's only just the beginning." Allen kisses Shanice's stomach as he is thankful to GOD for all he has done for his family. Due to that, his unborn son will not have to worry about any generational curses and have a safe, healthy adventure on his pathway to his goals and dreams.

Jukwan Brooks　　286

A Special Message to Everyone

First and foremost, thank you for reading this amazing book. I hope and pray that you gained a lot of wisdom while reading "The Adventures a High School Scholar". One of the main takeaways I hope you take from this story is to believe in yourself and go for what you want in life. Anything that you vision in your mind can come to path. Don't let nobody talk you out of, on what GOD has put in your heart to do. Because you never know, just by you following what GOD put in your spirit to do, you can change someone's life for the better. Stay believing in GOD, yourself, and work hard for what you vision in your life. In the famous words of the late great The Notorious B.I.G "Sky is the Limit".

Acknowledgements

First and foremost, I thank my father GOD in heaven for blessing me with the gift to write inspirational novels like "The Boy That Comes From Nothing" and "The Adventures of a High School Scholar". With Jesus Christ by my side, I know I can do anything that I put my mind to.

To my brother and illustrator Joshua Allen, we did it again! Thank you for the love and support you have always shown me. You have a great gift in illustration, showcase every gift that GOD has blessed you with. Love you, my brother.

Second, special thanks to Steve Seward, for your great editing skills and your love and support. Stay showcasing everything GOD has poured into you. You are an amazing person, I'm thankful for everything you have done for me. Stay being a great vessel for GOD, Love you my brother.

Thank you to Michael Newton Jr aka Uncle Phil, thank you for your guidance and support you have shown me. Always stay spreading better knowledge to people. Always stay listening to what GOD says to you. Love you, my brother.

To my good brother Devon Harris, it has been an honor helping you out with your ministry. Shoutout to everyone in Full Circle Refuge Ministries. Being around you has helped me be a better leader and mentor to people. What you have done and still are doing is transforming lives and families. Thank you for pouring into me and giving me great advice. I'm thankful for our friendship, stay being a great vessel for our Heavenly Father. Love you, my brother.

To my fellow Thomson native, David Mew, GOD is doing amazing things in your life brother. And it's only just the beginning for you and The Manhood and Womanhood Tour. Shoutout to everyone in The Manhood and Womanhood Tour. I'm honored to call you a friend of mine. Seeing the life, you have made for yourself with the help of GOD inspires me. Stay trusting in GOD, stay believing in yourself, and know the work you're doing right now is helping save lives. Love you, my brother.

Finally, to my fans and supporters I love you with all my heart. Thank you for the love you show and your support. We are doing great things at Better Knowledge (formerly named Bossman Kwan). Grateful to you all just know we are going to stay levitating. Peace and Blessings to you all, and remember you are a star that is destined to shine bright.